ARCTIC GREEN

ARCTIC GREEN

A MIDCOAST MAINE MYSTERY

ALLISON KEETON

To the Maine Snowmobile Association, the dedicated snowmobile clubs, and the generous landowners who all make snowmobiling in Maine a fun and accessible sport.

And to Tom and Dan's sledding bromance. Long may you ride!

Praise for Arctic Green

"Keeton has done it again! Another great cozy Maine mystery, where quaint little towns hide secrets that some will kill to protect."—**Jon Lewis**, author of The Ageless Series

"The magic of this novel is the rich smorgasbord of (the) inhabitants of the town, the tight bonds of love and friendship, and the rugged but exquisite setting in a winter wonderland of pristine grandeur."—award-winning author **Matt Cost** of the Modern-Day Chronicles of Max Creed

Chapter One

Raven Ouelette sighed and unzipped her old, duct-taped down jacket, unsure whether to blame the store's temperature or her frustration for feeling overheated. She scanned the paint shelves for Oceanic Blue in a satin finish. If Wolf Marine didn't have it in stock, Karl Wolf, the store owner, could order it, or she could drive the thirty minutes to the hardware store in Eelsboro, the closest town to Secretly, to check their stock.

She shouldn't even be looking for the paint. Her contractor, Craig Fisher, promised months ago to finish the renovations and repaint her rental cabins, Pine Acres. That was the whole purpose of paying the big bucks, but like many Maine handymen, Craig had more work than he could handle. With Valentine's Day weekend less than two weeks away, and five cabins already rented, Raven had no choice but to take matters into her own hands. An incoming snowstorm along the coast signaled the perfect time to paint while being snowed in.

She took a deep breath and pulled her long black hair into a bun as she studied the rows of paint cans on the shelves. There was no rhyme or reason—quart-size mixed among the gallon ones. Satin, semi-gloss, and matte finishes jumbled together. New, unopened ones sat next to lightly used, tinted ones, proven by a colored paint dribble down the metal front. Wolf Marine had it all, and it was all for sale. Well, the store really only had what it had, and either Raven could compromise on her color choice or try the hardware store. She really didn't want to do the drive. Before giving up, she had one more area to search.

Kneeling on all fours, she reached way to the back of the bottom shelf. Tiny pebbles from the mud- and sand-speckled floor dug into her knees, even through her jeans, the remnants of the dirt brought in by the multitude of offshore lobstermen who trekked in all day for boat parts, overalls, or other fishing gear that Karl jammed into his small store.

"Winter White. Lobster Red. Arctic White. Sunshine Yellow." Raven softly spoke the colors out loud as she pushed the cans out of the way. She was grateful for the flexibility of her thirty-five-year-old body, which let her stretch from her crouched position on the floor.

The front doorbell jingled, signaling an incoming customer, and the old wooden floor creaked under the new arrival's footsteps as the person walked into the store.

Karl's deep baritone boomed out. "What are you doing in here? You have some nerve showing your face in here and anywhere around town!" His voice echoed around the store's walls and made her jump.

She listened for a response to his outburst from whoever had just entered. The answer from that person came too quietly for her to hear it. A murmur. Her nosiness got the best of her, and she crawled to the end of the aisle, poking her head around an end cap of marine charts. A display of old, faded postcards in a rotating stand at the front of the store blocked her view, and she could only see scuffed-up Bean boots near the counter, their size not giving a clue to the person's gender. Karl's voice exploded again.

"I don't care what changes you've made. Nobody in town cares."

Another low murmur. Raven pushed a fallen strand of hair behind her ear and angled her head to hear better, facing the wall in front of her to concentrate. She stared up at an old dusty-framed print of two women rowing that had hung there forever. If it were for sale, no one had ever bought it.

Even by sitting very quietly, Raven still heard nothing. Darn it. If Marcel walked into the store at that very moment and saw her straining to eavesdrop, he'd shake his head in disappointment but without surprise. Her husband of ten years, Barrett County's lead sheriff, was always telling her not to get involved in other people's business. Could she help it if her curiosity got the best of her?

The Bean boots angled toward her. Raven, not wanting to look foolish, scooted back into the aisle as Karl yelled again. "Out. Get out! You're not welcome here. Ever."

The footsteps retreated, the front door jingled, and the shop fell silent. Raven scrambled to the paint cans in case Karl came her way, although he had to know she heard him. Sitting back on her heels, she thought of who in town would be judged harshly by Karl. Most of her fellow Mainers usually kept their comments to themselves. It had to be something big for Karl to show such wrath. She drew a blank. She thought back to what he had said about not caring about changes that were made. Gosh, that could apply to anything from clearing debris from a yard to keeping a dog on a leash.

The front door jingled again. Did that person dare to come back? She sucked in her breath. Oh, let the games begin, she thought.

This time, the voice floated over to where Raven sat on the floor, coming in loud and clear, not far from the door. Craig Fisher.

She grimaced. Why was she feeling guilty for buying paint for her own cabins? She didn't want him to feel bad that she was going around him, but, heck, he was behind on the work.

"Hey Karl, wanted to give you an update on the trails," Craig said. He was treasurer of SnowTracks, the local snowmobile club, and a master of trail maintenance in prior snowy years. The local paper even ran an article about the volunteer hours he put in one winter to keep the trails open and safe.

"So sorry, Craig, that I need to be here today. I'll close up early to help," Karl replied. He was the club's president.

The longer Raven stayed hidden, the more ridiculous it would be. She stood and poked her head around. Craig had remained by the door, his broad shoulders from his carpentry work filling the frame, his sandy-colored hair sticking out from a knit cap.

"Raven," he said. "I'm getting to you. I promise. Just not today."

"Oh, I get it," she said. "You need to take advantage of the snow while it's here." She gave him a thin smile. She did understand, but it still meant she had to do some of the work she was paying him to do.

"Thanks for understanding. Karl, I stopped in to see if you had any dollars to put toward more stakes and signs. It's too bad the state hadn't been funding us through those four years of no snow."

Karl smirked. "I can't believe the state gave our club money for the Aroostook County trails. We could have used those funds to fix the clubhouse steps or prep signage for a future snowy winter, like this one." His fifty-something-year-old face grew red and puffy with his shoulder-length, greying hair unfastened and wild around his shoulders.

Craig shrugged. "I'm with you, bro."

Karl nodded and went to the cash register, opened its drawer, and counted out a few bills. "For the good of the cause. By the way, you wouldn't believe who was just here. The nerve."

Craig reached out his gloved hand to take the money. "Who?"

Before Karl could answer, the door to the store opened again, and Mikey Dyer walked in. He lived on the road over from Raven, in a small, boxy house owned by his mother. She often saw him walking home, his stringy hair and dirty clothes, when he didn't have a vehicle in working order.

"Hey, Karl, I wanted to check if there was any work you needed done." His grease-covered coat hung on him, looking two sizes too big.

Mikey had a reputation for not being a very good worker for a young man of thirty, and she had heard that there wasn't a lobsterman within fifty miles who would hire him anymore. That said a lot since help was hard to come by. The words "lazy," "unreliable," and "argumentative" were just some of the descriptions used around town to paint a picture of Mikey.

"Nope, sorry, Mikey. Pretty quiet around here, being January and all," said Karl, his tone and volume even. "Bye, Craig. See you out there," he added as Craig left the store.

"Maybe I could sweep or unbox some inventory," Mikey said, not giving up.

"Many of the lobstermen pulled their traps months ago, and only the occasional offshore fisherman comes in. Unless you want to be a debt collector. I'm just about to post the debt owed to the store."

"On your website?" Mikey's voice said in a flat tone. "I don't know computers."

"On the front door. For all to see," said Karl, moving out from behind his counter.

Raven had returned to her paint can mission and heard a soft "oh" from Mikey. She was surprised to hear about the debt list. A couple of years ago, Karl had posted a similar notice on his door, listing various lobstermen's debt owed to him for the credit he had extended them throughout the season. It took only a week for those on the list to pay up or risk becoming the town's ridicule. She wondered who had made the list this year.

"How about after the snowstorm comes through? Will you need help shoveling out the gas pumps or the parking?" Mikey tried again to get some cash.

"Let's see if we actually get a storm. When are the weather guys ever right?" Karl's voice was muffled. Raven assumed he had turned his back on Mikey, a hint for him to leave. Mikey obviously wasn't good with hints.

"But you're betting on it, right, Karl? I see your Arctic Cat sitting out front."

Karl chuckled. "Well, I can be hopeful."

Raven had noticed it too when she parked in the lot. Karl's bright green Arctic Cat snowmobile was off to the side. He must have brought it up from his house to get it closer to a trail entrance.

"You still head of the snowmobile club? Is there still a snowmobile club? We haven't had enough snow in years to be on any of those trails." Mikey was now trying to be Karl's friend, Raven thought. Maybe the next sentence would be a straight-out ask for money. Raven wondered whether he had ever asked Karl for money.

"Yep. Still the president, and yep, there's still a club. The few members we have are busy out there fixing the trails as fast as they can right now. I'll go help as soon as I close up shop. If you're looking for something to do, they could use more volunteers."

"You gonna ride 'first on the trails' too?" said Mikey, ignoring Karl's suggestion of doing something for free.

"Hope so, I'd love to keep my record. This year's going to be epic, Mikey.

Mark my words." Karl's voice was buoyed by the prospect of finally getting on his sled without having to trailer it to another part of the state.

Raven smiled. That was the thing about New Englanders who loved snow: they doubted the forecast one minute but hoped it was right the next. She got it. She loved a real Maine winter, too.

The door jingled again, and Karl greeted another customer looking for bags of ice melt. Raven turned back to the paint cans and reached for the last two quarts in the back of that bottom shelf. One was white, again—Ivory White—but the last can in the whole store that she touched was "Oceanic Blue." In a semi-gloss. Close enough.

Chapter Two

For once, the weather reports were right. Raven watched snowflakes gather on Dukie's black, wavy coat as he ran ahead of her in the yard. Lily, their chunky English yellow lab, hid any snow accumulation in her fur, but the little that had landed on the hemlock bushes fell on Lily's nose when she burrowed under their branches. Dukie, an energetic Portuguese Water Dog, brought back the bright orange ball for Raven and left it at her feet to throw again.

"You just wait, Dukie." Raven bent down for the ball and underhanded it into the field behind their house. "You will have to plow your way through two feet of snow tomorrow to find this ball."

The reports were now saying the wind had shifted, and for the first time in many years, the coast of Maine might actually get a record-breaking blizzard.

Marcel's sheriff Jeep barreled up their dirt driveway and parked in front of their cedar-shingled Cape-style house and next to Raven's forest green Mini Cooper.

Dukie forgot all about his ball and raced to say hi to his dad. Lily trotted behind him, her thick yellow tail waving a hello before she got there. Marcel opened his vehicle's door, and Dukie stood on his hind legs to reach in and plant a wet kiss on Marcel's handsome face before Lily nudged her way in for her attention.

"Storm of the Century, they're now saying," he said to Raven, finally able to step out of the Jeep. He gave her a kiss as a hello, and then slightly brushed her ear with his lips. He tossed snow off her black hair.

She pulled up her hood, leaving only the ends of her long hair to stick out. "I think they announced that last year, and we only got rain."

"Well, this time, Southern New England is already getting hammered. They suspect its full arrival here will coincide with the full moon and high tide. We need to prepare for flooding and other damage, especially in Whale Harbor and other shoreline communities. I asked everyone to be on call for the next forty-eight hours. I just hope we don't lose any houses to the sea."

In the short time Marcel stood outside, snow also accumulated on his salt-and-pepper crew cut. If he hadn't stood nine inches above her, she might have brushed off his hair, too, although at five feet eight inches herself, she probably could have.

"Houses falling off into the ocean? Really? The waves could get that high?" But it made sense. The tides were already ten feet or more on a normal, calm day, and the ocean was a mighty beast.

Raven continued. "I was at Wolf Marine today. Karl is ready to snowmobile to keep his First-in-Town title. His sled is out front."

"The green one or the black one?" Marcel loved snowmobiles and had just secured two Ski-Doos for the county sheriff's office, arguing they could assist the game wardens with search-and-rescue missions.

"The green one. The one that has that cougar's face on it with the teeth. Like a sabertooth tiger." She showed her own teeth and raised her fingers in a claw shape as if to pounce on him.

"Meow," Marcel pulled her close again for another kiss, his greying five o'clock shadow gently scraping against her cheek. Raven snuggled in. The distance that she felt between them in the fall seemed to be gone these past couple of months. It helped that she hadn't heard Shannon McGrath's name in weeks. Either Marcel wasn't working much with the new county district attorney, or he was keeping quiet about it. Regardless, she and Marcel seemed back to normal as a couple, relaxed and happy. She hoped she was right. As her mother always said, "Don't invite trouble in."

He released her as he said, "I saw a couple of folks carrying brush out of the trails, and Craig was hammering in the signs to follow, bringing the trail in and out of the woods."

"He and Karl just had a pow-wow at the store. Craig said he promised he'd be back here soon to finish his work."

Marcel nodded. "I'm sure he will. Eventually. You can't blame him for being excited to use the town trails, although I would think with the ground being frozen, it'd be hard to pound in those stakes. I did see one of those cement drills lying in the back of his truck. That should help."

Raven turned toward the house to go in. The cold wind had picked up. She dug her bare hands into her pockets. "The club was probably too disappointed with the lack of snow year after year to do the work earlier, I guess."

Marcel nodded in agreement. "I think everyone on the coast had given up on snow. Now, I wish we had a sled too."

Raven smiled. She had loved snowmobiling in town as a kid. Then she thought of the town's trail route. "What are they going to do to get around Riverview Farm this year?" she asked, turning back to him.

The farm was smack dab in the middle of the snowmobile trail network and an integral part of getting from Secretly to Eelsboro, and then further into the state, using the snowmobile trails groomed by other clubs. Technically, one could ride from Secretly to the Canadian Border, all on a snowmobile. Mr. Ellsworth, former owner of Riverview Farm, had been a member of the SnowTrack Snowmobile Club himself, but with his passing last year, his entire farm went to his granddaughter, Camille. She and her husband had moved up from Boston during the spring and started an alpaca farm. She refused to sign the community paperwork allowing the snowmobiles to cross her fields. She said the sleds would disturb her animals, and her husband, Jared, even wrote a letter to the editor, saying how selfish the club was asking to use their property, and asking to use it for free. The town's anger was real and visible. Small signs dotted lawns all summer with large red print saying "Go AWAY" and "Bring back Old Maine." Those were the nicer signs.

Marcel put his arm around her waist as they walked. Her trim frame fit well against his muscular body. "It's a struggle throughout Maine as land changes hands. I heard there were new negotiations with Camille, but I didn't ask for details or whether it resolved anything. Sometimes being the county sheriff is a drawback. I didn't want to learn what methods they were using to persuade her to sign."

Raven chuckled. She doubted that anyone would do bodily harm to Camille or her hoity-toity husband, Jared. Camille had grown up summers in Secretly, and, prior to this bump in the road, had been well-liked in town. Raven also believed Camille loved the area as much as she did, but Jared walked around in his shiny shoes and tight city jeans like he owned the town, making sure everyone knew he was named after his great-great-great-great-grandfather, Jared Sparks, Harvard President, blah, blah, blah. No one cared.

Marcel opened the door for them to enter the house, and the dogs ran in first. "I guess we'll all hear how it all plays out in a day or two if this snow really does arrive. If I were Camille, I'd play it safe and keep the llamas out of those back fields for a few days, just in case, signed paperwork or not."

Before Raven could correct him by saying "alpacas," Marcel's radio on his belt went off. Fist fight at Wolf Marine.

Chapter Three

Tom Pinkham, a sheriff deputy, arrived at Wolf Marine before Marcel or any other sheriffs. He careened into the small parking lot and hopped out of his SUV just as "Lunchbox" Lennie Putnam took a swing at Ethan "Johnny" Johnson, Raven's father. Johnny, a tall, thin man in his late 60s, blocked the punch and stepped aside, causing Lennie, a former classmate of Tom's, to trip forward and smash the side of his face on the pavement next to the unleaded gas pump. Tom heard Lennie cry out.

"Cool your jets there," said Johnny, acting cool himself as a retired Boston cop. A fist-throwing lobsterman wasn't the same threat as a gun-wielding gang member, Tom thought.

"Pay up or leave my premises!" Karl Wolf stood with his arms crossed in the doorway of his store.

Lennie, leaning in his fleece-lined flannel shirt, pulled himself up by grabbing onto the pump. A large red scrape showed on his right cheek with a few strands of blood starting to trickle down his jawline.

"Not until you take my name off your door, Karl." Lennie pointed toward the store entrance and took a step toward Karl. "It's a violation of my privacy!"

"It'll be public knowledge when I take you to court," Karl bellowed back.

"Stay where you are, Lennie," Tom said, approaching, touching his hand to his holster. "Please." He stood half a foot shorter than Lennie, half a foot or more shorter than most men, but he succeeded by using his calm demeanor and humor to defuse a situation.

"Tommy, this idiot says I owe him $30,000." Lennie wiped the blood away from his mouth.

Karl growled. "You do. You probably owe me more than that. I saw on my cameras you getting gas one day and not coming in to have it recorded. You probably owe me $50,000! Maybe $150,000!"

Tom put his hand up to signal Karl to stop. The goal was to diffuse the situation, not throw gasoline on it, so to speak. Karl either didn't see the signal or didn't care. He continued.

"It's hard to believe you could rack up that many bills and not even be lobstering anymore!" The last comment was a nail to hammer home Lennie's failure to pay for his boat, too. *Red Tail*, a thirty-six-foot wooden Downeast, was repossessed in the fall by a local bank.

It worked. Lennie's face turned purple. Tom could also hear the countdown to the explosion. He stepped between Karl and Lennie. Johnny moved to stand beside Tom.

Tom noticed movement to his left. Mikey Dyer stood in the parking lot to the side, next to Karl's Arctic Cat snowmobile. "Go home, Mikey," he yelled over to him. "You don't have a dog in this fight."

Clark Christensen's Dodge Ram pickup truck stopped in front of the pumps. He got out and walked towards the group. Safety in numbers, thought Tom. Unless Clark was on Lennie's side too, like Mikey would be, he assumed. The lobstering community stuck together. Also, Clark's name might be on Karl's posted list, and he'd have his own reason to be here and to be mad.

"What's this? A party and no invite for little ol' me?" Clark, not little at all with his broad shoulders from pulling his own lobster pots, grinned but soon changed to a serious face. "Looks like a bad time. I just came to give you this, Karl. I heard about the list, and I'm sorry for forgetting to pay earlier." He handed a sealed letter-sized envelope to Karl, who remained rooted on the stone step in front of his door, his burly arms still crossed.

Karl accepted the envelope gingerly. "No problem, Clark. Sorry too for being impatient." He swallowed and continued. "I'm sure you heard about the posted list, but you're not on it, Clark. Only those owing $5,000 or more." He glared at Lennie.

Tom couldn't believe Karl was naive enough to extend so much credit to folks, but it was only when one got burned that the ways of doing business changed.

Lennie's purple face shaded to deep red all the way to his blond roots. "You're going to regret this, Karl."

"Whatta ya say we go and get a soft drink over at Lane's Market?" Johnny said to Lennie. "My treat."

The light snow started to accumulate, and Tom saw panicked shoppers running into Lane's up at the next corner. The small local store had everything and, like with Wolf Marine, saved residents from having to drive further to shop. Tom always thought it was funny how a little snowflake could suddenly make everyone need bread, milk, and cereal. And probably beer. Definitely beer.

Karl started to speak, but Johnny had moved in front of him. Tom saw Johnny's elbow jab Karl in the thigh. Karl kept quiet.

"You look like a ginger ale kinda guy to me," said Johnny again. "How about takin' a walk with me. I sure know I could use one."

Between Clark's arrival and Johnny's light demeanor, the heat in the air dropped around them, and Lennie's color returned to normal. Tom saw Marcel walking up from Lane's toward Wolf Marine. How long had he been standing there, quietly acting as backup without causing the situation to escalate?

"You're right. I could use something to drink," said Lennie, putting a hand up to his cheek.

"Sounds good," said Johnny, "and we'll get some ice for that face." He smiled as he approached Lennie and gently touched him on the arm. Lennie spun around, glancing just once over his shoulder at Karl, and the two of them walked towards Lane's. Marcel nodded to them both as they passed. Johnny stuck his hand out to Marcel, who readily grabbed it with two hands and smiled. Tom knew Marcel's fondness for his father-in-law, a fondness that Raven herself hadn't yet adopted since Johnny's return to Secretly a couple of years ago. She was still mad at him for leaving her and her mother when she was around five years old, even if he did come back sober.

"She'll get there," Marcel always said, "or else." Tom had taken the "or else" as a joke when Marcel first said it, but now he wondered if Marcel was growing tired of Raven's stubbornness to let her father more into her life. Johnny was truly a great guy, but Tom also didn't have a history with him.

Tom turned back to Karl.

"Could there be a different way to collect your debts other than posting them publicly?" he asked.

Karl sighed. "Trust me. I've tried. It's January, and I've been trying since September. Emails, snail mail, texts, shutting off the credit line, putting reminder notes under windshield wipers when I saw them parked at Lane's, not allowing them to get gas, lines, etc., etc., etc." He threw his hands up in the air. "There are five who owe me over $5,000, and, yes, Lunchbox Lennie owes me the most. I know I will never see a dime from him unless I take him to small claims court. And even then, I doubt he'll pay me. Hard to pay a bill when you do not have a job."

Clark cleared his throat. "Again, Karl, I apologize for my tardiness in paying you."

Karl waved him off and finally let his shoulders relax, lowering his arms to his sides. "Clark, I truly don't worry about you paying your bills. Don't give it a second thought."

Tom studied Clark. He definitely was a handsome man, despite his crooked nose and gap in his front row of teeth from an accident on his boat. Were the rumor mills true? Was he really fooling around with Tom's sister, Rachel? And why was Clark months late on paying his bills anyway? Tom's eyes narrowed. Was Clark struggling financially? Did Rachel actually foot this bill? Was he using her?

Then Tom remembered Mikey on the sidelines and looked over towards the green-and-white snowmobile. No Mikey. Thankfully, he had listened, this time, and left, hopefully for home.

The snow came down more heavily as the day's light waned. Tom wasn't looking forward to driving in the dark, with the dizzying snow and the bevy of accidents bound to happen.

"Time to lock up, Karl, and get some rest if you're going to keep your streak as the first sledder in Secretly, out on the trails tomorrow." He tapped Karl on the arm.

"Is that a challenge, Tommy? You think your Polaris could do better?" Karl finally smiled.

"Not a challenge. And I'm on duty. The trails are all yours. By the way, did you guys reroute around Riverview Farm, or did that finally get settled?"

"We're in talks."

Tom shook his head. Sometimes people from away should stay away. "I don't know why the state doesn't make it a law to add the snowmobile trails to the deeds. You buy the land, and you're agreeing to let the sledders through, without worry of liability or insurance."

"Boy, wouldn't that be nice," said Karl. "In this case, I'm just waiting to hear if Craig picked up their signed paperwork today. Let's just say I refuse to re-route a century-old trail. And speak of the devil."

Just then, Craig Fisher's shiny burgundy-colored pickup truck, with "Carpentry by Craig" painted on the doors, pulled up next to the store. Karl walked over to the driver's side door as Craig rolled down his window.

"What? Another new truck?" he said, leaning in to talk to Craig. "Your last one wasn't even broken in."

Craig chuckled. "You know Stella. She won't ride in anything from last year."

Tom shook his head at that comment. Sometimes being single was definitely a blessing.

Clark waved a good-bye to Tom and lumbered off in his truck in the direction of Jane Eats, Rachel's diner. Of course, he could simply be going in the direction of Eelsboro too. Tom was just suspicious.

Chapter Four

Johnny knew how it felt to be down and out. Heck, he had hit bottom more times than he remembered, each time thinking it would be his last. If he could help a fellow down on his luck, he would. He always would.

He glanced over at Lunchbox Lennie as they stood staring at the cold beverage selection at Lane's Market. Lennie's cheek had stopped bleeding and was starting to turn from dark pink to dark purple. At least his breathing had slowed, and his hands had unclenched from their fist position.

If Lunchbox truly owned Karl that much money, he might be hungry, too.

"I didn't have lunch today," said Johnny, "so let's make sure we grab some sandwiches to go with our drink. Can't face a nor'easter on an empty stomach." He chuckled. Lennie didn't respond or look at Johnny.

Craig Fisher came up behind them. His black-and-red wool checkered coat was littered with small sticks and leaves. His face was ruddy. Not like Johnny's used to be from excessive drinking. More from working too much outside in the cold wind and sun. He looked older than his forty years, probably from the weather exposure or worrying about owning his own business.

"Excuse me, fellas. Mind if I squeeze past you two for an Arnold Palmer?"

The words roused Lennie out of his trance, and he stepped back. Craig reached forward to pull on the large glass door.

"You guys covered a lot of ground in a short amount of time," Johnny said to Craig, acknowledging the manpower needed to clean up the snowmobile trails. "I'm impressed. Especially pounding those stakes into the frozen ground."

Craig gave Johnny half of a smile.

"Work that we should have done in November. Four years ago. But hard to get volunteers to care about trails they can't use. We've been snow-deprived for so long."

"Yes, yes, I get it," Johnny answered Craig, but kept his eyes on Lennie. "Well, sounds like you'll be able to get the groomer revved up this time."

Craig shook his head to show he wasn't sure. "Too bad it's so old. Hope it starts. In fact, I'd better get back home to work on it pronto."

"I thought the State gave each snowmobile club an annual stipend. Wouldn't that also cover groomer repair?" Johnny thought of the SnowTrack clubhouse with its peeling paint and a storm door hanging on one hinge. The club obviously wasn't using it on cosmetic touches.

"The stipend is based on the volume of snow from the year before. Kinda like a reimbursement. We haven't spent any money in years because we've been barren. So, we haven't gotten any State money either. And on that note, I'd better get going. My queen, Stella, needs some crackers and ginger ale. She caught a bug at the hospital and hasn't held down any food in a couple of days. Hope I don't get it."

Johnny grinned and took three steps backwards away from Craig, throwing his hands up in surrender. "I don't want it either! I hope she feels better."

"Thanks! Oh, almost forgot. Gotta get a new bottle of Allen's Coffee Brandy. Wouldn't be snowmobile season without it!" Craig disappeared down the liquor aisle, an area Johnny avoided like the plague, literally.

Through the whole conversation with Craig, Johnny observed Lennie, who had stood motionless with his back against a display of cola and root beer cans.

Johnny studied his face—vacant, defeated. Lennie's eyes were open but closed off to the world. Pulling up his most positive voice, Johnny asked, "Did you decide what you'd like? Remember, my treat."

"Why are you being nice to me?" Were Lennie's eyes filled with tears?

"If the shoe were on the other foot, I bet you'd do the same for me. One of these days, it can be your treat, okay?" He touched Lennie's arm.

"Don't hold your breath." Lennie didn't look at Johnny but directed the emotionless comment to the space in front of him.

"Listen, I know we don't know each other," said Johnny in a low voice, pulling Lennie down the paper goods aisle and out of the traffic of the refrigerated goods. "But I know what it's like to think there's nowhere to go but further down a dark hole. I've lived down at the bottom of that hole more than once. If I can crawl back to the surface, so can you."

For the first time, Lennie turned toward Johnny and studied him.

"I mean it," Johnny continued, his voice growing thick as he now choked back tears. "I lost my family. I lost my job. I thought going away would cure me. It didn't. It wasn't until I took a step back and decided that I wanted a better life for myself that I finally moved forward. I don't know if you have the same demon at the bottom of a bottle that I had, or if it's something else, and you don't have to tell me if you do or if you don't. I just want you to know that whatever has caused this crack in your life, you have the power to repair it. Now, let's grab some soda and sandwiches and hit the road before it gets too bad out to drive."

Lennie didn't move. His gaze shifted to the floor, and then he raised his eyes back up to stare into Johnny's. He finally nodded, and they headed over to the pre-made food. Lennie picked out an Italian sub for lunch. Johnny threw cellophane-wrapped, store-made chocolate chip cookies into the basket, too, along with two bags of potato chips and some other staples that Johnny thought Lennie could eat later.

On their way to the registers, they passed Mikey Dyer in the canned soup aisle. His eyes were wild, synthetically induced, Johnny thought, the kind he had seen too many times, as a cop, on heavy drug users. Mikey's hair was matted from lack of bathing, and his coat, the heavy-duty type for working outside, had oil stains and rips. He ignored Johnny but gave Lennie a long look and a nod. Were they friends, Johnny wondered? Was Lennie involved in whatever had led him down the wrong trail? Mikey was definitely someone that Lennie shouldn't be around if he hoped to come out of his hole.

The line of customers for the store's only two registers snaked past the shelves of liquor bottles, into the bread aisle, and then circled back to produce. As Johnny and Lennie waited for their turn, barely inching a foot in fifteen minutes, Johnny made small talk with Lennie about the impending snow, planting tulip and daffodil bulbs last fall, and how he debated adopting a dog, but he needed to make sure that it got along with Dukie and Lily, Raven and Marcel's two adorable pooches. Lennie listened but didn't contribute to the conversation. He didn't even nod his head, but he did look Johnny in the eye. That was an improvement.

Finally out of topics, Johnny asked him, "How did you get the name 'Lunchbox'?"

The woman in front of them, with her arms full of frozen boxed pizzas, turned around to see who was behind her and then quickly turned back, her face reddening.

Lennie shifted from one foot to another and visibly swallowed before answering Johnny.

"When I was six," he said, "my mother left me and my dad and my baby sister. I'd go to school without lunch. My dad had his hands full with my little sister and didn't think to make me anything or ask the school to help. So I started helping myself to the kids' lunchboxes. First, it was just in the cafeteria, where we sat. I'd ask if they had anything they could share. I'd end up with an apple, or peanut butter and crackers, or sometimes, just the crust of a sandwich. I'd eat anything they didn't want."

Johnny's heart lurched in sympathy for this man's childhood.

Lennie continued. "Then I had the idea to raid the lunchboxes before lunch. I'd sneak into our coat room off the classroom. That way I could get a sandwich or a whole stack of cookies. Something I actually wanted to eat."

Johnny reached out and touched Lennie's arm. "And now these same people torture you by calling you that name."

"Nah, most of these people only know it as my nickname now. I think Tommy Pinkham is the only guy from my class from that year who I see regularly. He was as kind to me then as he is now. Never turned me in for stealing. In fact, if I didn't hit up his lunchbox, he'd offer me half of his sandwich. I think it was some bratty girl who cried because her favorite ham-and-cheese was missing. 'Made from the Easter ham,' I remember her saying. I can still see her braids bopping as she cried. It did get me on the school lunch program, though."

They finally were at the register and checked out, with Johnny paying for it all. Outside their parked pickup trucks, Lennie stood with a brown grocery bag containing enough food to last at least a week, the sub sandwich peeking out of the top.

"Thank you, Johnny, for this," he said, jostling the bag in his arms. "I won't forget this." His voice cracked. Maybe he had a cold. Maybe Johnny had made a lasting impact, or at least a small dent.

Johnny shook his head. "No need to thank me, Lennie. Just be good to yourself, and stay safe."

Johnny sat in his truck and watched Lennie drive off. Everyone had a story if you had the time to listen. "That's why God gives you two ears and one mouth," his grandmother used to say.

He had sugarcoated his own progress a bit, making it sound like he had the power to correct everything in his life, everything that he had ruined, but he didn't. He lived with regret. He had never made amends with Julia, the best wife anyone could have asked for, and he still had a long way to go with his little girl, who wasn't that little anymore. Raven was softening, he told himself. If icebergs had the ability to break apart, so did her frosty heart.

Chapter Five

Betty smoothed her hand over the soft yarn of the pink mittens and turned the price tag over. Fifty dollars! Who was buying these around here? Maybe in the summer when the town was flooded with people from away, passing through on their way to the beach at Whale Harbor, but no townie would pay that price, not even her, with her Connecticut retirement dollars.

She chuckled at that last thought. Actually, the retirement dollars really belonged to Howard, her husband, for his decades of service at a boring insurance company in a boring actuarial job, although he always claimed it was interesting. She doubted that. It sounded boring to her. After over forty years of marriage, his retirement money was hers anyway, especially since he never spent a dime of it himself.

But fifty dollars? That was outrageous, even for her.

"Finding anything you like?" said Camille Sparks, the proprietor and alpaca farmer. She was a slim woman with the kind of high cheekbones Betty always longed for. Her wispy blonde hair was casually tossed back in a clip. Her skin was smooth and flawless. But what thirty-something didn't have great skin? Betty touched a hand to her own sixty-eight-year-old cheek, feeling the roughness of aging and the lack of regular facials since moving to Maine. She used to miss all that pampering when they had first moved up, but had now grown accustomed to the ease of life in Secretly.

"Oh, I do love these, but my husband would kill me for paying that much." Howard would never know, but Betty felt a tinge of guilt. She was getting soft in her old age.

"They're handmade with alpaca wool. Light but super warm, and if they get wet, they dry quickly." Camille took the pair off the hook on the rack. "Next year, we'll have our own wool, and we'll be able to lower the prices here. Plus, I'm looking for local knitters. Do you knit?"

Betty did, but not at the level to ever sell any of her misshapen pieces.

"I'm more of a crochet artist," she said, fibbing.

Camille smiled, showing beautiful, ultra-white, straight teeth, the kind that could glow in the dark if the lights were dimmed. Too much home-bleaching, Betty knew. She had been there herself years ago.

Camille continued. "Crocheted items are my favorite! Can I sign you up as a "co-producer"?"

"Co-producer?" Betty's eyebrows scrunched together.

"That's my term for the team who will partner with me. My plan is to have the name of the knitter, or crochet artist," Camille winked, "on the tag. I believe people should get credit, don't you?"

"Oh, most definitely." Betty smiled, picturing her name on a mitten tag, and then people in Lane's Market, commenting to her about how much they admired her work.

"So, can I sign you up?" Camille's smile broadened as she stepped closer.

"Actually, I'm kinda in a latch hook rug phase, at the moment. Maybe down the road. Thanks for the offer, though. I'm definitely interested."

"Ok, just so you know, when you do join, you'll be in good company. Marie Claire, from the library, has already signed up as my first one."

Betty bit her tongue. Of course, Marie Claire was already a part of this. How much activity did a one-hundred-and-twenty-year-old woman need? She didn't know why she felt such jealousy or competition with Marie Claire, other than the fact that she wanted that town librarian job and was chomping at the bit for Marie Claire to retire. To keep her cool, Betty looked out the window and watched the snow fall. Deep breath in. Deep breath out.

A door marked "Private" opened from the other side of the shop, and a man dressed for an Alaskan Iditarod race stepped in, his cheeks red. A few clumps of snow fell to the ground around his boots.

"Camille, can I see you for a moment?" he said, motioning with his head toward the door he had just used.

She excused herself from Betty and went over to the overly dressed man whom Betty recognized from town as Jared Sparks, Camille's husband. She had thought of him as wildly handsome and sophisticated when they first moved up, like a *GQ* model.

"You took down all the 'no trespassing' signs in the field, I see, without telling me." His voice was a hiss. If he didn't look like an overstuffed turtle, Betty would have thought of him as a snake.

"You know we agreed to let the snowmobiles ride through the property," she said, lowering her voice.

Betty was grateful the store was tiny. Even a whisper could be heard. She picked up a pair of light blue baby booties to pretend to study them while she eavesdropped.

"You mean, you agreed. I didn't." His anger floated up to the exposed brown-stained rafters and spread across the quaint shop.

"Jared, I want us to fit in." Camille's voice took on a pleading quality.

His volume increased. "You mean, you want to fit in. I don't care a lick about what anyone in this cow town thinks of me."

"Says the man who raises alpacas," Camille countered.

Jared spoke even louder. "Again, your idea, your problem! You know what I think of this whole matter!"

"Shhh." Camille's voice quivered.

Out of the corner of her eye, Betty saw Camille look over her shoulder in Betty's direction. Betty held the booties up to her eye to study the stitching.

Camille continued in a staged whisper. "You agreed to sell JavaTime and move here. Don't deny it." Now it was time for Camille to hiss.

Betty couldn't believe her luck. This was better than an old soap opera. She didn't dare look their way, but she pictured their faces becoming redder and redder, their noses an inch apart.

"Don't change the subject," Jared spat back. "Did you sign the paperwork with that snowmobile club, or not? Did they agree to our speed limit? Did they agree to stay on marked trails? Did they agree to avoid the pasture that runs alongside the barn? Did they agree to no snowmobiling between the hours of 10:00 p.m. and 6:00 a.m.?" He ran out of breath.

Gosh, Betty grew increasingly grateful she lived with Howard. He might be dull or boorish at times, but he wasn't bossy. Poor Camille. No wonder she was starting a co-producing group. She needed friends.

Camille sighed. "Yes, yes, they agreed to everything. I talked to Craig Fisher, the treasurer of the club, myself. I just haven't signed an agreement with them yet. He's supposed to get the paperwork to me. With this storm coming, it was a make-or-break decision that they needed for today, okay?"

"No, not okay. You shouldn't have taken the signs down yet, and you should have told me that you decided to cave in. Just because your grandfather let them walk all over him doesn't mean we have to roll over and play dead."

Betty heard Camille's intake of air. She pictured nostrils flaring while Camille spoke, like a bull in a ring, preparing to charge. Go, Camille, go.

"My grandfather did not roll over! He was a happily active member of both the snowmobile club and the town. Something you might consider doing if you want to fit in here."

"Fit in? Why do you keep saying that? Why would I want to fit in with a bunch of rednecks?"

Rednecks? Betty adjusted her turtleneck. Besides not being a redneck herself, whatever that definition was, what was wrong with being a redneck, anyway?

"You know, Jared, I'm beginning to wonder if you belong up here. I'm beginning to wonder if I belong with…" Camille stopped talking.

Then there was silence. Long silence. Betty almost spun around to see if they had both left. Then she heard Jared's snarl.

"Don't. You. Dare. And. Don't. You. Ever. Say. That. Again. To. Me."

Betty sensed that if she turned now, she'd see Jared holding onto Camille's wrist and spitting the words into her face. Maybe even throttling her around the throat. She needed to help Camille, as a fellow woman.

"I'll take these," Betty said, speaking louder than she needed to and bringing the baby booties up to the counter. She didn't know what she'd do with forty-dollar baby booties, and she wished the mittens were still in her hand instead, but she didn't want to cross the store to grab them from the rack.

Jared, still tightly zipped up in his parka, with only his flashing eyes showing, stepped back from Camille. Camille whipped around to the other side of the counter and pulled out her order pad. Betty could see Camille struggling to regain her composure and keep the tears from spilling over.

"Looks like the snow has started," said Betty, pretending not to notice Camille. "I wonder if we'll get that blizzard they keep warning us about."

Camille didn't respond. Her hand shook as she wrote down the baby booties' number and description.

Betty prattled on. "And here I am casually shopping, and you might need to close up and run for supplies for yourselves or the llamas."

"Alpacas!"

Betty jumped. The sharp voice, correcting her, came out of the ugly man along the side. Jared was physically quite handsome, but Betty would no longer think him so. He was an ugly, mean man.

She swallowed and played along, partly to allow Camille time to recover.

"Oh, yes, alpacas. That's what I meant. I'm so sorry. Do they spit like llamas do?"

Without answering, Jared stepped back through the door marked 'Private' and slammed it shut. Both Betty and Camille leaped at the loud noise.

"Oh, my! Drafty in here," said Betty.

Camille nodded, without looking up.

Chapter Six

Dukie barked at the bang.

Raven moved aside the curtain and peered out the bedroom window, with Dukie by her side. They both watched Emil Bryant's backup lights. The heavy plow in front of his truck must have hit one of her wooden cabin signs, pointing the way to the office and the various cabins. They stood only about three feet above the snow and were buried beneath it. That was how much snow fell last night. Four inches an hour, Marcel said as he headed out the door around three in the morning to check on the region and his deputies, not that he had slept at all, keeping track of events via his laptop and radio, making their home act like Command Central.

Now, at seven o'clock in the morning, extra-large flakes floated down. Her grandfather, who had built Pine Acres, always said to watch for the large flakes as a signal that the storm was coming to a close. Someone forgot to tell Mother Nature that. The large flakes had been coming down for at least an hour.

With the driveway plowed, she could get out if she needed. Not that she had anywhere to go. She'd stay put and wait for Marcel to come home.

She ruffled the soft curls on Dukie's head.

"Might as well get started on my to-do list." Marcel would be gone all day, and her list was long.

She had already taken Lily and Dukie out for the morning bathroom break and fed them. The snow was too deep for any walk until she had time to shovel a longer path. Lily now snoozed in front of the warm wood stove, disinterested in the thought of venturing out again.

Dukie's eyes pleaded with her to include him in any plan she had. His hair didn't fly around as Lily's fur did. She decided to chance bringing him with her to the first cabin's painting project.

She gathered the newly acquired Ocean Blue paint can and brushes of various sizes she had already brought up from the cellar, and grabbed a large roll of paper towels. She didn't need a key to the cabin. She didn't lock them any more than she and Marcel locked their own home.

"We'll be back, Lil," Raven said to the snoring lab. Lily gave a snort back.

Outside, Dukie followed behind Raven, stepping into her boot prints. They crossed the back field, passing the smaller cabins, each named for a different tree—Balsam, Fir, Spruce, and Hemlock. Ironically, though, not all the cabins were named after evergreens. The largest and oldest cabin, the one her mother moved into when Marcel and she got married and took over the main house with the business, was known as Birch. That's where she and Dukie were headed.

After her mother died, she cleaned out anything personal from the cabin, refreshed all the linens, and added touches found in the other cabins, like buffalo-plaid throws and framed old maps of Maine. It was finally time to fully change the cabin. The Oceanic Blue was for the bathroom.

She used her boot to kick off the accumulation from the bottom step of Birch's entrance. Stamping the snow off her feet, she opened the door. Dukie, with clumps of snow clinging to the backs of his legs, rushed in to get off the frozen tundra.

The cabin was chilly, of course. She drained the pipes every year after New Year's and usually didn't rent until May, but this year she thought she'd see if there was an appetite for Valentine's Day weekend since that made-up holiday was on a Saturday, and indeed, she had five cabins rented, including Birch.

She turned on the gas fireplace to warm the space. She hadn't considered how cold it would be in the cabin, probably too cold for painting. Maybe that was another reason for Craig's delays in working on the cabins. She should have brought a small thermometer to make sure the cabin warmed to at least fifty degrees, and maybe an electric heater to push that temperature up. Well, she'd just have to trudge back out to get both.

But first, she sat in an overstuffed twill armchair facing the fireplace to let Dukie warm up before they headed back to the house. He gratefully settled by her feet with his paws stretched out towards the flickering gas flames, pulling the balls of ice from his legs. She had never spent much time in this or any of the cabins. Just to clean them and change the sheets and towels. Even Birch, despite her mother living in it for years, she hadn't visited. Her mother always came over to the main house to see them. Too bad she and her mother hadn't spent some quiet moments in the cabin. Maybe she could have learned different stories about her father as her mother mellowed and grew softer towards the past, stories that could help her move forward, accept Johnny into her life, and forgive him for moving away when she was a child.

Raven looked around the expansive room. She could see what the guests said about it in the reviews—the Maine "chicness" of it, with its rustic yet comfortable style. The fireplace was fieldstone, built from the rocks uncovered when the cabin was first built over eighty years ago. She had converted all the fireplaces to propane when she took over the business, allowing the renters to turn them on with a flick of a switch. No sense having a guest burn the place down by starting a fire with wood, and then leaving it unattended.

She studied the fireplace, letting her eyes trace every stone, row by row, from top to bottom, appreciating the layers in some and the sparkling flecks of mica and quartz in others. The hearth was high, perfect height for sitting on the slate top. More stones were around the base of the hearth.

"That's funny," she said, rising to examine a stone that seemed to be sticking out more than the others. When she touched it, it moved.

"Oh, dear, this is a hazard." Her mind flashed to the rock rolling into the middle of the floor, and a guest tripping over it and suing her. Or worse, the fireplace itself becomes unstable and crashes down into the room. She'd have Craig look at it the next time he came, or even Marcel after the blizzard rush was over.

When she touched the stone again, it was actually stuck in tighter than she imagined, but it still jiggled slightly. Her fingers were too small to get a good grasp of it to see if she could actually pull it out. She'd need large pliers or some kind of clamp, something she'd bring back with the heater and thermometer.

Her cell phone rang. Betty.

"Hey there. How are you guys doing? You guys make out okay?" Raven said into the phone.

Betty ignored the question. Her voice was elevated with excitement. "Wanna pick me up and walk the dogs over at Baxter Preserve?"

Raven puzzled at the urgency to walk the dogs as the blizzard wound down.

"Sure, maybe later," she said, hoping not to disappoint Betty too much. The snow was much too deep for the poochies. Betty should know that.

"May I suggest now, and you can't see me, but I'm making 'air quotes' around 'walk the dogs.' I know it's too much for them. I'm thinking just you and me, maybe on snowshoes."

Raven still didn't understand why Betty wanted to go right now, but there had to be a reason.

"And the purpose of going right now is…?"

"I saw a photo online, taken from across the river. A snowmobile was left in the backfield of Riverview Farm. Jared must be having a fit. He was so mad at Camille yesterday in the store for letting the trail pass through. To have one croak out back there must have him purple in the face. I'm just being nosey. I'm dying to see the drama unfold. I hope we get to it before he does."

The lightbulb went off for Raven. "And Baxter Preserve runs along the Baxter River, and from a couple of spots, you can see across the river and look onto the back fields of Riverview Farm."

"Bingo. I'd go alone, but we're not plowed out yet, and anyway, Howard would have a fit if I said I was going out alone. But if you call me and ask me to go, well, it'll look legit."

"I'm surprised you're not whispering into the phone," Raven said with a chuckle.

"I'm in the attic, and Howard is in the cellar on his radios. He's quite disappointed that the storm wasn't worse. He was hoping to help with emergency transmissions."

Raven checked the time on the phone. Only seven thirty in the morning. Even with the gas fireplace on, it still felt too cold to paint in the cabin, and Marcel wouldn't be home for hours. So, why not?

"Okay, I'll come get you in fifteen minutes. I have to clean my car off."

"I'll be ready!" Betty sang into the phone and hung up.

Chapter Seven

Finally, a snowstorm that lived up to its prediction, Tom thought, as he maneuvered his SUV around Secretly and on the curvy roads of Whale Harbor. Thankfully, most residents of Barrett County had heeded the warnings to stay home at night, allowing those who had to drive, like medical folks and himself, to travel without dodging those trying to get a good photo of the high tide crashing against the rocks.

And boy, did the tide come in. He and Roger Stanton, one of the new recruits, helped to evacuate a young mother and her two-year-old son from a one-hundred-year-old fishing shack-turned-home as the pier it was attached to disappeared into the icy surf, taking the shack with it.

"Pooh Bear!" cried out the little boy in his mother's arms. "I want my Pooh."

As the small family sat in the back seat of his vehicle, wrapped in blankets, waiting for someone to pick them up, Tom pulled out his cell and pulled up an online store.

"Is this your Pooh?" Tom turned around and showed the little boy the screen.

"Yes! My Pooh. My Pooh."

Tom got permission from the mother to purchase and send the yellow-stuffed bear to her parents' house. He selected next-day delivery, assuming "overnight" wouldn't work anyway in the aftermath of the blizzard.

"That's so nice of you," said the young mother, wiping her eyes. "I'll pay you back."

"No, no. My treat. I loved my Pooh too," said Tom, grinning at the young man. "Having a Pooh Bear is very important."

"Pooh!" said the boy in return and clapped his hands.

Besides the tremendous loss of that home, there were very few other incidents considering the seventy-mile-per-hour wind and rapid snowfall. Other than a couple of cars stuck before the plows came through, and a pickup truck in a ditch, it was a quiet night. At daybreak, Tom headed to Eelsboro to help direct traffic because the traffic lights were nonfunctional. Driving up the peninsula from Whale Harbor through Secretly, he passed Lane's Market. Christopher Lane, the owner, was shoveling the front steps, the American flag waving in the breeze from its holder on the side of the store, beckoning to shoppers.

Tom slowed and lowered his passenger window to yell a hello to Chris.

Chris, a robust man in his forties, stopped shoveling and came over to the vehicle.

"What's the good word, Tommy?" Chris's cheeks were red and swollen. Tom hoped they were red from the wind and not from exertion.

"All's well. You got up and running fast this morning."

Chris shrugged. Tom got it—it's just what one did.

"Coffee brewing?" Tom asked.

"Coffee's hot and steaming. Let me grab you a cup."

Chris returned quickly with a large paper cup with a lid. Tom leaned over to hand him a few bills, but Chris waved them off.

"On the house. Stay alert. Thanks for all you do," said Chris.

"Appreciate it. I'll catch you later, Chris. Off to the next thing."

Chris nodded and waved, picking up his shovel.

Tom took a sip from the plastic lid. Steaming hot was right. And black. Oh, well, he should have said "light and sweet" as he did through a drive-thru, but it would keep him warm and awake. From Lane's, Tom saw Wolf Marine. Karl's green Arctic Cat snowmobile wasn't in the yard anymore. He hoped Karl had kept his "first on the trails" town record and had fun riding the trails last night.

Approaching the store in his vehicle, Tom slowed and noticed the front door didn't look right. Neither the driveway nor the pumps were plowed out yet. He pulled the SUV over to the other side of the road and put on his flashers. Crossing the street, he stepped over the snow bank and sank into two and a half feet of fresh powder, the snow flowing over the top of his boots and down to his socks.

He didn't notice his shiver because the store's door held his attention. The reason it looked strange was that there was no door. Wolf Marine was wide open.

He radioed into his shoulder about the break-in, if it was a break-in. Maybe the wind blew the door open, or a deer ran through the glass. That happened once at a nail salon in Eelsboro as his mother was getting her toes done. The deer crashed through the picture window, jumping over a woman having her eyebrows waxed, and ran through the shop. A smart-thinking client, coming out of the ladies' room, opened the side door for it to run back outside. Hard to believe the deer didn't break its neck or leg or lose too much blood from the impact, but no dead deer had been found nearby. He doubted, however, that a deer had turned the knob of the marine store door.

He approached the doorway and saw that the door was intact but open, hanging on its hinges, with snow billowing onto the floor. No footprints or any animal prints were visible. He debated waiting for Roger to respond before entering, just as Marcel drove up.

"I heard your call as I was crossing from the other side of the peninsula," he said, getting out of his Jeep. His eyes had bags under them from lack of sleep.

"Like old times, boss, just you and me," Tom smiled as he pulled his gun out of his holster. "I don't see any prints, but I'd feel a whole lot better going in prepared."

Marcel nodded and did the same.

Tom poked his head into the store. It was a mess. Okay, so it always was a mess, but even by Karl's standards, it was a mess. Displays were knocked over; the orange cold-water survival suits were off their hangers and tossed around; and the dusty, outdated postcards littered the floor, stuck to the wood by the wet snow.

"Wow," said Tom, taking a step into the store. "The door must have blown open, and the wind had a field day."

Marcel followed him in and walked slowly to the back of the store.

"Paint cans still upright," he reported, "though the charts are scattered and some things were blown off the walls. I can see empty hooks."

Tom walked toward the counter. Karl still used an old-fashioned cash register. Its drawer was open and empty, but Tom assumed Karl left it that way every night. It only made sense to bring the cash home with him. Why chance leaving it in the store just in case someone got a bad idea?

He walked behind the counter and noticed that all the drawers from the small desk had been pulled out, and their contents were dumped on the floor. No wind would have done that. Was the store really burglarized in the middle of the blizzard? If so, why didn't the thief steal the expensive floating survival suits worth four hundred dollars each?

Tom's radio went off, and its signal echoed with Marcel's on the other side of the shop.

"Come in, please," said a dispatch operator. Tom recognized her voice.

"Pinkham, here, Arly. Whatcha got?" Tom responded.

"Hi, Tom. Riverview Farm in Secretly called in about an abandoned snowmobile in their back field," she said. "And, boy, is he mad."

Tom shook his head and smiled as Marcel approached him. They knew this would happen. He responded to Arly.

"Thank you. I'm on my way. I'm just a couple of miles from the farm." Better to go up for a few minutes to calm down the Sparks.

Marcel leaned over the counter, his eyes growing large at the sight of the jungle of loose papers, pens, and anything else tossed out of the drawers that now lay strewn across the floor.

"Someone was looking for something specific," he said.

"Like someone looking for the receipts of what he owed? You think it could be Lennie?" Tom leaned down and picked up an open spiral notebook with his gloved hand. It had paper fragments in the coil from where pages had been torn out. Only Karl would know whether it had been like that, or if someone else had ripped out the pages listing the debts.

Marcel shrugged. "At this point, anything is possible. You'd better get over to Riverview Farm before Jared loses his cool."

"Worse than he already does, you mean." Tom moved around the counter and headed for the door.

Marcel chuckled. "Exactly. I'll give Karl a call and ask him to come down. Maybe he'll be able to see what else is amiss."

Tom paused as Marcel pulled his cell out and dialed Karl. He could hear the call ringing. It rang and rang, and then went to voicemail. Marcel disconnected the call without leaving a message.

"Must still be out there ripping up the trails," said Tom. "Lucky duck."

Chapter Eight

Tom pulled into Riverview Farm's driveway and parked out of the way of the barn and the house. Thankfully, the entire parking area for the farm and shop was plowed out. Jared Sparks was outside, bundled up like a sailor on a 1800s Antarctica expedition. He only grew up three hours south in Massachusetts, but he was obviously one of those who assumed Maine winters were brutal beyond compare. Frankly, along the coast, Maine was warmer in the winter than inland Massachusetts.

"It's about time," Jared said before Tom had even shut his vehicle's door. Tom couldn't see Jared's mouth with a black scarf wrapped around it, but he assumed Jared's lips were in a tight snarl to match the flash of anger in his eyes.

How to win friends and influence people. Tom took a deep breath. Maybe he should order that book and have it anonymously delivered to the farm with Jared's name on it. He took another deep breath.

"How are you?" asked Tom, choosing his words carefully.

"I'm disgusted. That's how I am." Jared's red cheeks, peaking out above the scarf, got redder, if that was possible. "My wife foolishly let that stupid snowmobile club ride through our fields. Against my advice! And now we have one left, broken down, in the back field. So inconsiderate! We will need to use that field, you know." He caught his breath. "Maybe not today, but soon. But I'm afraid if the owner just lets it sit and rot back there and then chooses to get it when the animals are out, well, we could lose our investment."

"Your investment?" Tom knew that Camille had inherited the farm.

"In the alpacas!" Jared snapped. Tom wondered if Jared had treated Boston cops like he treated Maine sheriffs. No respect. No manners. No brains.

Camille came out of the house in a puffy white coat, pulling on a white wool hat as she walked. She looked like a sleek polar bear.

"Tom, hi. Thanks for coming. Sorry to bother you. I'm sure you have more pressing issues than a dead snowmobile. Honestly, it's nothing we need to handle today. Truly." She smiled as she zipped the coat up to her chin.

Jared gave her a look Tom knew all too well from his domestic-dispute calls. An anger management class might work wonders. Tom wasn't about to leave now without at least looking at the sled. He might be able to find out who it belonged to and help remove it, just to keep the peace between Jared and Camille.

"No trouble, Camille. Let me take a look at it. Which way to the field?"

Camille brought him over to a gate and opened it to let him in. Jared marched over to a fence to watch, probably to see if Tom really did go all the way down to the sled.

"Sorry for the manure," Camille said. "I know you can't see it, but you'll know when you step on it." She giggled, creating laugh lines around her blue eyes.

She really seemed reasonable, Tom thought. And gosh darn it all, she definitely was cute, sparkling, actually. What she saw in that loser of a guy, he'd never understand, but she wouldn't be the first nice person mixed up with an idiot.

Tom made his way through the snow-covered poop minefield outside of the barn, ducked under the top rung of the next wooden fence, and stepped into the back field. From his stance on top of the hill, he spied the sled, mainly the windshield and handlebars, due to the drifting snow, all the way down the long hill and across the field. Of course, it was at the bottom of the hill near the river bed, and he had about three feet of snow to slog through to reach it. At least whoever had ridden it had obeyed the club rules to stay low across someone's property.

The sled was well placed on an approved trail. From Tom's viewpoint,

Jared should cool his jets. Folks may not have run their snowmobiles for years, and unfortunately, this poor sucker's luck ran out on this back field. Probably had to walk miles back to a main road and flag down a passing truck. Maybe the snow was too deep, and the runners got stuck. Maybe it was old, bad gas in the line, or not enough two-stroke oil. Definitely not someone who maliciously planted a dead sled to annoy Jared. That seemed like something that Jared would do, however.

From where he stood, he also saw movement across the river among the trees. Along the banks, in the preserve, two people were trudging through the snow. Probably two snowshoers happy to have plenty of powder to use. They waved to him, and he waved back.

Tom wished he too had snowshoes on. The depth of the snow made the walk slow, despite his thirty-seven years, and considering himself in excellent shape, he paused a couple of times to catch his breath. He descended across the field at an angle to avoid having to go under another fence. Near it, on a post, a barbed wire fell slack against the wood. As he chose his footing, he noticed a long red scarf in the snow to the side of the sled. The wind must have blown it onto the property. No one on any snowmobile would ever wear a scarf.

Getting closer to the bottom of the field, he saw the front of the sled, an Arctic Cat, the same kind Karl had at the store. The top of the sabertooth lion peeked on the side. It probably was Karl's. Too bad. What a hike out of here. At least Tom knew that Karl was good for coming back for it. Probably hadn't run it enough, since it had been dormant for years. That was the problem with not getting snow. He was probably still asleep after that long walk home. No wonder he hadn't answered Marcel's phone call.

Tom looked up again across the field toward the preserve on the other side of the river. The two people he had seen earlier were standing on the river's edge, again waving to him. He heard his name called out.

He walked around the front of the sled and toward the river to get a better look at the people.

"Tom, hi!" said the shorter, plump figure. He squinted in the sunlight that had finally peeped out from behind the white, puffy clouds. Darn it all, he had left his sunglasses in the SUV. He raised a hand to shield his eyes, and the two faces came into focus. Betty and Raven. What were they doing here?

"Tom, hi!" Betty said again. "We're just being nosey." She laughed and then yelled across the river, answering his silent question. "We heard about the dead sled. I was hoping for fireworks from Jared." She laughed again. "Isn't that terrible of me?"

Tom shouted back. "Just go up to the farm. He's stewing up there like canned tomatoes in a hot water bath."

"More like ptomaine-poisoned ones exploding all over a ceiling when opened, I'd imagine," Betty shouted back.

"Whose sled?" asked Raven.

"I think this is Karl's." Tom's throat was getting dry from yelling. "Must have died as he rode through last night."

"Does that count for his town record?" Betty asked.

Tom grinned as Raven shook her head. He knew her head shake wasn't meant to deny Karl's record, but to tell Tom that Betty was in true Betty form. He guessed this trek into the woods was Betty's idea.

"What's all that red stuff?" Raven pointed behind Tom.

"I think it's a scarf," said Tom, not turning around to look at it.

"That's an awfully long scarf," said Betty.

Tom shrugged. He was cold, his feet were wet, and he had just started the second half of his day. He had no interest in talking about winter accessories with Betty. "Talk to you ladies later. I have to go back up to the farm and report back to the Sparks."

But he didn't make it back up the hill. When he finally turned around, he realized that Betty was right to question the scarf. The red scarf was not a scarf at all, but an incredibly large amount of blood mixed into the snow.

Chapter Nine

Raven realized she was looking at blood at the same moment Tom did. The red mass was behind the sled, and Karl must be lying in the snow, terribly hurt, if he could even survive that much blood loss. She saw Tom radio for assistance and pull out his cell, and she too pulled out her phone and called Marcel. Just habit.

One ring. Two. Three. Four. He didn't pick up. Of course, he's probably talking to Tom or dealing with something else. He was busy. She should know that.

Maybe Tom could use some assistance. She scanned the river. A few feet downstream, a fallen tree from the other side almost reached across like a bridge she could traverse. If she could find another trunk, small enough for her to drag, she could cross over to help Tom with Karl.

Betty stood watching Tom and then turned to Raven. "Want to go back and grab a bite at Jane Eats if they're open?"

Raven barely heard the question. She scampered in her snowshoes the best she could along the bank and realized that between the branches of the fallen tree and the frigid temperature that froze the water at the edge of the river, she could crawl across to the other side without adding another piece of tree. Raven removed her snowshoes and tossed them aside with her poles.

"Wait. Where are you going?" Betty yelled to Raven as she got on her knees and maneuvered herself onto the largest branches.

Raven knew the river wasn't deep, so it wasn't a matter of going under if she fell off the tree and through any ice, but she didn't want to get wet and end up with hypothermia before she could get home if the middle of the river wasn't frozen thick enough.

Betty yelled to her again. "Wait. Why are you going over there? Wait for me!"

The deep snow, even with snowshoes, slowed Betty's progress toward the downed tree. Raven was almost on the other side of the river when Betty reached the impromptu bridge.

"Wait. I'm coming with you," Betty said, searching for the best way to get on the tree, her snowshoes still attached.

Raven anticipated the scene with Karl's injury to be bad, really bad, if he had lost that much blood. She would be no help to Tom if she had to take care of Betty.

"Stay over there. Please. I'll be right back. I promise," she said, finally reaching the other bank and straightening up. Darn it. She should have brought her snowshoes. Too late.

Betty wasn't convinced staying put was the best idea. "What's happening over there? I thought it was just a snowmobile that stopped working?"

"That's probably all it is. I'll be right back." If there had been a path, Raven could have sprinted away from Betty's litany of questions, but the going was slow as her legs sank to her knees with each step she took, and Betty's inquiring voice echoed behind her. To save time and energy, Raven didn't turn around to answer any more of Betty's concerns.

She lost sight of Tom and the snowmobile as she walked along the tree growth. She stayed close to the tree line, since the snow was less deep there than out in the open. There didn't seem to be a fence to worry about. Either the alpacas didn't cross rivers, or Jared and Camille had been making a mountain out of a molehill about the snowmobile club using a back field that they didn't even use.

She no sooner had that thought when she almost snagged her jacket on barbed wire. New, shiny metal coils were wrapped around a tree trunk, the wire running on the other side, stretching into the field and toward the farm. She saw that someone else's jacket fibers were already caught by one of the barbs. She was surprised the Sparks would use barbed wire, knowing they wanted to harvest the alpacas' wool and spin it into yarn.

She dared to glance over her shoulder, across the river. Betty had walked back to the open spot where they had shouted across and was straining to watch Tom. At least that was what Raven assumed since she couldn't yet see Tom or the bloody patch of snow.

She squished through a forested area with young tree growth to avoid the wire and crossed into the open field, wading through the deep snow to stand in the wider tracks that the snowmobile had made. Her eyes followed the snowmobile tracks behind her through the rest of the field. She saw where the sled had popped out of the break in the woods. Raven squinted in the sunlight and in the glare from the snow and turned back towards Tom and the Arctic Cat. He was standing over a dark mound at the back of the sled. His face looked paler than the white snow. Maybe because the snow surrounding part of the mound was as red as a cooked lobster. He didn't seem to notice her.

She looked down to catch her breath and steady her footing as she ventured toward Tom and what must be Karl's battered body. Right in front of her was a large rock, nestled in a snowdrift. Maybe that is what Karl hit, and it tossed him off the sled, but no, as she got closer, she saw that it wasn't a rock. She studied the dark, round object and ventured another step forward, just to be sure. It too had red snow around it. As she edged nearer, the rock morphed into what it really was—a snowmobile helmet.

Chapter Ten

Tom heard Raven cry out before he saw her. She was standing next to another red section of snow.

"Don't come any closer," he said, raising his gloved hand in a stop. He didn't have to worry. She collapsed into the snow and was crawling on her knees away from him and bloody snow, using the snowmobile tracks as best as she could, still sinking in spots, but gaining traction. In other circumstances, he'd check on her, but he didn't want to disturb the crime scene anymore than he already had, simply by arriving at it.

And yes, it was a crime scene. Well, it could have been an accident, of course. There was always that. But, however it happened, Karl Wolf was dead, and it wasn't from natural causes.

At least Tom assumed it was Karl. The body didn't have a head.

No head.

Based on Raven's reaction, he assumed she had found it. He had already called Marcel, who said he had never reached Karl but would try again; a state forensics team; and the medical examiner. They were all on their way. He should warn the Sparks about the others coming. And to stay where they were.

He glanced up at the farm. The Sparks hadn't wanted sleds to come through their fields in the first place, yet Karl said that was solved. Was it?

"What's happening over there? Where's Raven?" Betty called from across the river.

"She'll be coming back your way soon enough. Stay over on that side," yelled back Tom. He needed Betty to stay where she was. He saw Raven retching on all fours, too hidden by the snow banks for Betty to see. "She'll be back soon. She's on her way."

As soon as she finished losing her breakfast, he thought.

He felt like throwing up, too, but he forced himself to hold his composure, knowing Betty was watching. When he first saw the body, he thought the head had snapped back and was buried under the snow, but as he stepped closer, even with the crazy amount of blood around the shoulders, he realized the head was missing. No head. He had to repeat it again to himself. No head.

He had struggled to operate his phone, even to pull it out of his pocket, with his fingers shaking, to call Marcel and the others. Tom had handled dozens of bloody accidents, from smashed cars to accidental shootings to a few real murders, but everybody he had seen, including the guy who was loading his replica Revolutionary War musket with loose gunpowder, all had their heads.

He also, obviously, didn't know everyone in the county, but whenever he did run across someone he knew, he felt his stomach lurch. The guttural reaction was a good thing, he thought. It kept him human.

But now, in front of him, was someone he knew. Someone he really knew well. Someone he had just talked to yesterday. Someone he considered a friend.

In front of him, in a large patch of red snow, was Karl. Ugh.

To keep his focus, he pulled out his cell again. He didn't have the Sparks' phone number, but Arly in Dispatch could connect him. The first number that she tried rang and rang until the voicemail picked up, giving him the store hours. He asked her to try again to find a house or cell number.

This time, Camille picked up.

"Camille Sparks." Her voice sounded tired with a catch in it. Some might think it was phlegm from a cold, but Tom assumed she had been crying. She should be crying. She lived with a brute.

"Camille, this is Deputy Pinkham, I mean Tom." He softened his voice to be less formal. "I'm calling from your field."

"Oh!" She paused. "Yes, Tom," she said in an even quieter voice. "Is everything all right?"

He inhaled. No, it wasn't, but she didn't need to know that yet. "I've asked some others to join me down here. I wanted to give you a heads up that they'll be coming up your driveway soon. Please direct them down towards me."

"Oh, okay. Are you sure everything is okay?" she said, still breathless.

"I just need some assistance," he said.

"To get the snowmobile removed? Oh, I see the Sheriff's Jeep now," she replied. "Mr. Ouelette is getting out. Let me grab my coat and greet him."

Tom continued. "Camille, hold on a second. I also need to ask that you and your husband stay up at the house, for now, and keep the animals inside. All the animals. Especially the alpacas."

He heard her draw in her breath. She finally choked out her question in a raspy voice.

"Is there a danger down there in the field?"

Tom paused and turned away from the body. Whatever was dangerous had happened, but they did need to make sure that whatever caused Karl to be decapitated was fixed so it wouldn't happen to someone else.

"Not so much a danger as a situation." Tom chose to be coy, and he needed the site investigated fully before word got out and potential evidence was lost.

"What the hell is happening down there?"

Tom heard Jared's booming yell over the phone, Camille trying to shush him.

"I'm going down there." Again, Jared, ignoring Camille.

"No!" Tom heard Camille, in a forceful voice, try to stop Jared.

"Nobody's going to tell me what to do on my own property!" Jared yelled again.

A rattling noise, like wind hitting the phone, came through the receiver. Camille must have moved outside.

"What is going on, Sheriff?" Again, Jared's angry voice. Camille must be standing right next to him, or she had moved the audio to the speaker so Tom could hear their conversation with Marcel.

Tom strained to listen, the wind muffling some of the phone's audio, but he could make out that it was Marcel talking.

Jared said, this time a few octaves lower, "Okay, thank you for explaining it. I understand. We'll wait here. Sorry for my outburst, but it has been a stressful day."

I'm sorry, but…. That was one of Tom's pet peeves. The insincere apology. A slap in the face in Tom's book, but Marcel was the master of diffusion and the king of misbehavior. He could handle anyone in any circumstance. Even a bully.

Chapter Eleven

Raven heard Betty's shout, looking for her. *Please, Betty, stay where you are*, Raven thought. She was still on all fours, on the trail made by the snowmobile, her mind trying to blot out what she had seen. What she assumed she had seen. She hoped she was wrong.

"Raven, where are you? Are you okay?" Betty called out again.

She knew Betty couldn't see her due to the snow's depth. She pushed herself up, almost into a downward dog yoga position, before straightening up.

"Over here," she called out as loud as she could, facing the river. Her throat burned, first from throwing up, and then from the dry heaves. She couldn't see Betty but hoped she was still on the preserve side. She didn't want to yell again.

"Are you coming back? Or should I come over?" Betty yelled.

Whew. Betty was not near the bloody mess, but Raven had to muster one final shout.

"I'm coming back to you," Raven coughed out. She searched for the path she made when she walked over from the river. Some of the wind had already drifted snow into her boot prints, but she still saw her original line. Tom was on the phone when she glanced his way. She didn't want to disturb him, not that she had much stomach or voice to talk at all. Plus, she had to think of a story to tell Betty.

Raven reached the river and saw Betty gleefully waving to her. She reversed her crawl on the fallen tree over the frozen Baxter River with Betty cheering her on as she crossed.

"Adventure Girl!" said Betty, extending a hand to Raven to help her off the trunk. Raven made sure she had her own footing before accepting Betty's hand. No sense two of them tumbling down.

"What's going on over there? Is it Karl's snowmobile?" Betty asked as Raven buckled her snowshoes over her boots for their walk out of the preserve.

The images of the blood in the snow and the helmet without a body flooded back. Raven coughed, trying to disguise her need to dry-heave again.

"We'd better get you out of the cold," said Betty, readjusting her mittens over her poles. Thankfully, Betty thought Raven had a cold and lost interest in the snowmobile. She switched her focus to Raven's well-being. Raven wanted to get them away from the area before Marcel and the State showed up. Betty would learn of the horrible accident soon enough.

"Good idea," said Raven, standing and grabbing her poles. "Let's go."

"And I know just the thing for you. Chicken soup." Betty headed off on the trail first, toward where Raven had left her Mini. The preserve parking lot had miraculously been plowed before they got there.

Raven turned back toward the farm. Marcel had arrived at the snowmobile scene. Whenever she saw him out in public, her heart fluttered. She was surprised, considering the events, that it still happened now. Her surge of feelings for Marcel matched what her mother always said: "You can't stop the locomotive of true love. Even if it seems at a standstill, its engine is still hot."

She ached to walk back over to the clearing by the river to wave to him, but she didn't want Betty to see her wave or wonder why Marcel also cared about an abandoned sled. She'd catch up with him at home. They'd both be back there soon enough.

Home. She ached to be home under a hot shower, not that she could wash away the images, but she sure as heck was going to try. Poor Karl.

But home would have to wait. Once Raven and Betty were back in the Mini, Betty asked for another favor.

"We need half and half for tomorrow's coffee, and I could use some carrots too for that chicken soup I'm promising you. Do you mind bringing me to Lane's on the way home? That way I don't have to go back out, in case Howard gives me a hard time about leaving, which I know he will."

Raven paused. Her dream of crawling into bed with the dogs after that long, long, hot-as-she-could-get-it shower would have to wait. The last thing she wanted to do was go on an errand, but she knew how much Betty worried about Howard chastising her. Raven didn't see Howard as critical as Betty did, but she knew how complicated marriage was. She didn't want to think about that in depth today either. She agreed to take Betty to Lane's.

On the way to the store, Raven knew they'd have to pass in front of Wolf Marine. She barely heard Betty prattling on about how she learned to make this particular chicken soup from her mother-in-law because Howard only wanted to eat his mother's recipes for everything when they were first married.

"And to make it worse," Betty said, "his mother would tell me, 'my sons only like to eat my Mac and Cheese,' or whatever dish it was that I had just made. Anything to put me down and raise herself up. I think Howard and his brothers told her they liked her cooking only to make her happy—because she was quite the miserable lady—but I do like her chicken soup recipe. I will give her that. The secret is the parsnips."

Raven said, "Sound good." Not that she really ever ate parsnips. She couldn't even think of what they tasted like. Thinking about something as trivial as parsnips helped her breathe better. Maybe this errand was a good idea after all, except for having to drive in front of Wolf Marine.

She inhaled as the white peak of Wolf Marine's wooden structure came into view. A store without an owner. The last of the Wolf legacy.

As they approached the building, Raven saw a couple of pickup trucks out in front. One was getting gas at the pumps. Maybe the high school girl who worked there on weekends had opened the store since school was closed because of the snow. That might have been the plan arranged last night with Karl before he hit the trails. He knew he'd want to sleep in after his rip. And either folks in town weren't aware of the tragedy and were just out buying what they needed, or they had heard about Karl and were stopping by the store to pay their respects.

She slowed to peer over as she drove by, and she could have sworn she saw Karl at the pumps, his greying hair sticking out from the edges of a wool Nepalese hat. The ghost of Karl. She probably would always visualize him at the pumps for the rest of her life. The mind was a powerful entity.

Wait. Was that really Karl at the pumps?

She slammed on her brakes in the middle of the road, and Betty's seatbelt clicked in to hold her tight, with Betty bracing her arms against the dashboard. Thankfully, no vehicle was behind her. She hadn't even looked in her rearview mirror.

"Whoa!" said Betty. "What happened?" She crisscrossed her arms across her chest with a large sigh.

"Sorry about that," said Raven, quickly throwing the Mini into reverse and backing up, right on the road.

"What is it?" Betty looked from Raven to the marine store.

There was enough room for Raven to park between two pickup trucks, her front-end up against the snow bank that was created when the driveway was plowed out.

"Wait here," she said to Betty, who immediately unbuckled herself and opened the passenger door.

"I don't know what is going on, so I'm coming with you." Betty was standing outside the car before Raven could protest further. Fine. Raven had tried to protect Betty, but Betty might learn more than she wanted to know very soon.

Raven glanced around. The truck that had been getting gas had left, and the man whom Raven thought she saw pumping the gas wasn't near the pumps or anywhere else outside. Maybe it was a trick of her mind after all, or a wishful hope.

Betty was by her side. "Okay, you were weird at the preserve, and now you're being even weirder here. What is going on?"

Before Raven could answer, a man came out of the store and hopped down the two short stone steps.

Raven drew in her breath.

It definitely was Karl Wolf.

Chapter Twelve

Johnny plowed his driveway a couple of times throughout the night to keep up with the snowfall. He knew his small plow and his almost bald tires wouldn't be much of a match for three feet of snow if he waited until the end of the storm.

Now that it was sunny, even though it was also quite windy, he decided to drive around town and see how the rest of the folks had fared. He might even swing by Raven and Marcel's house, although he suspected Marcel would still be out and about. Raven had become tolerant of him just dropping by. Any day now, he knew, she'd be welcoming him with open arms. He hoped. He certainly had Marcel in his corner.

He took the long way around to the Ouelettes, driving along the Baxter River, and up towards Riverview Farm. At first, he thought they were having a party at the farm. Or a huge sale on yarn, he chuckled to himself. Both events would be odd on the day after a blizzard. Then he recognized Marcel's Jeep in the parking lot. He slowed to a stop on the road. No cars were coming in either direction, and that gave him time to study the parking lot. Tom's SUV was there too. Geez, he hoped Camille and Jared were okay.

As he sat in his truck in the middle of the road, a car with State of Maine plates approached from the opposite direction and also turned into the farm's entrance. The lettering on the front driver-side door said "State of Maine Forensics."

He whistled and couldn't resist turning into the farm's driveway himself. Once a cop, always a cop, he knew. Something was definitely wrong at the farm.

Before he could even park, he saw Clint from Forensics pull his kit out of the trunk. Clint had worked on previous sites in Secretly in the fall. A super nice guy. His partner today, a tall, regal woman with striking, long, blonde hair, probably in her thirties, was unknown to Johnny.

"That's a good thing that I've never seen her before," Johnny muttered out loud. "How many crime scenes do we need in Secretly?" Obviously, this was one too many for January. Not a good way to start the year.

He stayed in his truck, letting them get a head start to wherever they were going. He was curious. Okay, he was nosey and had nothing else to do, but maybe he could help, too. At least that is what he told himself to give himself permission to stay.

Clint and the woman didn't head towards the house, though. They also went straight past the barn. After seeing them duck under the fence, he figured it was no-harm-no-foul for him to peer into the fields, too.

Just then, Jared appeared next to his driver's side window and knocked, a bit too hard, on the glass. More like pounded.

"No media," Jared yelled, wagging a finger at him as Johnny lowered the window. "No trespassing either," he added, his face growing red with his teeth clenched.

"I'm not with the newspaper," said Johnny, rolling down his window. He was glad to see Jared was okay. But what the heck kinda greeting was that? Camille rushed toward them, her winter coat unfastened and flopping open as she ran, probably to catch up to Jared to stop him from making a fool of himself. Too late, but good to see that she, too, was okay.

Slightly out of breath when she reached the truck, she said, "You're Raven's father, right?"

Small town. She probably knew his whole story, too. Johnny wondered what angle she had heard. "He abandoned his family." Or worse. It was nearly impossible to move forward from the past, he was discovering. But he was heck going to try. He took this mention of Raven, though, as a chance to get out of his truck. He pulled on the door handle, and both she and Jared stepped back.

"Yes, that's right," he said, extending his gloved hand. "Ethan Johnson.

Please call me 'Johnny.' I understand you folks moved up from Boston last year. I was a Boston cop for years. Just retired a few years ago and moved back up to Maine."

He slid that in about Boston to get Jared to calm down and trust him. They both nodded at him without taking his hand. Maybe they were just cold, or shell-shocked for whatever happened on their farm that brought two sheriffs and a forensics team, or maybe they were always rude, stuck-up SOBs. Before he could speculate more, an ambulance pulled in with the medical examiner's van behind it, followed by another sheriff's vehicle and a state trooper's car.

"Geez. How many people are needed here to move a damn snowmobile! I demand answers! Now! What is happening down there?" Jared stomped his feet. "If I don't get answers and fast, I'm going down there myself!" His face turned from red to grey when the words 'medical examiner' must have registered. He went silent.

Camille's hands flew up to her mouth, also seeing the words on the van. "Oh, no. What has happened down there? Is someone dead?"

Jared's moment of calm disappeared. "I'm done with being told to stay up here. If someone died on my property, I demand to know about it. I can tell you one thing, it's their own fault," he said, and turned towards the path the forensics team took. Johnny placed a hand on his shoulder.

"If Marcel and Tom asked you to stay here, I'd listen to that advice." Johnny's voice was low and soothing. He assumed the Sparks were told to stay at the house. Otherwise, Jared wouldn't be hell-bent on going down the field.

"And just who are you to boss me around on my own property?" Jared's eyes narrowed.

"Jared!" Camille said. Her face flushed pink.

Johnny had a feeling that Camille spent half of her day managing Jared and his tongue. What an exhausting life.

He responded. "You're right, Jared, I'm a nobody, but I've seen a lot of things that I wish I could forget. I don't know what happened down there, but I think it is better for you to wait for Marcel to tell you than to see it for yourself. It might be something that you can never 'unsee.'" Johnny's memory flashed to accident scenes that haunted his dreams, especially the brutal way men chose to end their lives. He was betting someone used a 12-gauge shotgun on himself in the field, and they were picking up the pieces. What else could it be?

"You said you were a cop. In Boston," Camille stated.

Johnny knew it was her attempt to give him credibility with Jared. Not just the cop part, but the Boston part, too.

Johnny nodded. "For twenty-five years. Retired now."

She continued.

"And you're Sheriff Ouelette's father-in-law."

He nodded again.

"So, maybe you could go down there as our representative. You could find out what is happening, and let us know?" She was twisting her mittened hands in front of her. "That way we can stay up here, but still know."

He didn't want to interfere in an investigation, yet he saw how this could diffuse the tension a bit with Jared.

Johnny nodded again. "Okay, I think I could do that. At least get an overview for you two."

Her shoulders relaxed. "Thank you. That's great. Right, Jared? Thank you."

Jared shrugged and huffed. He walked towards the house like a man who had given up, shaking his head and muttering. Camille ran after him. Johnny only caught a couple of words she said. She asked him if he had seen anything while he was out in the blizzard. Whatever else she said caused him to stop walking and turn back towards Johnny.

"Seriously, thank you, Mr. Johnson. We appreciate the support."

Chapter Thirteen

Tom watched Clint and his bundled-up forensic partner make their way slowly down the snowy path they'd made with their boots. He was pretty sure both had worked on more gruesome scenes than he had, but even for them, would those prior incidents have prepared them for this one?

"Tommy! My man!" said Clint. "Fancy meeting you here."

Normally, Tom welcomed the banter to alleviate the strain of the situation, but with this being Karl Wolf and the brutal way he met his demise, Tom couldn't even wave to Clint. It was all too sad.

Tom noticed that Clint took the somber mood in stride and matched it. Marcel, who had been standing near the front of the snowmobile to stay out of the way of the crime scene, moved toward Clint, too. And yes, this was a crime scene. One didn't just fall off a snowmobile and become decapitated.

"Hey, Clint," Marcel said. "Once you two capture what you need, we'll need to walk around this area to see what else we can determine."

Clint nodded, his eyes wide at what was in front of him. Maybe this was one of the worst situations Clint had been called to work on. Tom saw Clint regroup and turn to his partner, a woman whom Tom hadn't met before.

Clint cleared his throat. "Where are my manners? This is Margot. Margot Gilbert. She just came up from the Portland area to Midcoast. And before that, who knows?" He winked at her and chuckled at the last part. Tom realized that Clint had to make jokes for his own sanity. He understood that. "She's working with me for a few weeks, but she really is in the ME's office."

"A new medical examiner?" said Marcel. "That's great. Welcome."

Margot looked at Tom and Marcel. Her long blond hair flowed from her hatless head, and her eyes were a dark brown, the kind Tom could fall into and enjoy being lost for a while. Tom also knew what he needed for his own sanity: to allow himself this moment of attraction, despite the circumstances of the morning. Gosh, she was darn pretty.

"Nice to meet you both. I look forward to working with you." She had a low, quiet voice and a small smile. Not small in the way some who are really disinterested and dismissive are. This smile felt like it came from a place of modesty and respect for the dead. Tom bet she could run circles around him in the smarts department.

Clint cleared his throat again. "So, what do we have here?"

As Tom opened his mouth to explain, he noticed Johnny up on the hill. Too far to hear their conversations, which was a good thing. Not that Johnny would spread the word on Karl before they were ready, but the longer they could keep the news to themselves, the less real it felt.

To steady himself, Tom turned to formal language. "It appears that a sledder came through last night on the old snowmobile trail and came across something that decapitated him."

Margot's eyes widen. "Decapitated? Did you find the head?"

Tom nodded and motioned toward the dark, round object with the red snow around it just a bit further down the trail. "I think that is it. I didn't want to disturb anything by going over there to confirm." He also didn't want to look at himself.

Clint whistled. "Any idea of who it is?"

Tom swallowed. He couldn't find his voice. Marcel spoke up.

"We believe it is Karl Wolf. I've verified the registration number on this sled as his, and he had this same Arctic Cat Sno-Pro out in front of his store yesterday, which is no longer there. He's the president of the local snowmobile club and holds the town record for first out on the trails after every storm. I haven't been able to reach him this morning either. I also called his girlfriend, who said he wasn't there. She assumed he was sleeping at his house after snowmobiling last night."

"He definitely was ready yesterday to keep his title," Tom added with thickness creeping into his words.

"Gosh, I'm so sorry to hear this," said Clint. "I know Karl. He's a good guy."

Tom and Marcel nodded. Yes, Karl was a good guy. Poor Laurie. First, her husband died, and now Karl. He was sure Marcel hadn't told her yet, however. She wasn't officially "next of kin," and they didn't yet know for sure if it was truly Karl.

"So, what do you think happened?" asked Margot.

Tom answered, "I'm not sure. I haven't looked around yet because I didn't want to make more footprints until you guys came."

Marcel pointed to the newer-looking post in the field, the one that Tom had also walked by, and noticed the barbed wire hanging from it.

"It might have something to do with that. It seems out of place, that new wood."

The others turned toward the direction of Marcel's raised arm.

"I noticed that too on my way down," said Tom. "I believe I saw barbed wire flapping on its side."

"We'll go check that out while you get to work here," said Marcel. He and Tom walked sideways across the slope, toward the new post.

The visible wire shone, showing it was as new as the post. Marcel shook his head.

"You're thinking that Jared put this here to keep out the sledders?" Tom leaned in closer to check the wire for blood. If this truly was the murder weapon, the wire with the blood was buried in the snow closer to the track made by the snowmobile.

Marcel rubbed his chin. "I sure hope not."

"Could someone be naive enough to think the wire would only scratch the snowmobile or fray a sledder's clothes? Like he put it up to annoy the trail users, but not to harm one, at least not fatally."

"If the wire was low, like a trip wire, then I might buy that." Marcel looked out across the field, shielding the sun with his hand. "But considering how high up it is on the post, it looks calculated to do just what it did. Probably attached to another post along the forest edge."

"Or a tree on the other side of the field. Why pound two posts into a frozen ground if you don't have to?" Tom added.

He squinted, looking across the field. With the drift, it was impossible to tell where the other end of the wire might have been attached.

"Marcel! Tom!" Clint called out. They glanced his way and saw him and Margot standing by the helmet. "Can you come down here?" he asked.

Tom wanted to say no. He hadn't been by the helmet yet and was hoping to avoid it altogether. He didn't want to look like a wimp in front of any of them, however, especially the new girl.

Marcel and Tom followed the trail they had just made, then walked along the edge of the yellow crime tape Clint had put up.

"What's up?" asked Marcel when they got closer.

Clint scrunched his face, glanced down at the helmet, and looked back up. "I haven't seen Karl in a year or so, but I don't think this is him."

Tom scrambled over the snow to get back on the packed trail, his heart pounding. "What? Really?"

He came to an abrupt halt, however, just shy of seeing the helmet, now covered with a forensic sheet, up close. He breathed deeply to keep his consciousness. He still couldn't look.

"Let me," said Marcel, from behind Tom. "Don't worry about it."

"I can do it, too. I'm all right," said Tom, more shaken now, wondering who it was if it wasn't not Karl."

They waited while Margot pulled back the sheet. She kept the neck covered, and with a surgical-gloved hand, she lifted the helmet's shield. A whole face appeared, pale white, with eyes closed.

"Mikey Dyer," said Marcel, stepping back. "I'm pretty sure this is Mikey."

Tom exhaled. "Yes, I agree. It's Mikey Dyer."

Mikey Dyer? What the heck was he doing riding Karl's snowmobile? Tom couldn't believe that Karl would loan it to him or anyone.

"Okay, we'll be sure, of course, to get a formal identification, but thank you for the preliminary one," said Clint.

Before any of them could speak further, a loud *brapp-brapp* sound came out of the woods, from the same direction the Arctic Cat sled had come during the night. Another snowmobiler was headed their way.

Tom moved past the group, waving the sledder to a stop and attempting to turn him around. The red, white, and blue Polaris slowed and then stopped. The rider got off the sled and walked toward the group. With a helmet on, Tom didn't know who the driver was until he flicked the helmet's shield up. It was Craig Fisher, the snowmobile club's treasurer.

"What's going on, Tom?" he asked, and then saw the blue sheets over Mikey's body and helmet as well as the blood-stained snow.

"Oh no, Karl. Karl!" He rushed forward, but Tom held him back. Everyone in town knew Karl's Arctic Cat. Craig let out a gasp and asked. "What happened? Jared did this, didn't he? That jerk! He didn't want us back here. Oh, no. Karl!"

Marcel stepped forward. "We are just beginning our investigation. I need to ask you to turn back, Craig."

Craig's voice cracked. "Karl. Poor Karl." He buried his helmeted head into his hands.

Tom saw Marcel swallow, then saw his face decide.

"Craig, we've just started our investigation," Marcel repeated, "but I can assure you this isn't Karl."

Craig's head whipped up. "It's not?" He teetered, almost losing his balance.

"It's not," Marcel confirmed.

"Are you sure?" Craig tried to look over Marcel's shoulder.

"Yes, I'm pretty confident that it isn't Karl," Marcel responded.

Craig's chest heaved. "Oh, thank goodness. Wow. Thank goodness." Then he paused. "If it isn't Karl, then who is it?"

Tom knew the small-town talk would start the moment Craig drove off. "We need you to keep this incident to yourself for now, Craig, okay? We have to notify the next of kin and follow the proper protocol. You will learn more soon enough."

"Oh yes, of course. Of course. I don't feel too good. I'd better get home." He turned back to his sled and swayed.

"Can we bring you home, Craig?" said Marcel.

"No, no, I can ride home. I'd rather ride home." He climbed back onto his sled. He carefully turned the snowmobile around, taking three or four tries to back up a few inches, then pull forward a few inches. Tom was grateful Craig had enough wits about him to not get stuck. Digging out a sled was the last thing they needed to do right now.

"Did you hear what he said about Jared possibly doing this?" asked Tom.

Marcel nodded. "We need to give the Sparks an update anyway. No time like the present to talk to them."

Chapter Fourteen

Raven finally exhaled. She hadn't known she was holding her breath. Betty, who never realized that Karl was supposed to be dead at the Riverview Farm field, strode up to Karl, leaving Raven frozen in her tracks.

"Hey Karl," said Betty in her friendly voice as if she were his best customer. Raven assumed that, other than the one time when Raven had brought Betty to the store, Betty didn't shop at Wolf Marine on her own.

"How are you ladies today? Everything okay at your houses?" Karl talked as he made his way back to the gas pumps. He carried a shovel and used it to remove snow that the plow had pushed between the pumps.

"Oh, yes. All good. On our way to Lane's. I'm glad to see they're open." Betty gestured down the road to Lane's Market. Their American flag flapped in the post-storm wind.

"He was open this morning before I even got here," Karl spoke as he shoveled. "I'm just glad I can stand up today. No fun spending the night with the stomach bug I had."

Raven came closer and noticed that Karl looked paler than usual.

"Oh? You were sick last night after your snowmobile ride?" Betty talked like a snowmobile subject-matter expert.

Karl, being sick, could speak to why his sled was in the Sparks' field if he had left it there and walked, somehow, home, but that didn't explain the body near it.

"I never went out last night. I closed up the shop early and had planned to help the club finish the trail signage, but Craig and his crew were already done, and he said he didn't need help repairing the groomer. Imagine if we had actually gotten money for the club these past few snowless years. Besides buying a better groomer, we could have insulated the clubhouse walls, even if we used the cash as the insulator!" Karl chuckled and continued his story. "So, I had an early dinner. Maybe it was the three-week-old crab cakes I had in the fridge that got me, but I couldn't move away from the bathroom until about an hour ago."

Raven saw Betty's face twist in reaction to the spoiled food. Even her own stomach did a flip.

"Then who rode your snowmobile last night?" Betty's question was an innocent one. "They left it on a trail."

"You've seen it?" He pointed to the spot where it had been the day before. "It wasn't here when I got in this morning. I was wondering who took it to ride last night. Maybe someone thought that it was the sled with the record, not the rider." He grinned and then shrugged. "Oh, well, I broke my streak. What a shame after all the work Craig did to get the trails ready for me, too."

"Yes, I think it's the one stuck in the field at Riverview farm," Betty said.

"Riverview Farm?" Karl clapped his palms to his head. "Of all the places for it to be. I don't think we even have the signed paperwork to ride there. I never got a chance to verify with Craig. I'll have to crawl on my hands and knees, with the firstborn I never had, to get Jared to give it back to me. I can just see him making me buy it from him, especially after I threw him out of the store yesterday."

Raven nodded to herself. So it must have been Jared who Karl threw out of the store when she was looking for paint.

Karl paused and leaned on his shovel's handle, rubbing his chin. "I wonder if the sled's disappearance is connected to the break-in."

"What break-in?" Raven was finally over her initial shock of seeing Karl, quite alive and well enough. He certainly looked better than whoever was lying in the field.

"When I got here this morning, I could tell someone had gone through my desk behind the register. Must have left the door open to make it look like the wind and snow had made the mess, but I'm pretty sure no Nor'easter can open up heavy oak drawers! Here, let me show you."

Karl walked up the stone steps and went into the store. Raven and Betty followed. Two men clad in heavy, lined flannel shirts stood talking inside.

"Hey, Raven," one of them said.

"Hi, Clark. Hi, Frank." She could tell Betty wanted to be introduced, but this was not a social call to Raven. She still wanted to be home, showered, and buried in her covers even if it wasn't Karl who had died by the sled. Somebody else did. She followed Karl to the cash register.

"Just take a look over the counter," he said, moving out of the way. The wooden drawers he spoke of were open, and papers were strewn everywhere—stuck to the floor and piled up into the corners.

"And take a look at this." He held up a spiral notebook, its coil holding tiny scraps of white paper from the pages that had been ripped out. "This is the ledger where I keep the credit I've extended. All the notes are gone. Ya think this was all orchestrated by Lunchbox?"

"Lunchbox?" Betty asked, glancing at Raven and then back at Karl.

Raven was also in no mood to get into town nicknames and changed the subject. She also didn't know why Karl had even mentioned Lunchbox Lennie, and she didn't want to know.

"I'm sure Marcel will be happy to come over and write a report when he's done at Riverview Farm." Raven fussed with her coat. She wanted to go home.

"Marcel's at the farm?" Betty turned toward Raven. "I only saw Tom."

"Gee, that's a lot of manpower for one dead sled." Karl leaned his back against the counter. "Marcel was already here once this morning. He must have driven by and seen the door open. He left a voicemail on my phone. I was finally asleep and didn't hear it. I'm glad he gave me a heads-up. Made the surprise less surprising. I gotta call him back."

Raven felt her legs grow weak and needed to change the subject from the sled, the field, the blood. She steered the conversation back to the store break-in.

"Was there anything else stolen or destroyed?" She asked, stepping away from the counter and surveying the store. It wasn't neat on its best day, but it definitely looked like a place that had been 'tossed.' At least now the faded, outdated postcards, destroyed on the wet floor, would be thrown out.

"You know what's funny? The only other thing I've noticed missing is the old paint-by-number." He gestured toward the wall to the side. Betty walked over, and Raven followed. The outline of where a frame hung was obvious. Raven had just stared at the picture yesterday. Two women rowing, if she remembered correctly. Why would someone want that?

"Did it just blow off because the door was open?" Raven glanced around.

"I thought that too," said Karl. "But I haven't come across it yet."

"Was it a map? Like something antique?" Betty asked.

"Nah, it was a nice enough picture of people in a rowboat. My grandfather had accepted it years ago as payment for gas. The story was that some guy from away, I think from Boston, needed gas desperately. We didn't, and still don't, take any credit cards. He didn't have cash and asked my grandfather if he would take the painting as collateral for the gas. He promised to come back up with the cash within a month. The other funny part is he wanted to make sure my grandfather would be willing to give him back the painting once he paid him." Karl smiled. "Like my grandfather actually wanted to keep it. Maybe if it were a painting of a lobster boat, he would have."

"I saw it hanging here yesterday. I'm guessing the Boston guy never came back." Raven managed a small smile.

"Nope. Never. My dad, who inherited the store, always said that since his father had promised to give it back, we could never throw it out, just in case the guy showed up. He didn't mind keeping it. It gave him a story that he loved telling to anyone who asked about the painting. And then I grew to love telling the story, too. It became kind of a fixture of the store. Every once in a while, someone says it looks familiar." Karl laughed again. "Hey, if someone really liked it and had to have it that badly, more power to them. They could have just asked for it, though. No need to make a mess to take it."

Raven again observed Betty's face, wondering what mess the burglar had actually made and what was left messy over the years.

Raven's mind ached—a stolen print, a destroyed ledger, a dead sledder— her stomach did flips again, and her arms felt heavy. She feared passing out.

"I need to get back for the dogs," she said as an excuse to go home.

Betty's face showed surprise and hurt. "Oh, I thought we were going to Lane's? Do you still have time for that?"

Raven sighed and nodded, not trusting her voice. As long as she could close her eyes and wait in the car.

Chapter Fifteen

Tom was relieved it wasn't Karl in the field, but he still felt bad for Mikey. What a way to go. Seems like Mikey never got his life together. Tom always thought of him as a drifter, someone who could have made something of himself if he had a father, even a mentor, around to guide him.

He and Marcel walked back up the snow-covered hill to talk to the Sparks. With all the other law enforcement officials now buzzing around the field, the path was worn down, and the climb was made easier, though now a little slippery.

"I wonder why Karl let Mikey take his sled out?" Tom mused, mostly to himself.

"Knowing Mikey's history, I'd wager he helped himself." Marcel said from behind Tom. "I'm just surprised Karl didn't call it in as stolen."

Tom nodded about Mikey and the sled theft. He hadn't had the most stellar town reputation. A few OUIs, an accusation that he took firewood from a neighbor, and a suspicion that he was acting as a middleman for some locals who were known for drug possession. Tom was barely touching on the list of Mikey's sins.

"Do you think someone saw him take the sled and did him in? To get back at him for stealing or not fully paying for something? Something drug-related?" Tom asked. "There's only one route on the snowmobile trail, in and out of town. It'd be easy enough to anticipate his direction and path."

"Well, whoever did it definitely did it with the intention of killing someone," Marcel responded.

They had reached the top of the hill and crossed under the fence. The alpacas, about ten of them, were now out in a pen that had been shoveled. They rushed away from Marcel and Tom and hovered as a group in a corner. Most were brown, with a couple cream-colored. They sure were cute. After passing the animals, Marcel and Tom stood in the driveway, facing the Sparks' white farmhouse.

Tom sighed. "Can't delay this any further, although I sure would like to."

They approached the house, and Tom stepped up on the stone step. Johnny answered his knock, wearing his coat and hat.

"I was just leaving," he said, stepping out but holding the door for Tom. "Good luck," he whispered as he passed by.

Right behind Johnny was Camille, her face pale and her eyes squinting as if the sun hurt them, or she had been crying too long.

"Are you leaving now?" she said to Tom and Marcel. "Is everything okay down there?"

Jared moved her aside—literally moved her—to get in front of her and to face Tom and Marcel. "I demand to know what is going on." His face was still flushed, his hair, from its time under a hat, was matted and moist.

Marcel asked in a low voice, "May we come in?"

Over Jared's shoulder, Camille said, "Yes, of course, please do."

When Jared didn't respond, in word or movement, she said, "Jared, please let Sheriff Ouelette and Deputy Pinkham in."

Jared stood frozen in place, and then, with a large sigh, his face relaxed, and he stepped back, allowing Tom and Marcel to enter the hallway of the old farmhouse.

"Let's go into the kitchen, and don't worry about your boots." Camille led the way through the house.

Tom followed, with Marcel bringing up the rear, sandwiching Jared between them. No more pushing Camille around in their presence. He then chuckled to himself about Camille's comment of keeping his boots on, as if any law enforcement person would take their boots off at a crime scene just to save a person's carpets. People were funny creatures.

The kitchen had a beautiful blue-enameled cookstove, the kind fed with wood, that served as both a heat source and a functional oven. It warmed the whole room and made the place feel cozy. The topic, however, that they were about to discuss was not cozy and would ruin the serenity and comfort that this kitchen gave, probably ruin it forever, Tom thought.

"Can I get you something to drink? Coffee? Tea? Hot Chocolate?" She stood before a row of mugs on a shelf.

"I'm all set," said Marcel, "but thank you."

Tom simply shook his head, saying, "No thanks."

She poured herself a glass of water from the tap and held on to the glass with both hands as if it were her last drink ever.

"What's the big secret down there?" Jared said in a bark. "Are you going to finally let us in on it? It is our property, you know."

Camille's eyes widen as if she were trying to telepathically tell him to be quiet. Or respectful. Probably both.

Marcel took over the conversation.

"Mr. and Mrs. Sparks, why don't we please sit down, and we'll update you on all that has happened."

Jared was about to utter another remark, but Camille, standing next to him, elbowed him in the ribs. He tossed a glare at her but kept quiet. How she got mixed up with him, Tom was dying to know. A powder keg waiting for one tiny match. Perhaps that flame ignited him last night.

They all sat around a small kitchen table, just large enough for its four wooden chairs. Tom noticed the blue woven tablecloth was similar to the one his mother had, made locally.

Marcel began. Tom watched their expressions carefully. Especially, Jared's, if Craig's comment had any bearing.

"I'm sorry to share this news. Unfortunately, a snowmobiler has died in your field."

Jared pounded his fist on the table, causing Camille to let out a squeak. A splash from her glass of water leaped out and landed on the tablecloth.

"I knew it was a bad idea to let them use the back field. Now, we're going to be sued!"

Camille set her glass down next to the stain. Her hands flew up to her mouth with her eyes filling with tears.

"Someone died? How? How did it happen?" she murmured.

Marcel continued. "We're still looking into that."

"So, the body is still down there?" Jared's head swiveled toward the window.

Marcel nodded. "For now. After the forensics team is finished, the medical examiner will take it away for further examination."

"Forensics team?" Camille's eyes squinted. "Why would you need a forensics team?"

"Was he shot?" Jared asked. The redness was gone from Jared's cheeks. He looked genuinely concerned after his initial outburst.

Camille swayed in her chair, her whole head now in her hands. Jared put an arm around her and kissed her on the side of her forehead.

"It's okay," he whispered. "You were just trying to be a part of the community. You didn't know someone would get hurt in our field."

Tom considered the switch in Jared's demeanor. Was it to hide something, or did maturity finally kick in? Did he finally realize he was acting like a jerk? Could he actually have a compassionate side?

"Why would you ask if the person was shot?" Tom asked.

Jared shrugged. "Seems like everyone rides around here with their shotgun. I've never had a gun living in Boston, but up here, I'm thinking I need to own one just to level the playing field."

It was off-topic, but Tom had to know. "You feel less safe here than in Boston?" He tried to take the incredulous tone out of his voice, but he couldn't help it. He knew Boston was safer than other large cities, but much more dangerous than Maine overall.

"I do feel less safe. It's dark up here. No street lights. Fewer people around to witness a crime. People eye us suspiciously, like we're the enemy. Look at what just happened here in the middle of a blizzard? If this were Boston, a video camera probably would have captured the event, and if someone was involved, he'd be identified easily. I can assure you there are no cameras in our field to help you."

Maybe Jared had a point there, but the incident in the field was a one-off,

Tom thought, and sadly, as with most murders in Maine, the crime was probably committed by someone who knew the victim. He noticed Marcel taking in all of Jared's comments.

"So, what happens next?" Jared asked, his arm around Camille, who still sniffled into his shoulder.

Marcel picked up the conversation. "We'll need to get the sled out of there, too, later today. I'm going to ask that you stay out of that back field for now, too, if that's okay, in case we need to go back down later or in a few days, as we continue to investigate." Marcel had such a gentle way with people. Tom couldn't have learned from a better role model.

"Of course. Of course," Jared said, and then paused, "Do you think the town will blame us? For this person's death? We were just trying to be neighborly."

For all of Jared's anger, and the known fact that he did not want anyone back there, the shift to being a good neighbor raised an eyebrow on Tom. Maybe it was the sight of Marcel, in uniform, that made Jared back down.

Or maybe he had something to hide after all.

Chapter Sixteen

Raven ended up going into Lane's after all, and then reminded herself to never go grocery shopping with Betty again, at least not when she was emotionally exhausted and just wanted to be home.

Betty, who had claimed that she only needed carrots and a carton of half and half, perused the aisles of Lane's as if she were a tourist at a foreign store. Thankfully, there weren't many aisles to peruse.

"Oh, they have Needhams back in stock," Betty said, picking up a chocolate-covered, plastic-wrapped square of candy. "Who would think potatoes could taste this good?" she chuckled as she tossed four into the plastic basket.

"Do you mind if I wait in the car?" Raven didn't wait for an answer. She needed to sit down quickly and headed outside.

"I'll be right out," Betty called after her.

Fifteen minutes later, Betty sat buckled in next to Raven.

"I just want to thank you for the great morning," said Betty, adjusting her hair in the visor's mirror as Raven pulled away from the curb. They passed again in front of Wolf Marine. No one was out front this time.

Raven let out a long sigh. Yeah, a great morning. If Betty only knew. She'd know soon enough.

As Raven drove up Betty's snow-packed driveway, she could see that the Harts were now fully plowed and shoveled out. Betty's husband, Howard, a tall, distinguished man in his late sixties, opened up the side door. He was in stocking feet.

"Where did you go? Mount Katahdin? You've been gone all morning." He called out to them as they alighted from the Mini Cooper. Raven took one of Betty's grocery bags.

Betty muttered under her breath to Raven as they walked toward the house. "Heaven help him make his own lunch!" In a louder voice, she said, almost sing-songing, "I'll be right in to make your lunch, darling."

Betty kissed Howard hello at the door and went into the house. Raven followed, and Howard gave her a peck on the top of her head.

"Thank you for getting her out of the house. She was driving me batty," he whispered.

Raven gave a weak smile and set the bag on the counter. She had known Howard and Betty for years now, meeting them when they moved up to Secretly from Connecticut. Howard had retired as an actuary, a word she had learned when she met him. Betty had dabbled in teaching for a while before raising their three daughters. Howard had dragged Betty to Maine—Betty's words—but Betty had settled in nicely by starting a garden club.

"Okay, Betty, I should get back to the poochies and the wood stove." Raven turned to leave.

"Oh, don't go yet." Betty flicked the burner on and placed a kettle full of water on it. "Help me tell Howard about what we saw in the woods."

What we saw in the woods, thought Raven, isn't really the whole story, and she didn't feel like reliving it at the moment.

"Karl Wolf's snowmobile died in the field at Riverview Farm," said Betty, with a laugh. "That Jared must be exploding right now. He was so mad at Camille for agreeing to let the club use that field."

"How do you know this?" Howard eyed Betty.

She fumbled with the ceramic mugs. Raven knew it was to get him off the topic of her shopping at the farm. "What kind of tea did you want, Raven?"

Howard rolled his eyes at Raven. He knew Betty's tricks as well as she knew his, Raven thought.

"Chamomile, if you have it," said Raven.

A car door slammed outside. Howard looked out the window.

"Make that four mugs. Johnny is here."

Raven was getting used to Johnny showing up wherever she was. Her breath and heart rate no longer quickened. She was also getting used to accepting him back into her life—as her father—but this morning she didn't feel like a generous daughter. She still needed to watch her every expression and word to make sure she was kind, forgiving, accepting, and whatever else Marcel had suggested that she be towards Johnny. This morning, she barely had any energy left to forge a smile.

"He's the only parent you have left, Raven," Marcel had said to her one night after Johnny left, and she had been less than patient with him, again. "He's trying. Can't you open up your heart a little? And, remember, forgiveness helps the forgiver more than the forgiven. I remember your mother saying that all the time."

Had her mother forgiven Johnny for leaving? Did Marcel say that because Raven had become bitter? Cold? Even towards him? Was he saying that about her and her suspicious of his relationship with this former girlfriend, Shannon McGrath, the new county district attorney? Was it he who needed to be forgiven, too? Not that she had told Marcel that she was wondering about the two of them. She had no proof of him stepping out on her, but she knew she had become quieter, watchful. And Marcel was right. She needed to open her heart.

She shook off all of those thoughts and prepared to welcome Johnny. A new leaf. Why not?

Howard opened the side door.

"Quite the morning in Secretly," Howard said, shaking Johnny's hand. "Come in and have something hot to drink and join our kibitzing."

"Thank you, kindly. You'll never hear me say no to a good chat," Johnny said, taking off his boots. "Do you have any coffee, by any chance?"

"Happy to make a fresh pot," said Howard, hanging Johnny's winter canvas coat on a hook by the door. "Betty, put the coffee pot on too while you're in there."

Betty scowled and then smiled. Raven knew Betty was thinking, "Why can't you do it? You just offered?" but Betty was well-trained as a hostess from her Connecticut childhood by a stay-at-home mother and would never let a guest feel unwelcome, even if she was annoyed at Howard.

"Yes, happy to," Betty said, pulling a bag of ground coffee from the freezer.

"We walked the Baxter River Preserve this morning," she said in between counting scoops. "Karl Wolf's snowmobile was dead on the other side of the river. Right in the Sparks' field. I hope that still counts for Karl as 'first on the trails.'"

Johnny shifted on his feet and wiped his mouth.

"Yeah, I saw the snowmobile."

Betty jerked her head around with a surprised look on her face. Raven knew it crushed Betty to not be the town's main source of news.

"We didn't see you at the preserve," she said. "And only Tom Pinkham was at the sled. I'm sure Jared called it in to the sheriffs' office with a huff."

Johnny nodded. "Yeah, he sure is wound tight. I wasn't in the preserve. I had seen the medical examiner pull into Riverview Farm's driveway, and got nosy. You know me." He shrugged and smiled.

"Medical Examiner?" Betty's eyes were now wide, the pot of water for the coffee maker clutched in her right hand. "Why would a medical examiner be there? Nothing happened to Karl. We saw him this morning."

There was no avoiding it now. Betty was about to learn a gruesome truth, not that Raven knew who was lying in the field, but someone definitely was dead. It was whoever had taken Karl's sled.

"Let's sit down for a moment," Raven said, lifting a mug of steaming hot herbal tea off the counter with both of her hands. She felt frozen to her core and hoped the tea would thaw her.

Betty didn't seem to read the serious tone in Raven's voice. She responded jubilantly.

"Oh, great. I'm glad you're going to stay. I love company. We haven't had anyone over since Sally visited over the holidays."

Howard grunted. Raven figured it was at the mention of Sally, their middle daughter, and the wannabe actress who flew in from Los Angeles whenever she was low on cash or housing. A dreamer, Howard always called her, when Betty was out of earshot.

Betty frowned at Howard and then seemed to catch herself about the solemnness of the situation. "Good to have you both here, even if it is to talk about something serious."

She led the way into the family room adjacent to the kitchen. Raven always loved this room—the cozy, floral prints of the cushy chairs and the way the sunlight streamed in all day. It was now brightly lit with the rays coming in from the Northwest from both the sky and the reflection off the snow. The comfort of the sun countered the events of the morning, and she relaxed with a sigh into a plush armchair.

Johnny, always seeming like he was ready to bolt, fidgeted against a door frame, nursing his mug of black coffee that Betty managed to produce. Howard, his face showing eagerness to learn about the morning's events, sat in his normal leather chair, his laptop close at hand on a tray table, and Betty took her normal floral print armchair on the other side of Howard's chair, a small wooden table between them.

"Can I go first?" Betty asked Raven, which took Raven off guard. Did Betty know more about the death at Riverview Farm than she realized?

"Why, of course," said Raven. She felt like she was joining Howard, who appeared to be at the edge of his seat.

Betty actually did sit at the edge of her cushion, her back straight to command attention, her excitement obvious.

"Karl Wolf's store was robbed last night," she pronounced to the room.

"Really?" said Howard and Johnny in unison.

Raven let out a breath. Betty must have brushed off the medical examiner's comment in order to take the floor, and that was fine with Raven. The longer the delay in revealing the accident, the better. Raven paused her thought. Was the death out in the field actually an accident? Yes, it had to be. Just a mistake by the Sparks and their fencing.

Betty nodded. "Yes, robbed, and they made a mess. Tossed around his office. Well, the drawers behind the register. They were dumped out."

Johnny's eyebrows moved together. Raven saw his brain whirling, the cop's mind at work

"What are you thinking?" she asked her father.

He took another sip before asking his question. "Was the notice about the debt still posted on the door?"

Raven shrugged her shoulders. Betty said she didn't know.

"He didn't mention it," she said. "I don't even know what your question means. Why would Karl post debt he owed for the world to see?"

Howard cleared his voice, a habit Raven knew he did when he was about to one-up Betty. "Not what Karl owed. What people owe Karl. He did that a couple of years ago and created chaos down there. I'm surprised he'd do it again."

"Wow," said Betty, sitting back against the cushion. "That's definitely a statement. Why would he do that?"

Johnny brushed her question aside with his hand. "Not important at the moment. Go on, please. I'm happy to hear that Karl is okay."

"Oh, yeah. Fine. Except for his stomach. That wasn't very smart of him to eat such old shellfish. And he's angry, of course, for the mess and the violation and that someone stole his snowmobile and his town record, and that he has to grovel to Jared to get his snowmobile back," Betty added. "But he seems good other than all that. So, get this, other than the paper mess, and maybe that debt poster, the only other thing he can't find in the store is an old framed print!" She bounced her hands on her legs in a show of finality to her news.

"I'm sure he'll find more things missing as he goes through the store," said Howard, dismissing Betty's statement.

She wrinkled her face. "He already went through the store. He said that was it. You always have to contradict me. You weren't even there."

Howard raised his hands in surrender. "You're right. You're right. I was just thinking out loud, and not to contradict you, again, but that wasn't a framed print. It was a painting. Did you ever actually see it, Betty?"

Raven thought back to the framed print, painting, whatever it was. Karl called it a paint-by-number. It was a fixture in the store for as long as Raven could remember, always dusty and hanging crooked. The longest she ever looked at it was yesterday, when she was eavesdropping. Two women in a rowboat. Kinda dark, like it was a dawn or a dusk scene with a stream of light coming from the unseen rising or setting sun. The only color was a pop of red in the girls' outfits as they sat in a small white boat. Nothing remarkable to Raven. Kinda bland. She closed her eyes for a moment to remember more details: a gold frame with a few missing pieces along the edge, a cobweb in the upper left corner, and, of course, not quite straight on the wall, but why would it be? It was a piece of junk, her mother would have said. But kinda perfect for Wolf Marine. Part of the charm of the store.

"Okay, so, not a print. A paint-by-number, then," said Betty, not answering Howard's question and quoting Karl. Raven knew that Betty was frustrated that she hadn't paid attention to it last fall when she was in the store with Raven.

Betty stood up like a shot. "Who needs more tea and coffee?" And before anyone could answer, she headed into the kitchen. Clinking of ceramic on ceramic floated into the family room, followed by a few clanging pans. Betty was upset.

Howard sighed and gave Raven a small smile. She was sure neither Howard nor Betty was easy to live with, especially after over forty years together. She assumed she and Marcel didn't appear the same way to others, but maybe she was naive. For the last couple of years, Raven had struggled with her mother's death, her father's return to Maine, and then those dang suspicions of Marcel reconnecting with his high school girlfriend. If only Marcel didn't have to work with Shannon. "Don't invite trouble in," her mother always said, and Raven had been trying day by day to let her fears go. Why was she worried about her marriage? She had no reason to be. She and Marcel were solid. Right?

Johnny had stood quietly through the exchange between Howard and Betty. "I'm still wondering about the debt sign on the door."

"I don't know why Karl would do that again after last time. Being humiliated can lead to more trouble," said Howard.

"It's definitely a mistake by Karl, that's for sure, although I do get the need to be paid." Johnny turned to look out the window.

Raven hadn't realized that Karl had posted the debt owed to him by the local fisherman and lobstermen. That must have been the reason for the fight at Wolf Marine yesterday. Howard was right. When Karl had made a similar announcement a few years ago, it caused a ruckus in the town, complete with whispering and actual pointing at community events like the annual March town meeting. She understood Karl's need to collect the money owed to him, but to embarrass people didn't seem like the wisest move in a small town.

"Who was on the list this year?" Raven asked.

Johnny shook his head. Raven knew he wasn't going to spread the gossip.

"I need to get going," he said. And with that, he put his mug on the tray table and was out the door, in his truck, and backed out onto the road before Raven could even say good-bye.

Chapter Seventeen

Johnny couldn't stop thinking of Lennie, or the scene at Riverview Farm, or the fight at Wolf Marine the day before.

He didn't exactly know what had happened at the farm, but he saw the blood in the snow, the forensics team, the medical examiner, and Karl Wolf's sled. He could surmise that someone below was dead. He had thought it was Karl, but hearing Betty's story and knowing Karl was alive—thank goodness—his thoughts now drifted to who tossed the store and possibly tried to eliminate Karl. Or who may have stolen Karl's sled to get back at him, and that person was now the victim. He headed to Lennie's, hoping he was home.

He had an idea where Lennie lived. That was the thing about living in a small town. He rarely went to anyone's house except for Raven and Marcel's, but he paid attention to whose truck was parked where. He assumed everyone else did the same. He thought he knew where he had seen Lennie's parked.

Johnny knew he shouldn't get involved, but he told himself it wasn't about Marcel's investigation skills. Marcel was excellent at his job and could hold his own against the State Police, too. This was about reaching out to a person in need. He wished he had had someone looking out for him in his earlier years. Maybe it wouldn't have taken half of his life to get his act together and another quarter to earn the guts to fully confront his own past.

One day at a time. No judgment. Just live for today. Just today.

He pushed away the dissecting thoughts about his morning at the Harts. He and Raven were becoming closer, he felt. It just took time, although he wasn't sure how much time he had left. Hopefully enough.

He drove down the peninsula in the direction of Whale Harbor, the neighboring town that boasted a white sandy beach, a rarity in Maine, and its famous Whale Harbor lighthouse, depicted in multiple movies, although the town was mad when Hollywood once pretended it was a North Carolina scene. Lennie, however, lived just at the town line in Secretly, on the state road. His pale yellow ranch-style home, purchased in financially better days, was barely visible from the street.

Johnny stopped at the bottom of Lennie's unplowed driveway. Lennie's pickup truck wasn't in the yard, meaning he didn't sleep in his house last night. Johnny's heart skipped a beat. Tire tracks would be visible if he had left in the middle of the night, Johnny thought, and he definitely couldn't have driven out this morning with the two to three feet of snow on the ground. Maybe Lennie had support after all—his sister, a girlfriend—and he was over at their house. Perhaps Johnny was an intruder, an interloper, and he should back off. He hadn't gotten the sense, though, at Lane's that Lennie was going home to anyone with his bag of groceries or had anywhere else to go.

Johnny still had his small plow on his truck. The least he could do was clear Lennie's driveway, making it easier to reach his house when he returned. Hopefully, Lennie returned. Johnny took his time plowing up to the house, plowing a little, and backing up, and then repeating the process until it was clear, including a carved-out spot for Lennie to park his truck. The snow was sinking in its density with the passing of time, and he was glad to forge a wide path for Lennie. Seeing the amount of snow on the steps confirmed for Johnny that Lennie hadn't been home through much of the storm, or at least not the heavy, fast accumulation toward the end. Thinking back to the incident at Riverview Farm and the break-in at Wolf Marine, Johnny wondered if Lennie was gone for good.

"Doesn't hurt to do a wellness check," he muttered to himself. Of course, it wasn't a wellness check. A snowed-in driveway. No truck. No Lennie. He knew darn well that no one was in the house. But just in case, he should check, he thought, while he was there.

Johnny parked his truck and pushed his way up the snow-covered steps. He peered through the small window of the front door. The kitchenette was to the right. Pretty neat for a single guy. Like his place. He tried the knob. The door, of course, was unlocked.

He stamped the snow off his boots on the inside mat.

"Hello?" Johnny called out, just in case. "Lennie?" Silence.

He eyeballed the counter. He saw the remains of the cookies he had bought for Lennie yesterday, wrapped in plastic, saved for later. The garbage can held the empty sandwich container; the sandwich had probably been fully devoured. He opened the refrigerator. Not even a can of beer or a bottle of ketchup. Definitely tough times. A cabinet held a box of butter crackers and a can of tuna, along with the cans of soup and hash that Johnny bought him yesterday. Johnny would definitely offer Lennie a job working on his land as soon as the snow was gone, not that he had a lot of extra money himself, but his Boston cop pension kept him comfortable, and he liked to share.

In what Johnny would call the living room, there was one ratty recliner with oil stains and a couple of tears in a faded blue fabric next to a table with a lamp on it. The thin lampshade was stained too with a slight film of dust. The television was large, not in width but in the size of the old-fashioned wooden case with legs. Decades old. Probably wasn't even compatible with cable if Lennie could have afforded it. Johnny wondered if it even turned on.

Walking down the narrow hall, Johnny poked his head into the first room. Small and dark. He flicked on the light switch, and the overhead bulb flooded the room with light. Cardboard boxes marked "Christmas" and "Photos" were stacked on one side. Johnny paused to consider. Maybe that was the only inheritance Lennie received from his parents. Sentimental guy if that was what it was.

The small bathroom had a bath towel hanging to dry over the shower curtain. The full-size bed in the last room was unmade, the sheets and blanket all knotted up in a ball on one side. From restless sleep, Johnny assumed. Besides the bed, the room had one short dresser and a wooden chair with a pair of jeans and a flannel shirt flung on it. Again, just an overhead light, no lamps.

Johnny didn't notice anything that pointed him to Lennie's current whereabouts or his involvement in the Riverview Farm incident. He returned to the front door and debated leaving Lennie a friendly note, saying he'd stopped by and hoped he was okay. No, too intrusive.

Back in his own pickup truck, Johnny took the long way home to drive the state road along the coast. The tide was high again, but more in control than how he heard it was during the night. The sun glared off the snow, causing Johnny to almost hit a white pickup truck that was leaning in a ditch. Lennie's!

He pulled behind it, keeping his wheels flat on the road, and hopped out. Holding his breath, he walked toward the cab. The snow had covered the windows, both from the storm and from the passing plows. He gingerly climbed down to the cab window to brush off the snow and look inside. The crust of snow was thick, probably from the spray of the plows clearing the road. He banged against it with his fist, cracking the top layer. He pulled off the icy top with his fingers and then used his glove to clear off the rest of the window. He cupped his hands around his eyes as he pressed his head against the glass and held his breath, unsure of what he might see inside.

He quickly saw that the cab was empty. No Lennie. He relaxed for a moment, glad not see Lennie hurt or worse, but he was no closer to knowing where Lennie was or why Lennie was out during the storm.

He pulled open the driver's side door. Like the house, it was relatively clean. A travel mug, the kind with free refills from a local convenience store up on Route One, sat in the cup holder. A white eight-and-a-half-inch by eleven-inch piece of paper lay on the passenger seat. Even without picking it up, Johnny knew what it was. Karl's posted list of debts. Damn.

Chapter Eighteen

Tom stretched his back. The wooden chair in the Sparks' kitchen wasn't made for long conversation, probably by design, but for whose benefit? He couldn't imagine many people wanting to talk to Jared for long. Camille, on the other hand.

"Just a couple of more questions," said Marcel. Tom hid his disappointment. He was hoping to leave. Jared was too guarded to let anything slip, and Tom also wanted to get back outside to talk to the new forensics person. What was her name again? Marilyn? Madeline? Margot. Miss Margot. He assumed she was a Miss, at least he hoped so. He was so predictable.

"More questions?" Jared's eyes flared again. His temper was back. "You think we had something to do with this? How could you even think that?"

Tom witnessed Marcel ignoring the snap. Camille, however, didn't, and jabbed Jared again in the ribs with her elbow, in full view of them all.

Marcel continued, ignoring both the outburst and the jab. "Did you hear anything last night? Anything unusual?"

"Just the wind. It rattled the windows. I was afraid the barn's roof would blow off. We haven't had a chance to replace it yet," said Camille, twisting a paper napkin in her hand. She had aged since the first time Tom had met her months ago. Last summer, the Sparks asked for help blocking traffic on their road for the alpaca delivery. Traffic. He sat there waiting for the cattle truck for two hours, and one car had passed him. At the time, Tom thought of her as luminous, like a sprite floating along the river. He'd known her from the summers she spent visiting her grandfather, and meeting her in person did not disappoint. He glanced at her now and saw deep creases in her brow, with pale, dry skin and red-rimmed eyes. He knew a sprite was still in there somewhere.

Jared scoffed at Camille. "That roof is fine. I've told you that a hundred times. I'm not sure why you worry about those damn animals so much. They live in the mountains outside elsewhere."

Camille blinked and dabbed her eyes with a tissue. Tom studied Jared's face. Maybe if he smiled, he'd be handsome. Scowls always made others unattractive, he thought. There had to be something redeeming about him if Camille married him. She seemed like a nice, normal person, and certainly her grandfather was the salt of the earth. What had he thought of Jared?

Marcel asked more questions. "How about the snowmobile? Did you hear it or other ones in the field?"

Jared spoke this time, more composed, shaking his head. "No, I didn't. I was surprised to see it in the field this morning, because I thought I would have heard them go through last night." He turned to Camille, putting his hand on her knee. "Honey, did you hear them?"

"Them?" Tom asked. "Why are you saying 'them'?" Tom also wondered why Jared was now being nice to Camille in front of them by calling her "Honey." He had never witnessed such mood swings.

"Them as in the snowmobiles. I had assumed more than one went through. That the guy on the broken one had gotten a ride home from someone." He paused. "But of course, it now sounds like only one came onto our property, if I'm reading you right."

Tom did not need Jared "reading him."

Marcel kept going. "Where were you two last night?" he asked.

"What? Where do you think we were in the middle of a blizzard?" Jared snapped, withdrawing his hand from Camille's leg. Angry Jared was back. He was unbelievable.

Camille shifted in her seat, eyes down. Was it Tom's imagination that she looked like she wanted to give a different answer? Or was it just embarrassment over her husband's constant rudeness?

Marcel, undaunted, continued. "You were both together the whole night? Can you both confirm that?" He said that as a statement, not a question.

Camille nodded as Jared said, "Of course, we were!"

She rose, holding her empty water glass. It shook a little. "Can I get anyone something else to drink?"

Jared answered Marcel, ignoring Camille. "The only time we weren't together was when I went out to check the barn doors around two o'clock. To make sure they were latched. That wind was something fierce."

Camille whipped around in surprise. Either she slept through Jared's field trip, or she was surprised he was worried about the animals. Tom was definitely confused as to why Jared would chastise Camille for her zealous care of the alpacas and then brave the blizzard to check the door. Tom had assumed Jared thought the animals were a waste of time and money, based on how he reacted to the idea of a new barn roof.

Or maybe Camille knew he had gone out but thought he had gone somewhere else. That seemed more likely. Regardless, she should never play poker. Her face told too much, even if Tom couldn't fully read it.

"I'd like to check out the barn, actually, now that you mention it. Camille, do you mind showing me your alpacas?" Tom stood. He felt Jared's eyes on his back as he and Camille left the kitchen. Maybe if he got her alone, she'd share what she knew.

Once outside, Tom and Camille chit-chatted about the snow and how much fun it was for her as a kid to come up on Christmas break and use an old toboggan to sled down the steepest hill.

"My grandfather had to bribe me to come in with the promise of hot cocoa with as many marshmallows as I wanted." She laughed, and then paused to swallow back the sentiment. Tom saw the love for her grandfather in her face. Franklin was an amazing man and was so missed by the town.

Tom finally tried to broach the topic. He said to Camille, as he helped her slide open the heavy wooden barn door, "You seemed surprised to hear Jared say he was out at the barn." He let the words hang in the cold air.

She stopped pushing and turned to Tom, her breath coming out in puffs of clouds from the cold air.

"No, no. I'm sure he did check the barn. He must have done that before...." She let her voice trail off. Tears streamed down her face. Tom waited.

Camille brushed off her face with her mittens. She took a big breath. "We didn't have a good night last night. He was so mad at me for signing the paperwork that allowed the snowmobiles into the back field. I don't think it was just about them being on our property, or about the alpacas, or about liability. It was more about him not being consulted, not being included in my decision. It's hard for him because this is really my farm, in so many ways. I'm the one with the memories here. He left behind a life in Boston that he really loved, but he moved here because he wanted to live here. He did it for me. We just need to figure out how we can both be happy here."

"What did you mean that he went to the barn before he did something else?" Tom watched her closely.

"Oh," she stammered. "I just meant, before he came back in the house."

Tom didn't believe a word she said, but he let her continue.

"I woke up around two o'clock. He wasn't in bed, so I went downstairs. I wondered if he was stewing in the TV room since he had stormed off to bed fully pissed, but on my way to check, I noticed his Bean boots were gone. I was so afraid he had gone down the field to wait for snowmobilers to come through, and for a moment, when Sheriff Ouelette had said someone had died back there, and then Jared asked if the person was shot, it made me wonder if he had actually gone out with my grandfather's rifle and shot the person. But no one was shot, right?"

She shook. Tears streamed down her face. Tom shoved his hands into his pockets to stop himself from comforting her. He wanted to tell her what probably killed Mikey, but he couldn't.

"We don't really know the cause of death." They suspected it was the barbed wire, but maybe the ME would find a gunshot wound, too. Not for him to speculate, and not for him to let Jared off the hook yet for stringing that wire at two o'clock in the morning. It was possible, and the timing probably worked.

"Oh no, I hope he didn't do anything stupid. He wouldn't hurt anyone. Really, he wouldn't. I know he wouldn't. He's a hot head and gets angry at the slightest things, but really, he is a good person at heart."

Tom hadn't seen much of the good person side of Jared to believe Camille, but there had to be something good about him, he hoped, for Camille's sake. They were still standing in the barn doorway when the side door to the farmhouse opened. Marcel and Jared stood on the stone step.

Tom and Camille walked toward them. He felt that Camille wasn't sharing something else that happened last night with Jared. He'd come back this week and talk to her again, without Jared looming nearby. Camille joined Jared on the stone step as Marcel stepped down to stand with Tom.

"Oh, and one more question," said Marcel, turning back to them.

Jared and Camille, looking like a sheet wrung through the washer, nodded and seemed like they didn't have any energy left for one more question.

"When did you install the barbed wire in the back field?" he asked.

"Barbed wire? We don't have any barbed wire on the farm. It would get caught in the alpacas' coats and ruin the fiber." Camille's tone and her face looked genuine.

"Maybe it was left over from Camille's grandfather's days of farming?" Jared suggested. "Was it down in the back? To be frank, we haven't used those back fields for livestock yet. I should have thought of that as another reason to caution the snowmobile club's use. There could be all sorts of hazards down there."

Marcel nodded. "Thanks for the time. Folks should be clearing out of here in an hour or so. Again, please stay out of that field until we give the okay, both you and the animals."

Tom walked next to Marcel. "That barbed wire looked new to me."

Marcel nodded. They both knew what that meant. Either Jared and Camille were lying, or someone else had been on their property before the snowmobile had come through.

Chapter Nineteen

Lily and Dukie sniffed around the driveway as Raven carved a wider path near the front steps with a shovel. It felt good to be outside with the dogs, in the crisp air and bright sunshine. She loved snow and snowstorms, but this one had taken on a dark, heavy feeling, making her wish winter was further along. Even though it was comforting to know that Karl was safe, someone else wasn't. Prayers for that poor soul.

The barks of the poochies alerted her to the vehicles coming up the driveway before she even saw them. Marcel's Jeep came first, with Tom's SUV close behind. The dogs knew enough to stay out of the way to let them park, and then barreled toward them as soon as the engines were shut off, Dukie rushing to Marcel's open door, and Lily waiting impatiently, with her butt wiggling, for her boyfriend Tom to alight from his vehicle. Raven also met Marcel at his Jeep, pressing close to him as he kissed the side of her face at the temples. She was sure Tom had told him what she had seen earlier that morning.

"We came home for a quick lunch, and then to go back out there," he said into her ear. She pulled back, and he lightly kissed her on the lips. "Tough morning. You okay?"

She wanted to say she was fine so he wouldn't worry. She didn't want to tell him that she couldn't get the image of the helmet and the blood out of her mind. Instead of answering, she asked if he knew Karl was okay, alive, and well.

"I don't know where Karl is," Marcel said, still holding on to her. "But I do know that it wasn't Karl in the field."

"Yes, I know. That's what I meant. I saw Karl at Wolf Marine."

"You did?" Marcel pulled back. "When was that?"

"About two hours ago," said Raven. "Betty needed to go to Lane's after the preserve, and gosh, I did not want to go—I hadn't told Betty what was really happening—but I'm glad we did because we saw him out front pumping gas. We stopped, and he told us about the break-in. I didn't say anything about a body, but Betty told him his sled was at Riverview Farm. Do you think whoever broke in also stole his sled?"

She saw Marcel's gears clicking in his mind. "I'm not sure what has happened. A developing story." He released her to greet Lily, who had now made her way over to him. "Well, thank you, Lil, for giving me the time of day. I know it's hard to pull yourself away from your darlin' Tom."

Tom, close behind Lily, chuckled. "I can't help it if I'm so charming."

In the kitchen, Raven pulled out cold cuts, sliced cheese, condiments, lettuce, and rolls for Marcel and Tom to assemble what they wanted for lunch. A bark from Dukie caused Raven to glance out the front windows in the living room. Johnny was already out of his truck and heading to their front door. She heard the door open. The dogs rushed to greet him.

"What a morning!" Johnny said, entering the kitchen.

Marcel and Tom nodded, mouths full.

"Make yourself a sandwich," said Raven, waving her hand toward the counter.

"Thank you! I will take you up on that. I'll tell you, my head is spinning—the snowmobile in the field, thinking Karl was dead, learning Karl is alive, dealing with the Sparks."

"How did you know it wasn't Karl in the field?" said Tom.

"Oh, I assumed it was Karl until I went to the Harts and Betty shared going to Wolf Marine. Glad to hear Karl is a-okay. Do you know who died in the field?" Raven saw concern wash over Johnny's face as if he was bracing for the news.

Marcel lowered his sandwich to the plate and wiped his mouth. "Yes, I'm sorry to say it was Mikey Dyer."

"Mikey!" Raven thought back to him coming into Wolf Marine and looking for work. Did he take Karl's sled because Karl didn't give him any money?

Johnny exhaled a long whistle. "He was eyeing the sled yesterday during the argument."

"Yep," said Tom. "He was standing right next to it when I told him to go home. Must have seen the key in it." He wiped the corner of his mouth with a paper napkin.

Johnny leaned against the counter. "I saw him right after that in Lane's, when I was in there with Lennie. He was looking…well, not to speak ill of the dead…but he seemed to be stoned or something."

Marcel nodded. "He has always given his mother grief. I think he had earned the 'most suspended from school' superlative when he graduated high school."

Johnny shook his head. Raven knew that Johnny understood how hard it was to fight demons. It was probably near impossible to come out the other side alive. Somehow, Johnny did. Mikey did not.

Johnny stood in silence at the counter, not making a sandwich.

"Something on your mind, Johnny?" asked Marcel.

Johnny rubbed his chin and nodded. "I was just thinking of how quickly life can be extinguished. Also, I came across Lennie Putnam's pickup on the side of the road. Any report on what happened to it or to him?"

"Really? I didn't see it near Whale Harbor when I did my rounds." Tom made his way over to the counter to make a second sandwich.

"Past that. On the way to Eelsboro. Towards my house. I was on my way back home, but I took the long route. You know me, I'm nosey, and I wanted to see the shoreline damage."

"Ah, I was on my way in that direction when I saw Karl's front store door open. I would have seen it then if I hadn't stopped at the store. Let me make some calls about Lennie." Tom set down the mayonnaise knife and went to a corner of the living room to talk on his cell phone. Raven heard his low voice but couldn't hear what he was saying.

Marcel asked Johnny, "What were you doing inside the Sparks' house today?"

Raven knew by the tone of Marcel's voice that he wasn't interrogating

Johnny but genuinely curious.

Johnny shook his head. "Ah, I was again nosey and saw the ME and the forensic cars pull in, so I did the same. Jared and Camille ran over to my truck and sort of asked me to find out what was happening. Besides my own curiosity, I thought it might help Jared relax. He's a cannon, ready to be lit. I think you saw me on the hill at the top of the field. I didn't think it was my place to "report back" what I saw, as Jared had asked. He was not pleased with me when I said I thought it was a matter better left to the authorities. I was glad 'the authorities' were there to pick up my slack when I left." He winked at Marcel.

Marcel nodded, smiled, and gulped down his milk.

Johnny continued. "I'm sure you've both run across people like him before. His anger is a shield protecting something."

Marcel nodded again. Raven also knew the layers people carried within them, often without realizing it themselves. She had even been surprised by herself in recent months.

"One thing that I did want to share from my Sparks encounter: I had knocked at their door when I came back from the field. I waited a few minutes and knocked again. I finally opened it a crack and yelled 'hello.' No one came, but I heard yelling in the back of the house, which I later learned was from the kitchen. I overheard Camille say, 'Tell me where you were last night!' I didn't hear a response from Jared. Her question is the same one I thought I had heard her say to him outside, as they were walking away from me. I hustled back to the front door and knocked on it again. This time, Jared came and let me in. His face was flushed with anger. That goes without saying."

Tom added, rejoining the group. "That fits with what they told us about Jared checking on the barn. But it doesn't fit with Jared's style. I think Camille knows that, too, but isn't sharing everything with us. I wonder where he really went. I'm suspecting he left the property."

"I agree," said Marcel. "We'll go back and talk to them. But first, let's check on Karl and then Lunchbox once we find him, since he and Karl had words yesterday."

"Did you learn anything about Lennie?" Johnny asked.

"I did. He's okay but has a nasty bump on the head. He's still at County Hospital. The responding officer reported that Lennie said he was run off the road by an out-of-control, speeding vehicle. He didn't see anything but heard it bang into his truck. Next thing he knew, he was in the ditch. "

"What time did this happen?" Marcel asked. Raven saw his brain whirling through the timing of the night's events.

"I'm thinking it was when I was helping that family whose house went into the ocean. I knew there were a couple of vehicles off the road elsewhere. So about two o'clock? One thirty or two thirty?"

"Yes, I heard those reports, too, about cars and trucks in a ditch. I didn't connect the dots that one could have been Lunchbox." Marcel stood up. "Well, that doesn't cross him off the list. He could still have tampered with the wooden post and the barbed wire before getting stuck in the ditch. We also need to break the news to Mrs. Dyer about Mikey. I think we should do that next."

The poor mother, Raven thought. No mother should ever hear that her child died, especially the way Mikey did.

"I'm going to just check on Lennie at the hospital if that's okay with you guys." Johnny put his coffee cup in the sink.

Raven saw both Marcel and Tom raise their eyebrows, probably wondering what Johnny's interest was with this local, but they both just nodded their okay.

She saw Johnny read them, too. He shrugged to try to answer their question, she guessed by saying, "Kindred spirits." And with that, he went to the foyer to don his boots and winter coat and left.

"I knew this blizzard was going to be a lot of work, but I didn't think it was going to take on this dark vein," said Tom, also placing his dishes into the sink. "When will we be talking about something light and fun? We need a party or something!"

"You know, I was thinking the same thing," said Marcel. "Remember, babe, when we used to have Sunday dinners? When your mom was still here?"

"I loved them!" Tom said. "Can I be back on the list? When's the next one?"

Raven smiled. Memories of her mom making her way over from the Birch cabin, sometimes with an apple crumb or her famous whoopie pies. Betty and Howard came too, and an occasional wayward friend from town who seemed like they needed a meal surrounded by good company. All of that stopped when Julia was diagnosed with cancer. At that time, Raven could barely breathe at the thought of losing her mother. Then Johnny showing up just after Julia died also didn't cause Raven to restart the dinners—Marcel would have insisted that Johnny be invited—and she hadn't been ready for that. Maybe Marcel was right. A little socializing would be a good thing again.

"What about next Sunday night? A small dinner party to kick off the 'Sunday Night Gatherings.' I think that is what your mom always called them," said Marcel.

Raven smiled at the image of her mom saying that in the kitchen. "I'm here for the Sunday Night Gathering," she'd call out from the foyer, giving a warning shout, she said, because she was always afraid she might catch Raven and Marcel in a compromising position despite Raven telling her over and over that they were expecting her for Sunday night dinner and would definitely have their clothes on.

The other soft spot in Raven's heart was that next Sunday was actually Raven's birthday. She didn't expect Marcel to remember that at the moment, with all that had happened at Riverview Farm and Wolf Marine. Also, she knew that he was terrible with remembering special dates like birthdays and anniversaries—the day they first met, their wedding day, the day her mom passed away. He would remember if she asked him, "Do you know what today is?" because he would pause and consider the calendar. She wasn't going to prompt him on the special nature of next Sunday. Not yet. Even if she was planning her own birthday celebration, it could be fun to have the Harts over, and Tom, and even Johnny this time. It would be her first birthday party with him, since she didn't remember any of the ones before he left her for Boston.

"You're on," she said. "Cook's choice, by the way, but I'm sensing lobster mac and cheese in our future."

"Don't have to invite me twice!" said Tom with a big grin, his bright blue eyes sparkling. "Consider this my RSVP."

"Speaking of inviting, what do you think of having Shannon McGrath attend? The new county DA that I went to high school with?"

Raven froze in the kitchen at the sound of Shannon's name. She knew darn well who she was.

"It's time you two met." Marcel kissed a speechless Raven. "See you in a bit, babe." And on that explosive moment, out of the house he and Tom went.

She stood paralyzed. Her heart picked up its rhythm, and tears formed along the rims of her eyelids. She didn't want to meet Shannon, let alone have her in her home and on her birthday. She thought her worries about Marcel and Shannon reconnecting were over, that she had been overreacting and misreading their friendship. She now wondered if she was being played as a fool. Was he being sly in inviting Shannon to come over right under her nose? Or was it simply an innocent invitation, as in he truly was just friends now with DA McGrath and wanted to show off his wife to her? Regardless of the reason, there was no way she was inviting Shannon to her own birthday dinner. She had a week to wiggle out of it.

Chapter Twenty

Still wiping her tears, Raven trudged through the snow drifts back to the Birch cabin, leaving Dukie behind this time. She hoped that keeping busy would help distract her wandering mind from Marcel's comment about Shannon McGrath coming for dinner and all that it might imply.

She knew Marcel wasn't good with special dates. Whenever he surprised her by bringing home a bouquet of flowers or her favorite cinnamon bun, he said it was to make up for all the missed moments. She had never cared if she didn't have a birthday or Valentine's Day card from him. Her mother always said, "Every day is Valentine's Day when you're in love," and that was the truth.

Her mother had many good sayings about love. Fascinating from a woman who had been burned by her own marriage to Johnny. Somehow, her mother had been able to keep her perspective on it all.

Raven followed the path she had taken earlier that morning. Hers and Dukie's prints were visible, despite the wind filling in the gaps, but the overall break in the snow pile had held, making her trek easier than when she walked it in the morning. She was glad, though, that she had left Dukie in the house with Lily, their bellies full, in front of the wood stove with their favorite bully sticks.

In the cabin, the gas fireplace still flickered. She had left it on low when Betty suggested their preserve walk, but then she had forgotten about it. She was glad, however, because now the cabin was warm enough for painting a wall or two. She deposited her boots by the door on a mat and put on the slippers that she had brought, stuffed in her pockets, to keep her feet warm. Before starting on the bathroom painting, however, she wanted to check on that loose stone. If it wasn't easily fixed, she felt it would be too risky to rent this cabin anyway over Valentine's Day weekend, and she might as well save her painting efforts for another cabin.

She stepped back and studied the stones, easily spotting the loose one again. It protruded inches out past the others. How had she never noticed this before, for all the times she cleaned this cabin? Too much rushing, probably. She knelt down in front of the hearth. Should she really try to pull it out? What if it was the crux that was holding up everything, and the fireplace collapsed on top of her?

"Now that is the silliest thought ever," said Raven out loud. "Stop living in fear."

Yes, stop living in fear. Fear of the stone. Fear of the fireplace collapsing. Fear of loving Johnny. Fear of losing Marcel. Fear. Fear. Fear. It was eating her alive at times, eating away her life, her own limited time on earth.

"You can at least get rid of the fear of the fireplace collapsing on a guest by having it collapse on you," she said and laughed to herself. Marcel's mention of her mother coming for Sunday dinners brought her mother to life in the cabin. Of course, Julia was with her always. Where else would she be?

"You're right, Ma. I have nothing to fear but fear itself. Yes, I know Roosevelt said that first. But it's such a good quote, I'm going to use it!" And Roosevelt was right. Fear is the enemy more than anything else.

"'Screw your courage to the sticking place.' That's another good quote, but I can't remember where it's from other than something I learned in high school lit class. If I can come up with enough quotes, I will have this stone out in no time." Raven wished she had brought Dukie back with her to the cabin. At least all of her talking out loud would seem less crazy to anyone peeking in the windows. Not that a soul was out there. Just her own mixed-up mind.

She lay on her stomach, propped up on her elbows, to get a closer, eye-level view of the stone. It was about the same size as the others—about five or six inches across—and almost a perfect rectangle. She noticed the cement wasn't fully sealed at the bottom. She just needed something thin and flat to pry it out.

"A butter knife. I wish I had brought one with me. Wait. A spatula for the wood putty." She jumped up and headed into the bathroom, where she had left her painting supplies, including a small spatula to smear any putty needed to patch holes or dents in the wall. Going back to the hearth, she again laid down and angled the metal spatula under the rock. It moved, but not much.

She rose to her knees to use her weight against the handle. Pushing down on the stone moved it slightly. She bounced the handle up and down and saw the stone moving out of its hole.

"If I could get a grip on the rock itself, I could yank it out and figure out what I'm dealing with. Hopefully, nothing that some new cement can't fix." She hoped she wouldn't find rotted wood behind the rock. There were no termites in Maine, but large black carpenter ants were plentiful.

A couple of more bounces of the handle, and she heard a suction sound. The stone moved out four inches.

"Wow, now I'm getting somewhere."

Still on her knees, she was able to get a grip with her fingers and pull on the stone. It moved toward her. Her hands were too small to fully grasp the whole stone, but she wiggled it to the left and the right, and finally, it popped out. It wasn't as deep as she thought it would be. In fact, it was only two inches thick. Was that thick enough to hold up the hearth? She assumed whoever built the structure had used it only as decorative stone, not as a practical one.

She shone the flashlight from her cell phone into the hole, looking for rot, and praying a mouse didn't pop out at her. While the stone wasn't large in depth, the hole itself was. Stretching almost to the firebricks of the fireplace. The light picked up a glint of metal.

She was afraid to reach in—again with this fear! She picked up the spatula, which had a lip on one side, maybe for cleaning the rims of paint cans, and gritted her teeth as she reached inside the hole. The lip caught on something, and with a tug, the sound of metal came closer to Raven. She showed her flashlight app again into the hole. The side of a grey metal box came into view.

She reached in and pulled it out.

"Who put this here?" she asked out as if the rafters would answer.

The box was about three inches high and under a foot wide. That is why it was sideways in the hole, which was only six inches across but deep enough to hide the whole box. It wasn't rusty or old in appearance, just dusty. Could a guest have put it here? If so, to hide what?

There was a built-in lock that had a keyhole, but Raven tried the latch anyway. It sprang open.

She fell back and gasped at the contents. The box was stuffed with money. One hundred-dollar bills lay on top of yellowing envelopes. Based on the box's size, there must be thousands of dollars inside if all the bills were the same.

She brushed aside the bills and picked up an envelope. It was addressed to her mother. No return address in the corner or on the back, but the postmark was a couple of months before her mother's death. From Boston, Massachusetts.

She opened the envelope and found a small folded piece of paper inside.

"Dear Julia, Here is this month's payment for you and Raven. I've officially retired from the Boston Police. I won't have as much income to keep sending the same amount, but I will continue to send something. Actually, if you'll have me, I'd like to move back up to Maine to get to know Raven, and of course, to see you, my love. I could get a small job too. I do hope that one day you will forgive me for everything. Love, Johnny"

Raven sat frozen for the second time that day. Again, her heart raced in her chest. Her breathing became shallow. "Love, Johnny."

"In. Out. In. Out," she coached herself to keep from passing out.

She looked back at the metal box and dug through the rest of its contents. Hundreds of one-hundred-dollar bills and dozens of envelopes. The bottom one was postmarked the year she was ten. They were all from Johnny.

He actually had been trying. All this time. His whole life. He must have assumed that she knew about the money. He must think she was the coldest-hearted person in the world, the most ungrateful. More tears streamed down her face. It was all too much.

Johnny had never abandoned her and her mother. Marcel had been right all along. Johnny had to leave and face his demons alone, but he never stopped caring about her and Julia. A wave of relief mixed with gratitude washed over her, followed by guilt for how she had been treating him. She looked down at the metal box and wondered what Johnny's reaction would be when she showed it to him.

But then a dark thought entered her mind. Why did Julia hide this information from her for all of those years? She let Raven think that Johnny had vanished, that he didn't care about either of them. She had encouraged Raven to rely only on her for emotional support. Was her mother really that selfish? Or just hurt beyond repair? Was she protecting herself, and not Raven, all this time?

Chapter Twenty-One

The part of the job Tom hated most was notifying family members when something happened to a loved one. In his career, two cases stood out. The first one, telling an eighty-five-year-old invalid woman that her husband of over sixty years didn't survive his heart attack in the produce section of the grocery store, and the second involved a foul baseball that hit a fifth grader in just the wrong spot on his head in little league practice. He could still hear the parents' sobs.

And now, he thought, I'm adding to the worst experiences by telling a mother her son was probably murdered. It was hard to think of the barbed wire as an accident, especially when the Sparks insisted they never used that type of wire. But there it was, hanging at the scene, on a relatively new post, and near a tree across from it. They had found the other part of it in the woods and now had a fiber sample as well. Most likely, a search warrant for the Sparks would be requested to match those fibers. Whether it was them or someone else, the fibers would help with a conviction.

Of course, there was a slight chance that Mikey could have committed suicide. He had heard of young men doing similar deeds that caused body parts to roll around train tracks and such, but it would have been a difficult feat with the blizzard and knowing if he had the opportunity to use Karl's sled. Certainly, if he wanted to kill himself, he could have found an easier way. No, Tom didn't think that Mikey took his own life.

Tom swung his SUV into the driveway of Mrs. Alma Dyer's home. She had been a teacher's aide when he was in grammar school. A kind woman, with eyeglasses taped at the bridge, because she couldn't afford new ones.

That was how he remembered her.

He glanced over at Marcel, who had been silent their entire ride. Plotting out the details of the case, Tom assumed. If it were truly murder, it would, of course, point to a local. A murderer among them. Always tough in a small town.

When Tom cut his engine, Marcel looked over at him and gave a small, thin smile.

"Never gets easier," he said.

"No, it doesn't," Tom agreed. He saw a curtain move in the front window of the small house. The house was the size of a large square white box with black shutters, surrounded by birch trees. Their white and black striped trunks complemented the house. Mrs. Dyer had seen the sheriff's car drive in, and he knew her heart was beating to hear why they were there. Of course, she'd assume that it had to be about Mikey. What could she have possibly done to warrant a visit from the sheriff's office? She was used to Mikey getting in trouble.

The driveway had been plowed, but the front steps weren't shoveled. Someone must plow her out but not get out of the truck to clean the stairs. Probably a cheaper bill that way. The black front door opened before they reached the stairs. A broom came out first, and then Mrs. Dyer, a short woman in her fifties, showed up on the stoop without wearing a coat or hat.

"I wasn't expecting company. I'm so sorry my steps aren't shoveled." She quickly pushed the top layer of snow off the first step. It had already settled and become heavy.

"Let me get that," Tom said, rushing forward. He held out his hand to receive the broom. He looked at her face, wrinkled, worn, tired, but without the pain he and Marcel were about to lay upon her by telling her that her only child was dead.

"Tommy, you've always been such a good kid," she smiled. "Hi, Sheriff Ouelette. How are you? Pine Acres made out okay with the storm?"

"Yes, thank you. I'll tell Raven you were asking about it." Marcel smiled at Mrs. Dyer.

"Good to see you both," she said. Tom marveled at her attempt to make small talk and to put them at ease. "Come in out of the cold, please."

She stepped back into the house, and Tom and Marcel followed her into the tiny foyer. Her salt and pepper hair was cut close to her head in a slightly uneven style, as if she did it herself and couldn't see the back of her head to even it out. She was wearing a blue plaid flannel shirt with elbow patches and what his mother even called "Mom Jeans." Her television was tuned to the weather channel. On a brown-clothed chair, she had left knitting needles with variegated yarn already worked on them. It looked like it would end up being a scarf. He hoped she wasn't making it for Mikey.

"Can I get you a cup of coffee? Some cinnamon raisin toast?" She smiled, but her hands shook.

She hadn't asked why they were there. Tom knew it wouldn't be the first time someone from the sheriff's office had been in her driveway.

"We're all set," said Marcel, answering for them both. "Mind if we sit down?"

She swept her hand around the small living room. "Please do."

A loveseat matching the chair's pattern held a snoozing tabby cat on one cushion. "Tabitha, gotta move, sweetheart, for the gentlemen."

Tabitha didn't even open one eye.

"Let me just put her on my bed." Mrs. Dyer gently picked up the sleeping cat in her arms, keeping it curled up, and left the room, returning quickly.

Tom and Marcel waited for Mrs. Dyer to sit before they did.

Marcel started. "Mrs. Dyer, we have some sad news about Mikey."

Her face flushed, and without knowing what it was yet, tears burst out of her eyes. She ignored them rolling down her cheeks, as if tending to them would be impolite.

"I figured. I don't know what it is about that boy. Always getting into trouble. If his father were alive, I think he would have turned out differently. I don't know why I couldn't handle him." She gripped the arms of the chair to steady herself for what she was about to hear.

Marcel cleared his throat. "You're not responsible for the actions of another adult, Mrs. Dyer. Even if that adult is your son. In this case, he appeared to be at the wrong place at the wrong time."

Her eyes grew large. It seemed to dawn on her that he wasn't so much in trouble as injured.

"Yes?" She said in a shaky voice, sitting up straight in her chair. Tom noticed her grip had loosened because her hands were vibrating too quickly.

"Last night, Mikey went out for a snowmobile ride," Marcel said in a low voice.

"A snowmobile ride? I don't think he has a snowmobile." Her voice shook.

"He…borrowed someone else's." Marcel tactfully explained to her.

"Oh. Is he okay? I'm guessing he got hurt. That's why you're here. Is he at the hospital?"

Tom's brain silently answered her. "No, he's at the morgue." He appreciated that Marcel had taken charge of relaying this news. It made him sick.

"I'm sorry to say, Mrs. Dyer," said Marcel, leaning forward, "that there was an accident with the snowmobile, and Mikey has died."

Her hands stopped shaking. She sat frozen, her mouth open. For a moment, Tom wondered if her heart had stopped and she had died too. Then her eyes blinked, and she fell back into the cushions, her mouth still agape. A loud sob escaped her lips.

"Where is he now? Can I see him?" Her arms crossed her chest, not in a holding her heart type of way, but looking like she was hugging herself.

"Is there someone we can call for you?" Marcel asked, skirting her question for now.

She nodded. "Yes, my sister. I'll get her number for you."

Chapter Twenty-Two

Betty pounded chicken breasts as thin as possible. She believed her chicken parmesan was the best anyone had ever eaten. She prided herself on her cooking. Her mother was an excellent cook, feeding her and her brothers gourmet meals nightly, whether or not her father was home from New York City to eat them. She hadn't realized how unusual it was to not have a father often home for dinner at their Connecticut house until she had married Howard and found him home like clockwork every day. Good thing she knew how to cook.

"Are those chickens not dead yet?" Howard yelled from the family room next to the kitchen. She wished the kitchen had doors to shut her in, like some older homes had to keep the servants away from the owners. She'd gladly sequester herself away to keep from hearing Howard.

"I need them as flat as possible. And even. So they all cook the same." Betty didn't know why she bothered to respond to Howard. He didn't care about what she was doing. She knew he was really complaining about the noise from her metal meat tenderizer hitting the wooden cutting board. She had given up expecting him to appreciate her culinary efforts.

With each slap to the chicken breast, Betty thought about Jared Sparks and his anger toward the snowmobiles going across his land. Well, it really was Camille's land. If Camille were smart, she wouldn't have added Jared to the deed, but would that matter in a divorce? Would it be common property anyway?

Look at what she was doing—breaking up a marriage without knowing all the details. If disagreeing was grounds for dissolution, she and Howard wouldn't have made it to their first child, let alone to have had three daughters and multiple moves to beautiful homes, not that this house was her favorite, but it had grown on her. And she certainly didn't see the locals the way Jared did. What a snob he was.

"Rednecks!" she said with a bang against the chicken.

"That's what you're serving for supper?" Howard asked. "How do they taste?"

She hadn't realized she said it out loud. She left the kitchen for a moment, meat tenderizer in hand, and peered around the wall. Howard was in his leather recliner, feet up, glasses on top of his head, reading a book on how to invest like a millionaire. She thought they already had that much money from his retirement funds from his job as an actuary for a Hartford insurance company. Maybe she should look for a bank statement to be sure.

I guess one can always have more money, she thought. *More for the girls to inherit eventually since he definitely won't let me spend any of it.* She sighed.

He put down the book and lowered his glasses to his eyes. "Yes?"

"I was just thinking out loud. Jared called everyone in town a redneck when I was at the shop yesterday."

"So what? Those aren't exactly death threat words." Howard put his glasses back on, dismissing her.

"No, but he definitely has hatred for us all. He must not have seen me in my Mercedes convertible last summer." She felt like pounding Howard with the tenderizer. He was so rude to her.

Howard glanced at her, his glasses still on his head. "I can't believe he didn't. I told you that you'd stick out here like a sore thumb up here in that car."

She wagged the tenderizer at him. "I don't think I do. I no longer wear the chiffon scarf trailing behind me as I did in Connecticut. I keep a low profile."

Howard shook his head and lifted his book to his nose. She knew he wanted her to leave him alone. She wasn't ready to comply.

"I don't think he's very bright," she said.

"Who?" Howard put down his book. Now she had his attention.

"Jared."

"Why do you say that?" asked Howard.

"Nothing in particular other than him name calling, generalizing. That's usually someone who isn't very smart." Betty thought she didn't need to explain her reasoning to Howard. Her opinion should have been enough.

He shook his head. "Kinda like you thinking everyone who lived in Maine only wore flannel. I remember you saying that when I first told you I wanted to move here."

She pursed her lips. "That's not exactly what I said, and that is certainly not what I meant about Jared. I'm just thinking that he could be naive about barbed wire, especially coming from living in a city. He might have thought if he strung it across a field, it would simply stop the snowmobiles from crossing, not to kill someone. Like someone would see it and put on their brakes, signal others to stop, and so forth." She had learned after Raven left that someone had indeed been lying deceased in the farm field near the snowmobile, although she was missing the full details.

Howard had resumed reading his book and nodded without looking up. He did show that he agreed, however. "You got a point there. More like a lack of knowledge than stupidity."

"All right, if you want to say it that way," said Betty. "Yes, Naïveté. I'm positive he's the guy. It would be simple to find out. Tom and Marcel can get a search warrant and find receipts for barbed wire or even the leftover wire from the roll. It's probably in the barn."

"What difference could that make? He could claim the farm needed that wire."

Betty sighed. Howard might be as dense as Jared. "It's not just owning the wire, but where he put it."

Howard didn't give up. "If he bought it for sinister reasons, why would he save the receipts or the rest of the wire? He'd probably pay cash for it, too."

"Okay, then we could canvas hardware stores with his photo. We could ask to see camera footage."

Howard laughed. "Since when did Barrett County employ you in the sheriff's office?"

Betty stamped her foot. "I didn't mean me, per se. I meant 'the good citizens of Secretly' with Marcel and Tom as our representatives."

Howard pulled his book closer to his nose again. "What time is dinner?"

"Why do you always change the subject when I'm onto something? And I was also thinking about the robbery at Wolf Marine. Especially since it was Karl Wolf's snowmobile that was stolen. Now you've made me lose my chain of thought."

Before Howard could answer back, there was a knock at the side door, and Raven entered, not waiting for either Betty or Howard to say "come in." She looked distraught. Her hair was a mess, and her face was pale. She had been crying. She held a metal box.

"Oh, no," said Betty, eyeing the metal box. "Has something happened with you and Marcel? Are you moving out?"

Howard stood up. "Betty. Quiet. Raven, are you all right?"

Raven glanced at the metal box and then at them. "I don't know. I don't know any more."

Chapter Twenty-Three

After finding the money and notes in the Birch cabin, Raven shut off the gas fireplace and left the cabin, taking the box with her. Too much to digest alone.

She needed to show it to Marcel, but she didn't want to interrupt him while he was delivering the bad news about Mikey to Mrs. Dyer, or while he was speaking with Karl, Lunchbox, or anyone else connected to the case. The metal box wasn't an emergency, even though her throat was closing in and her breathing was shallow. No, it could keep until he got home.

But it really couldn't. Once back in the house, she stood in her kitchen, turning in circles, not able to focus. Did she want a glass of water or to lie down, or-or-or what? Lily and Dukie sat patiently staring at her. Being watched, even if it was by them, didn't help. She had lost her ability to concentrate. All she could think about was that box of money and the letters. Johnny had been supporting her and her mother. He had been checking in. And her mother hid it from her. She took it to her grave. Why? Julia knew she was sick. There had been time for her to tell Raven about Johnny's financial support and his desire to come back to Maine. She could have even told Raven where to look for the money. Why didn't she? Raven had to talk to someone about it.

"I'll be right back," she said to Lily, who had stood and walked over to Raven's legs, nudging her as a reminder to feed them dinner. "I know what time it is, but you two will need to wait. Stay here." Dukie's face looked crushed with disappointment, but he was always the gentleman and didn't complain.

She bundled herself up in her down jacket and boots, grabbed her car keys, and, of course, the box. She had to share it.

The good part of having older neighbors was that they were usually home. She could have walked over to the Harts, but she didn't trust her legs. She felt weak and dizzy, which meant she shouldn't drive either, but it was just down her driveway, a short turn to the left, and then up their driveway. She made it to their house in her Mini without incident, took a deep breath, then stepped out of her car and walked up the steps.

Inside, she saw Betty standing with a long-handled meat tenderizer raised in her hand as if she were about to pummel Howard. They immediately recognized that something was wrong with her and ushered her into a cushy chair. Betty ran to get a glass of water while Howard stood by her side. Raven drank half of the glass before speaking.

"Nothing's wrong. Well, maybe everything is wrong." She swayed in her seat. All she had known since childhood was now upside down.

"Why don't you start at the beginning?" Howard sat back in his chair, keeping himself at the cushion's edge.

She looked down at the metal box and ran her hands over the top. Opening it had changed her world. Did she dare open it again?

"I'm not sure if you ever heard my mother speak of Johnny's departure when I was little, and the decisions she had to make to keep me and her safe." She sniffled.

Betty, standing next to Raven's chair, answered first. "No, I can't say I ever had a personal conversation with your mother. More about lupines—she thought of them as a weed—or her favorite lobster recipe—lobster stew—which was really just half-and-half, a stick of butter and cooked lobster—not my cup of tea."

Howard cleared his throat.

Betty quickly added. "But you have told us, Raven, about the struggles, especially after your grandfather passed, to keep Pine Acres afloat."

A sob escaped from Raven. "It was all one big lie." She covered her face with her hands.

Betty knelt next to Raven and rubbed her back. "Oh, honey. I'm so sorry."

Raven cried softly for another minute. She knew she had much more crying to do, alone, but she didn't want to do it in front of the Harts. She needed to show them the money and the notes. She needed to hear what they thought of her mother's lies. Her mother's lies!

Howard had retrieved a box of tissues from somewhere in the house and handed her the whole cardboard box. She blew her nose a couple of times and stuffed the used tissues up her sleeve.

With one or two more sniffles, she straightened her back. Her long black hair had been falling into her face, and she pushed strands behind her ears.

"I was in Birch cabin today. I wanted to freshen up the paint for the Valentine's Day weekend guests. Heaven forbid I did this last fall instead of last minute."

Both Betty and Howard shrugged. Everyone knew it had been a busy time.

Raven continued. "Anyway, I noticed a stone on the hearth was off."

"As in loose?" Howard asked.

Raven nodded. "And you know my imagination. I visualized a guest pulling on it, and the field stone chimney collapsing on top of them."

Betty chimed in. "A scandal. A lawsuit. You're ruined. Marcel is fired."

"Betty!" Howard gave her the biggest, wide-eyed look he had.

"It's okay," said Raven. "Betty's right. That's exactly where my mind went too. I had just discovered the loose stone when Betty called this morning." She paused. She had enough wits about her to protect Betty's scheme to get out of the house. "And we decided to walk in the preserve, so I left it as is and just went back to see if I could remove it or fix it. I waited until after Marcel and Tom left to conduct their investigations." She paused, remembering Marcel's suggestion of dinner with Shannon. She'd tell them about that, too, in a bit. She remembered now why she had gone back to the cabin, more to get out of the house and to keep busy than to inspect the stone.

She caressed the box in her hand. "I was able to get the stone loose. To remove it."

"And the chimney is still standing," Howard said as a statement.

"Did it creak?" asked Betty. "Do you think it will fall down?"

Raven shook her head. "No, no. The stone was part of the hearth. Where you sit. Not part of the chimney, and nothing creaked or leaned or made any sound at all. In fact, the stone seemed more cosmetic than anything else."

"And when you removed the stone…." Howard obviously wanted to know what was in the box.

"I found this." Raven held up the box.

"The hole was that big?" Betty, still kneeling next to Raven, touched the box.

"Yes, perfect size for it. The box was placed in the long way."

Betty also caressed the box. "Wow, do you think your grandfather built the hearth that way on purpose. As a hiding place?"

Raven shrugged. "I don't know, or maybe my mother discovered the loose stone too, as I did, and just decided to use it."

"Your mother?" Betty and Howard asked the same question in unison.

Raven nodded and looked down at the box. "I'm assuming this was put there by my mother. Who else put it there?" She turned the box around so it would open up facing Howard and Betty. She lifted the lid.

Their reaction did not disappoint. Betty gasped, and Howard almost fell off his seat cushion.

"Holy crow," Howard said, gazing at the hundreds of hundred-dollar bills.

"Your mother saved a nest egg for you," said Betty. "Isn't that sweet?"

Raven shook her head. "She always said we had to be very careful with money because we were on our own, and yet," she lifted a yellowed envelope from the box, "this note is from Johnny. Reading these notes shows a pattern. He sent money monthly to us. No wonder he has been surprised at my disdain for him."

The tears flowed again down Raven's cheeks. Betty reached for one of her hands.

"It's not your fault. You didn't know."

"I know. I know," said Raven, "but I still feel bad."

Howard added, "Johnny will understand."

Raven nodded. "I agree with that. He will be okay. What I don't understand is why my mother lied to me. Even as an adult? Why didn't she even tell me about this when she got sick?"

"That is curious," said Betty. "I could see not sharing with you as a child. She may not have known how you'd take it, or she may not have trusted that the money would keep coming. But as time went on, why not tell you?"

Howard's brows squished together. "Do you think she was afraid she'd lose you to him? Like he'd look like a hero, and you'd move to Boston to get to know him?"

"I know my nickname came from him. She never called me 'Raven,' not once, because Johnny had given me that nickname. She even told me she thought I shouldn't let anyone call me Raven. Maybe if I wasn't an obstinate junior high kid at the time she told me to go by 'Elizabeth,' I would have wanted to please her, but that made me embrace the nickname even more."

Betty, now sitting in her favorite chair, asked, "If she didn't call you that, how did the nickname stick if Johnny no longer lived here?"

"My grandfather called me that." Raven thought of her grandfather calling her that across a room and her mother scowling. Why did her grandfather keep calling her the nickname that Johnny gave her?

"Your grandfather did?" Howard sat back in his chair. "Maybe he also knew that Johnny was sending your mother money."

It was Raven's turn to sit back, a wave of exhaustion hitting her. She could have closed her eyes right there and then and fallen to sleep. Did her grandfather know about the money? She tried to remember anything he may have said about Johnny. She couldn't remember anything, positive or negative. But Howard had a point. If he continued to call her Raven, he might not have had any animosity for her father.

Was her mother simply protecting her own feelings of hurt by not talking about Johnny? She and Johnny never divorced. Did they both hope to get back together one day? Why was marriage such a complicated thing? That thought reminded her of the dinner party that Marcel wanted to have.

"The other thing that happened today is Marcel wants us to have a dinner party next Sunday."

"Oh, for your birthday? How nice." Betty smiled at Raven.

"Nice of you to remember it is my birthday," said Raven. "I don't think Marcel does. Not that he ever does. It's just not his thing."

"Well, still nice to have a gathering. We can celebrate you even if he doesn't remember. What can we bring?" Betty clasped her hands together. Raven knew she loved a good party.

"You're assuming we're invited, my dear," said Howard, trying to give Raven a graceful out.

"Why wouldn't we be? It's Raven's birthday. Are you cooking? Want to have it here instead, and I could cook? Speaking of which, I think I left that chicken on the counter. Let me put it back into the fridge to finish later."

"You mean to finish me off later. It's probably spoiled." Howard called after her.

"If you let us heat the house at a warmer temperature, it probably would be spoiled, but since it's an icebox in here, anyway, I think you're safe," Betty yelled back, over her shoulder.

"If we have the dinner party, we'll have to have it at our house. Marcel wants Shannon McGrath to come."

"What?" Betty turned abruptly and came back into the room.

"Really?" said Howard. "Shannon McGrath? That hot district attorney we got a glimpse of last fall? I'm definitely coming next Sunday."

"Howard!" It was Betty's turn to now give him a wide-eyed stare.

"Yes, really," said Raven. She was grateful she was already ensconced in a plush chair. It comforted her.

"I thought this Shannon thing was behind us," said Betty.

"Us?" said Howard. "I have to say, I don't think there is anything to worry about. What man invites his mistress over to meet his wife?"

"A dumb man. An overly confident man. I think they do that sort of thing in France," Betty said over her shoulder as she returned to the kitchen and the chicken.

"You're not helping, Betty," said Howard.

Raven closed her eyes. Howard did have a point, though. She knew Marcel to be a kind and gracious man. He was an upstanding citizen beyond reproach. People don't change, as her mother always said. She thought her mother only meant that in a negative way, about her father, that people didn't change for the better, but Julia was right. People didn't change. And good people were always good people. The larger question now was, what side of the aisle did Raven now place her mother?

Chapter Twenty-Four

Tom parked the SUV next to Clark Christianson's pickup truck. He wished no one were at Wolf Marine, but with Clark in there, the rest of the town was bound to learn too much too soon.

Raven had said that Karl had cleaned up since the break-in, but the tipped-over postcards were still plastered to the floor. If Tom had to wager on the clean-up efforts, he'd bet that those postcards would never be picked up, but would, over time, wear off through normal day-to-day traffic. The store was as cleaned up as it was ever going to be.

Karl, leaning over his counter by the register, was telling Clark his story.

"So, I never got out on the trails. I finally stopped puking my brains out around nine this morning. I came here, and, voila, robbed."

Clark waved to Tom and Marcel as they entered, then turned back to Karl. "Gee, that's terrible. I'm so sorry to hear that. I figured, though, that you had gotten out on your sled since your Cat wasn't sitting in the driveway."

"Yeah, someone helped themselves to it last night. Can you believe that? I'm thinking they wanted the sled to keep the title even if I couldn't." Karl chuckled and handed Clark his change. Tom suspected that Clark had already eaten his purchase, a beef jerky stick, since his other hand held an open and empty plastic wrapper strip.

"Karl, do you have a moment?" Marcel had stepped forward. Tom knew that if Clark didn't get the hint and skedaddle, Marcel would move him along.

"Sure do," said Karl, not budging.

"I suppose you want me to leave," said Clark. "That's fine." He glanced at his watch. "I can just catch the evening take-out at Jane Eats."

Tom's eyes narrowed. Was that an innocent mention of the diner, or a subtle way for Clark to say he was going to see Tom's sister, Rachel? He hoped that Rachel was already home, feeding her husband, Dennis, and their kids. He didn't know why he worried about her as much as he did, but once a brother, always a brother.

After the door dinged as Clark's exit closed, Marcel turned and addressed Karl.

"We'd like to talk to you about the store break-in and also your sled. Mind if we start with the sled first?"

"Not at all. Shoot." Karl still leaned over his counter.

"You were planning on riding it last night?"

"Yep." Karl nodded.

"Who knew you were going to use it?"

Karl laughed. "The whole town, I suspect. I had it out front for a couple of days, and everyone knows my record of wanting to be first on the trails. Anyone who has lived here for at least five years, that is. I haven't had a chance to be on these trails in recent winters, as you know."

Marcel nodded. Tom studied Karl as he spoke. Nothing Karl said, nor the way he said it, gave the impression that Karl wasn't telling the truth. Marcel continued.

"And the reason you didn't use your sled last night?"

"Because I had my dinner coming out both ends, to be graphic. I think it was something I ate."

Tom jumped on a thought. "Food poisoning? Where did the food come from?"

"My fridge. I'm not known to waste food. If it was food poisoning, I did it to myself."

Tom pursued his line of questioning. "Did you eat from a container that was already opened, or one you had to open yourself last night?"

"Leftovers, baby. Crab cakes I had made a week or so ago."

Marcel joined in. "Do you keep your house unlocked?"

"Don't you?"

Marcel just smiled. Tom knew he did. He couldn't think of anyone in Secretly who locked their house. Well, if they were locals. People from away were used to being locked up tight, so it made sense that they would lock up tight here, too, at least until they relaxed into their new way of life if they had moved here full-time.

Karl straightened up. "Wait. Are you implying that someone deliberately made me sick? Like snuck into my house and poisoned my food so they could mess up my store? And then steal my sled for a joyride? I guess I could also have caught something from talking to Craig yesterday. From standing too close to his open window. He said Stella was throwing up. Something she picked up working at the hospital."

Marcel said, "We're just trying to cover all angles."

Karl cleared his throat. "Who took my sled anyway? Raven and that older woman who lives next door to you were here earlier today. They mentioned that my sled was up at Riverview Farm. Stuck in a field. Do you know who rode it up there? Did it break down?"

"We'll be able to return your sled in a day to two. We think it is running fine." Marcel shifted his stance.

"So why did someone just leave it there?"

Marcel paused. Tom took over. "There's been an accident. With the sled in a field."

"Really? Did the thief get hurt? I hope he did. But the sled is okay? Do you know who left it there?"

Tom knew that Karl would regret saying he hoped the thief was hurt when he heard that the thief had actually died. "We believe that Mikey Dyer rode it up there."

"That Mikey!" Karl banged his fist onto the wooden counter. "He came in yesterday looking for money, under the guise that he would work for it. I sent him on his way. Probably getting back at me for not giving him anything."

"Would he want to ride your sled so badly that he'd make you sick?"

"No, no, I can't believe that. Mikey is lazy and untouched by protocol, but I never knew him to be cruel. Wait until I get my hands on him, though. The last thing I want is to have to ask Jared Sparks for my sled back. That man is a menace to this town."

"Why do you say that?" asked Marcel.

"He thinks he is better than all of us, riding around in that fancy Range Rover of his. I've seen him bully Franklin's granddaughter, too, his wife, what's her name? Camille. She's a nice girl. Why she picked him as a husband is beyond me."

Tom had wondered the same thing too many times. Either Camille had a side that no one else saw, or Jared wasn't himself up here, because he was definitely a jerk when in town.

Tom asked, "Do you think that Mikey messed up your store, too?"

"Mikey? Nah."

Marcel asked, "What are your thoughts? Who do you think did this?"

"I know the obvious answer would be Lunchbox or anyone on the posted debt list, but I don't think any of them would do it, really, not even Lunchbox."

Then a glimmer flicked in Karl's eyes. It was obvious he had an idea, a suspicion.

Tom picked up on the change in Karl's face. "You think you know who might have had it in for you."

Karl stared into space for another few seconds and then shook off his stupor. "Nah, I just had a crazy idea. That's all."

"How about sharing your crazy idea with us, and let us judge how crazy it is." Marcel waited for Karl to respond.

"Nah. I don't want to get someone in trouble because I have an imagination. I'm sure it's nothing."

"Well, if you change your mind and want to bounce the idea off of one of us—"

Karl cut Marcel off. "Back to what I said. My only thought is about the guys on that debt list; the only thing really missing, as far as I can tell, is my ledger showing amounts owed to me. I expect all of them, except maybe Lunchbox, will easily pay me back in the spring once they get their traps back into the water. Let me get you that list of names if you want to talk to them."

Karl went around the corner, stepped out from behind the counter, and walked to the front door, where he had posted the debt list. He looked at the window. There was no list on it.

He opened the door, stood on the stone stoop, and looked around at the ground, covered in snowbanks on either side of the stoop. He shut the door and looked in the corner behind the door, inside the store.

"I guess it could have blown off when the door was left open. I had taped it on the inside of the window facing out." He looked closer at the window. "Even the tape is gone. You'd think if the paper had blown off, a corner of it would have still remained, taped to the glass."

Tom nodded. It certainly seemed like someone had deliberately removed the list. That same person probably stole the notebook pages, too, and if someone would go that far, maybe eliminating Karl altogether would complete the plan. Who had the most to gain with all of the records of debt erased? As much as Tom didn't want to admit it, all roads led to one person: Lunchbox Lennie.

Chapter Twenty-Five

aven went to bed early, too exhausted from the day's events at Riverview Farm, and the discovered metal box and all of the other pieces that made up the day. She had left a plate of dinner in the fridge for Marcel, and didn't even hear him crawl into bed, probably also early for him. She woke up, however, around four thirty in the morning to find herself cradled in his arms with both Lily and Dukie snoring at the bottom of the bed. She inhaled the calmness she felt. If only moments like this could be bottled and sprayed on like perfume in times of stress.

Before she had left the Harts yesterday, it was decided that she and Betty would go to Riverview Farm's shop to test out Betty's theory that Jared was to blame for the snowmobile accident.

"There has to be some evidence somewhere that Jared put up that barbed wire," speculated Betty.

Even Howard thought it was a great idea for them to go, and Betty was thrilled.

"For once, I think being nosey will be a good thing for you, Raven. Always good to be distracted from one's own life by nosing into someone else's," he had said with a twinkle in his eyes, followed by a wink.

"I agree wholeheartedly," said Betty, her eyes bright with being given the green light to shop, Raven knew, and to snoop. They had decided that, once inside the shop, and with Camille engaged with Betty, Raven would make an excuse to leave the shop to go out to the car, and instead, she'd pop into the barn to see if any remnants of barbed wire existed.

"Or receipts," reminded Betty. "You might be looking for something small."

It seemed like a good idea at the time, but this morning, in the coziness of the bedroom, Raven didn't have any interest in it, but she didn't want to disappoint Betty. She'd rally to go. It didn't have to take all day. Then she could tackle the Birch cabin painting project again, and at some point, even if not today, show Johnny the box that she found. He deserved to know.

She still didn't know how she felt about it all, especially the part about her mother hiding the support that Johnny had wanted to provide. She had also wanted to show Marcel the box and get his take on the contents. She knew he wouldn't say "I told you so," but he had been a champion of Johnny's arrival to Secretly, and the box of money and the kind notes that Johnny had written would only put an exclamation point on Marcel's interpretation of him. It was easier for Marcel to accept Johnny, she had always said, because he didn't have a history with him. But if she were honest with herself, she, too, didn't have a history with him. What did she really remember about him? The last disastrous Christmas when the tree ended up in the street, lights and all. Maybe it wasn't Johnny who threw it out. Maybe her mother had done it all. Her personal history was being rewritten, like it or not.

Her image of her mother was no longer clear. The edges had frayed, and a fogginess had settled in. She didn't like that thought either. She wanted to remember her mother as she thought she had known her. Oh, it was all too complicated and was giving her a headache.

She rose to grab some over-the-counter headache meds from a kitchen cabinet. The metal box sat on the counter. She had left it without a note for Marcel to see. She didn't know if he had peered inside. He may not have had the energy or interest when he got home. Seeing it now, it looked like a normal, small cash box for a tag sale or charity event. It wasn't worn—no nicks on the grey paint. Did her mother buy it specially to keep Johnny's money? It seemed so.

She ran her hand over the lid. Part of her wanted to open it up again and re-read some of the notes. She hadn't read them all—there were so many—but she had read enough to see the pattern of Johnny sending his love, updating Julia on his sobriety progress, and always hoping that one day they could be a family again. Gosh, wouldn't that have been nice?

The poochies pattered out to the kitchen. It didn't matter to them that it was earlier than usual for a morning bathroom break and breakfast. They sat quietly watching her, and when she finally glanced their way, both tails thumbed against the kitchen floor.

"Okay, why not? Let's go out." She donned her boots, coat, and hat, and they all went out into the yard, still needing to use the shoveled paths because of the snow.

The cold air helped clear her headache. She breathed in deeply and blew out a gust of air, a small cloud rising from her mouth. Both dogs came back to her quickly after doing their business, and now she knew it was her turn to feed them, keep them quiet, and let Marcel sleep.

She looked around the yard before going back inside. Snow gave a grace of peace, didn't it? How lucky she was to live where she did and with whom she did. Gratitude was a powerful tool, her mother always said. Was her mother saying that about having a war chest for a rainy day? For knowing that she hadn't chosen poorly after all when she married Johnny?

Howard was right. If her grandfather kept up the nickname given to her by Johnny, he must have known that Johnny had a good heart, and maybe even knew that Johnny was sending money to Julia. He had to get the mail some days, right?

She knew one reason her mother was successful was her resilience and stubbornness. While those traits can help with survival, they also can stop serving the user if they're blind to the truth. She didn't want her own brand of stubbornness to ruin her trust in Marcel. If he thought that she should meet Shannon, she would, and she would not even make a fuss that it was on her own birthday. She loved to cook and would be happy to show that skill off. Besides, she'd have her own friends there too. It would be fine.

Once the dogs were fed, Raven gave herself a chore to pass the time until she'd pick up Betty. She had just finished wiping down the stove top when Marcel emerged from the bedroom, his hair disheveled and his eyes looking heavy with sleep that they still desperately wanted. She had forgotten that he hadn't had any sleep the night before due to the blizzard.

"Morning," he said, his voice thick as he hit the button on the coffee maker.

Thankfully, she had placed a mug for him earlier under the coffee dispenser. Too many times, in a tired state, he started the drip without anything to catch the outpouring hot coffee, and the counter was soon flooded with the hot, dark liquid.

"Tom's on his way to pick me up." He stood in front of the fridge with the door open. Raven knew his brain was trying to remember that he needed the half-and-half carton. "We're on our way to Lunchbox Lennie's this morning. The hospital has released him."

Raven stopped her cleaning. "How did it go with Mrs. Dyer?"

Marcel stretched his arms over his head as the coffee ran into the mug. "As you'd think. Sad. She's the nicest lady."

Raven nodded. She remembered her as an aide in school. Very sweet. "She didn't deserve the heartache that Mikey dished out, over and over again."

Marcel agreed. "No, she didn't. No one does."

Raven glanced at the metal cash box on the counter. Was that an antecedent to her mother's heartache? No need to clog Marcel's brain with it at the moment. There was plenty of time to talk about it once his investigation was over. She almost told him of her own snooping plans for the day, but thought better of it. He'd tell her to stay out of it and to definitely stay away from the Sparks. Now that she was up and awake, the thought of going back to Riverview Farm with Betty did interest her, at least to keep her busy. What harm could really come of it anyway? She didn't think that Camille and Jared were really involved with Mikey's death.

Marcel poured his coffee into a travel mug, kissed her good-bye, and was out the door just as Tom's SUV pulled in. She got ready herself and headed for the Harts. Betty was in the kitchen when she entered the house.

"I don't think Jared is very agricultural," Betty said, sipping her coffee while leaning against her counter. "I can't imagine him stringing a fence, but that also means he probably wouldn't be in the barn either when you go in. Worth a peek, though, don't you think?"

"Sure, why not?" Raven glanced around the Harts' kitchen. The rooster motive was alive and well in every corner, on the curtains and the hanging dish towels, and on the bounty of magnets on the fridge, and she didn't think of Betty as very agricultural either.

The shop opened at ten o'clock, and Raven and Betty pulled into a spot next to the door a few minutes after ten. The "open" sign showed in the window. Camille must have been inside. So far, all was going according to plan.

Raven hadn't been to the shop yet. She hadn't been to many of the new places that had popped up in Secretly or Eelsboro over the past few years, as more and more people from away had moved in and brought their talents with them. It wasn't that she didn't want to support a local business. She was busy with her own business and didn't want to be lured into spending money she should use for Pine Acres' upkeep. There was always something that needed repainting or linens that needed replacing. That was where her extra money needed to go. Not on a trinket or a painting, or in this case, something made out of alpaca yarn, as practical as that was.

The shop was nice—bright, well-laid-out. A small, rotating kiosk held mittens on one side and nicely made cards of the alpacas in the farm's fields on the other. A few quilt racks held thick, colorful wool blankets that reminded her of the boiled wool one her grandfather had from the Army.

"Welcome!" said Camille when they entered. "Coming back for those mittens, Betty?"

"Oh, yes, I wanted to look at them again. Yes, that's right," Betty said, heading for the mitten section, sounding a little flustered and nervous. "I was telling Raven about how light they were. So tempting, right, Raven?"

"Do you knit, Raven? I'm looking to partner with local knitters or crocheters." Camille winked at Betty. "Once we have our first batch of wool ready later this year."

"Unfortunately, I don't. My mother would have loved to work with you, though. She did beautiful handiwork. I do not have her talent."

"You have other talents," said Betty, almost elbowing Raven. Raven got the hint to use her snooping talents pronto.

"Oh, I left my phone in the car. Let me go grab it in case Marcel is trying to reach me," she said, exiting the store. She saw Betty bring a pair of socks to Camille, probably with a question as convoluted as Betty could devise to keep Camille occupied.

Raven walked quickly past her Mini Cooper and headed toward the barn, which was next door to the shop. There didn't appear to be an easy door to use to get in. She pulled on the large one that was almost as tall as the barn itself and hung from a metal track at the top. She pulled and pushed to slide it open, and at first she thought it was locked somehow, but then realized it was just wicked heavy. Putting in more effort, she eventually slid it open just wide enough to squish through sideways. Once on the other side, she slid it closed in case Jared happened to look out into the driveway. No sense calling unnecessary attention to herself.

She paused before moving further to allow her eyes to adjust to the dim light. There were windows along the back of the barn, and the morning light, while not sunny, still reflected against the outside snow and bounced into the barn. She hadn't thought about the alpacas also being in this barn until she stood inside, but they thankfully weren't in this section. Not that she'd mind them, but she didn't want to disturb them or track poop around, although hiding evidence in poop probably was a genius idea. She heard a few bleats and some jingling from stalls to her right. They probably thought she was bringing them a lunch snack. Sorry, guys.

She knew she had to be quick. How long would it take for her to "get her phone," and just how many questions could Betty have about socks? She scanned the walls. Different items hung on nails—a harness, probably from when Mr. Ellsworth, Camille's grandfather, owned a horse. Various rakes and shovels and an old handsaw were also hung along the walls, but no smoking gun, such as a shiny, bright coil of barbed wire.

She walked to the left, away from the animals' sounds, and opened a door. She hadn't realized that the barn was also their garage. Only one vehicle was pulled in—Jared's white Range Rover. She pulled on the passenger door handle—it was unlocked—and leaned inside. No receipts stuck out from the cup holder. She opened the glove box. Nothing but the owner's manual, with registration and auto insurance information stuck inside. The armrest compartment was spotless and empty.

When she shut the door, she noticed the front right fender was crumpled. Peering closer, she saw that the front headlight on the passenger side was smashed, too. He had definitely run into something, and it had probably happened recently, since there were no signs of rust. Must have been a deer. Those poor things were always jumping out in front of cars, regardless of the time of year.

She turned to the back of the vehicle and had enough room to open the hatch door. Again, the back of his SUV was spotless. Did he even put a grocery bag back here? Before she shut the door, however, a tiny piece of something caught her eye. It was in the furthest spot from her, where the crease of the seats to fold down met the back of the trunk. She crawled into the trunk area and picked up the tiny piece. It was wood, about the size of a dime, and painted gold. It looked familiar.

"Hard to believe there would be anything out of place back here," she mumbled to herself. She pocketed the piece of wood, not because she thought it was important, but because she had touched it and didn't want to toss it back into his car, or if something did turn out to be amiss with the Sparks, she didn't want her fingerprints on it. Not that her fingerprints weren't all over the entire Range Rover, the barn door, and whatever else she might have touched. How foolish to not wear her gloves. She put them on now, even though it was probably too late.

Well, at least she hadn't found barbed wire. Nor had she found any receipts of any kind. She turned to head back to the shop and noticed a canvas tarp covering something in the corner, near the front-left tire. Maybe a leftover supply of wire? The size might be right.

She knelt down to peel back the tarp. It was stuck behind something. Definitely something was wrapped up in the tarp. She pulled it all out away from the wall and laid it on its side, unrolling the tarp to see what it was hiding. In front of her wasn't a coil of barbed wire. It was a frame. A gold picture frame. And it was framing the paint-by-number painting from Karl's store that she had just looked at a couple of days ago, and the one that was missing since the blizzard break-in. It was the only item taken from the store, except for the ledger. Why would this painting be here, and why would the

Sparks want it? Did they even know it was in their garage? Did someone else put it here?

"What are you doing in here?"

Jared's voice, loud and sharp, made Raven lose her balance from her crouched position. She toppled over onto the dirt floor of the barn and stared up at him. He glared down at her, holding one of the large metal shovels in his hands as he stood over her.

Chapter Twenty-Six

I n the gray morning, a lamp shone from Lennie's living room window. Tom parked the SUV near the front steps, and he and Marcel got out. Lennie met them at the door, a bandage still taped to the left side of his forehead, and wearing a flannel shirt and jeans. His hair needed a good wash. He held onto the door frame as if he were dizzy. Tom felt bad that they were about to make him dizzier with their questions.

"How are you feeling, Lennie?" Tom asked. "Mind if we come in?"

Lennie stepped aside without answering, and he and Marcel entered. The house was small and sparsely furnished, but it was clean and neat. He wasn't sure what to expect, and he didn't know why he equated people in debt with being hoarders. Obviously, Lennie's debt didn't come from purchases, unless it was the kind of purchases that went up one's nose. He didn't think so, though. Lennie just seemed like a guy who made some wrong business decisions. He hoped that was all it was.

"What can I do for you?" Lennie asked, now holding on to his counter once they were all in the house.

"Do you mind if we all sit down for a moment?" Marcel asked. Lennie motioned to the living area, where one chair was next to the table with the lamp. Tom grabbed the two kitchen chairs and brought them over to that one, forming a half-circle.

"You just got out of the hospital. You take the softer seat," said Marcel, motioning to the living room recliner.

Lennie didn't argue and sat in the armchair. The chair was situated perfectly for sitting and looking out the picture window. If he had had the funds, Tom bet to himself that Lennie would have had a bird feeder right outside the window. Without owning his lobster boat anymore, Lennie probably now had too much time to sit and stare at nothing.

"I'm glad to see you're okay. How did your accident happen, anyway?" Tom asked.

Lennie shrugged. "Bad conditions. Stupidity on my part. I was just driving around, and some idiot ran me off the road."

"About what time was that?" Marcel asked. Both he and Tom knew what time their colleague had found Lennie in the ditch, but it was always good to hear what someone had to say about their own timing.

"About two o'clock." Lennie looked out the window, his eyes vacant.

"In the afternoon?" Marcel said in a conversational tone.

"No." Lennie's face swiveled back in the direction of Marcel and Tom without looking them straight in the eye. "In the morning. Two o'clock in the morning. Sorry."

Marcel nodded and leaned forward. "And what would make you be out in the middle of a blizzard at two o'clock in the morning?"

Lennie shrugged again and turned away. "Just being nosey, I guess."

"Nosey about what?" Tom knew that Marcel hated pulling teeth, but Lennie was making them earn every answer, word by word.

"The tides, mostly. I wanted to see the storm in the middle of the big tide, the high tide with the full moon."

Marcel shifted in the wooden chair. "I see, but your truck was found driving away from the ocean."

Without turning back to them, Lennie answered. "I was just driving around to see the amount of snow."

Marcel let silence hang in the air, but Lennie didn't elaborate. Marcel then resumed his questions. "Were you at Wolf Marine during the blizzard?"

Lennie jerked his head quickly toward them, his eyes wide. "No, why would I be there?"

Tom thought, *okay, now we're getting somewhere.*

Marcel seemed to catch that, too. "Perhaps you were there taking Karl's notebook on what you owed him? Erasing your debt? You heard the store was broken into."

"No, I didn't know that, and I don't even owe Karl that much money that he claims." Lennie's face flushed, and he leaned toward Tom and Marcel, resting his elbows on his knees. "I don't know why he thinks I do. He's full of it."

Marcel continued. "Okay, did you happen to drive past Wolf Marine that night when you were driving around?"

Lennie sat up again and shifted in his chair. He took a moment to respond. "Yes, I did."

"Was the front door open when you drove by?" Marcel asked.

Lennie paled. It was almost hard to detect, considering how pale he already looked, but there was a slight color shift in his cheeks. He either knew the door was open because he had left it that way, or he had seen it open. Tom wondered if Lennie would tell them the truth.

Lennie swallowed and looked at his hands. "No. The door was shut."

Marcel stretched in the chair. Tom agreed that the chairs were uncomfortable. They should find out the brand and use them in the interviewing rooms at the sheriff's office

Marcel resumed. "I just want to confirm, after driving by Wolf Marine, you kept on driving around? Was this before or after looking at the tides?"

Lennie looked back at his hands, then he put his head into his hands and let out a loud sigh. Tom and Marcel waited. One minute. Two minutes. Finally, Lennie let his hands drop to his lap, and he spoke.

"No. I was at Wolf Marine before I went to see the tides. I stopped at the store. I got out of my truck."

Okay, good, Lennie. Keep the truth pouring out, thought Tom.

Marcel said, "Why did you do that?"

"I couldn't get that posted debt paper out of my mind. It was all I could think about. Why did he have to pour salt into my wounds? Make my situation public? I figured it was my chance to grab that paper. The one that Karl put on the door." His body shook in the chair. Tom watched to make sure he wasn't having a seizure or about to pass out. He braced himself to rush forward and catch him before he hit the floor.

Lennie's voice was thick. "Do you know how humiliating it is to have your name on a door?"

Marcel ignored the question. "So you went into the store and what?"

Lennie said, "Nothing. Nothing happened. I just opened the door and took down that piece of paper. The one with my name on it."

Marcel pursued. "And then knocked things off shelves, pulled out the drawers behind the cash register, and took Karl's notebook with the figures in it?"

Lennie sat up straight. "What? No, geez, I felt guilty enough taking the paper off the door."

Tom believed him. There was something in his voice and mannerisms that told Tom that Lennie was telling the truth. The break-in at Wolf Marine wasn't serious. Nothing of value was taken. If he admitted to taking a posted paper, why not admit to taking the ledger too? So, if Lennie didn't mess up the store, who did?

Marcel continued. "But you left the door open so the snow could blow in and cause a mess for Karl."

Lennie shook his head. "I did not. Absolutely not. In fact, I even pulled and pushed on the door to make sure it was shut. It's an old door and has a temperamental latch. I might owe Karl some money, and I might be super mad at him for publicizing it, but I wouldn't wish him any harm. I wouldn't wish anybody harm. No, I definitely shut the door."

Marcel did not look at Tom, but Tom knew what Marcel was thinking. He believed Lennie, too. The interview was about to wind down.

Marcel said, "I'm sorry to keep asking you the same things, but I just want to be sure I'm fully understanding. You didn't take anything else from the store, just for fun?"

Lennie again shook his head. "No, nothing. I swear."

Tom had a thought dawn on him.

"Was Karl's snowmobile still out front when you were there?" Tom asked. If Lennie was telling the truth about the time, and if the snowmobile was gone, then Mikey took it prior to two o'clock. They'd start to build a more solid timeline of the events in the field.

Lennie sat for a moment, thinking. "If it were, it would have been covered in snow. No, no, the sled definitely wasn't there. I'm positive it wasn't there. I had stopped my truck on that side area where Karl had it parked and walked toward the store that way."

Lennie sat and thought a bit more. "After taking the paper off the door, I got back to my truck and saw lights from another vehicle coming my way. I got out of there fast so I wouldn't be seen. That's when I drove down to the lighthouse and watched the tide coming in for a bit—gosh, it was scary, to be honest, I hope no one was out in that—and then I drove back towards home. That's when I got sideswiped and ended up in the ditch."

Marcel nodded. "Did you see the type of car or truck that hit you?"

"No, all I saw was white. The white out."

"Okay," said Marcel, and then looked at Tom. "Anything else?"

Tom shook his head. There were still a lot of holes in their investigation, but it didn't seem like Lennie had the answers they needed to plug them. Tom had known Lennie his whole life, and he knew the struggles he had as a kid. What would happen to Lennie now without a boat? Lobstering was all Lennie knew how to do. Then Tom had a thought. He'd let it simmer for a while, but it was a solid idea. Tom inherited his father's lobster boat, *Peggy Sue,* when his dad passed. Tom used it only as a part-time lobsterman, more as a hobby and an escape from the law enforcement job. *Peggy Sue* was in Whale Harbor, bobbing all day, probably wishing to be used more. It would be easy for Lennie and Tom to share it. Yes, he'd talk to Lennie about that once they wrapped up this case.

"Thanks for your time, Lennie, and for being upfront about Wolf Marine. We appreciate your cooperation." Marcel stood.

Lennie rose slowly, gripping the arms of the chair for support.

"I don't hate Karl. Believe me, I don't. I hope he maintained his trail record on his snowmobile."

Tom realized that most in town didn't know yet what had happened to Karl, to his sled, or to Mikey. Now wasn't the time to share. Not yet.

Chapter Twenty-Seven

"And they come in what colors again?" Betty glanced over her shoulder, hoping she would see Raven walking into the shop. Just how many more minutes could she spend on socks? She should have picked up a blanket or the knit-your-own kit. Camille must think she was an idiot for asking some questions three times.

To her credit, Camille maintained a nice smile and a professional tone. Betty would buy something as a 'thank you' for that graciousness. Maybe one of the beautiful blankets, even though they were five hundred dollars each. Howard wouldn't question her bringing home one of those on a day like today. Now was her chance.

"You know, I wonder if Raven ran off and left me." Betty giggled. "Do you mind if I check on her? I'll be right back."

Betty rushed out of the shop and instantly saw the barn door open. She had assumed Raven would be more discreet and would have closed herself in. Betty made a mental note to give Raven that advice for a future snooping episode. Discretion was nine-tenths of the law. Was that the quote? No, discretion was the larger part of valor. That sounded more accurate, although Betty didn't understand what it meant. Regardless, she needed to coach Raven to do better next time.

She reached the barn door and was about to call out when she heard voices. She stopped to figure out where in the barn they were coming from. The llamas were making noise too, little chirps or whatever a llama did, and kicking their stalls. Demanding little fellows, weren't they? She held her own breath, not that the barn smelled bad—it actually smelled nice with the hay—but to concentrate better on zeroing in on where the voices spoke. To her left, she thought. She saw an open side door further along the barn and headed that way.

"I asked you, what are you doing in here?"

Betty froze. A man's voice. She had only heard Jared once, a couple of days ago in the store, but it had to be him. Who else could it be? Was he going to kill Raven, too? Maybe he had barbed wire in his hand and was going to strangle her with it. Betty shivered at the thought.

She hadn't heard Raven answer. Maybe it was too late, but Betty had to act positively and fast. She had to save Raven.

She crept toward the door, hearing again a man saying, "You have no business being on our property. I should call the sheriff."

"Please do." Raven's voice, stronger than Betty would have anticipated, came through.

Whew. Raven was still alive. But for how long?

Betty looked down at the floor, covered in hay. She hoped there wasn't a creaking board, well, a very loud creaking board, that would give her away. She had to chance it.

Clutching her purse, she tiptoed as quickly as she dared toward the doorway. Leaning in to her left, she saw Jared looming inside next to his white Range Rover. She always liked those cars, even though Howard said they were impractical with the tight backseats and little storage space. They looked snazzy driving around, however, and how often would she have someone in the backseat anyway?

Jared held something in his hand. Betty couldn't quite see it. A wooden handle connected to something. Oh! A large metal shovel. She almost gasped out loud. He was going to pummel Raven to death.

Betty was too far away to do anything like run back for a rake or some other tool. It was too late to just call Tom or Marcel. First off, it would take them too long to arrive. Second, Jared would hear her and probably beat her to a pulp, too. Marcel and Tom would know he did it since it was on his land, and his fingerprints would be all over that shovel handle. Even if he wiped it down, he'd miss one or two. Betty was confident about that. But both she and Raven would be dead. What good was that? She needed a better plan, and quickly.

She had no choice but to get closer. Taking a step into the room that was being used as a garage, she saw Raven's face change. She was sure Raven had seen her, but Raven was wise enough to keep her eyes on Jared so as not give it away. At least now, Raven was being discreet enough not to alert Jared. Gold star, Raven.

"Why did you take this painting?" Raven asked.

Jared shook his head. "I didn't take it. Karl gave it to me. He was going to throw it away."

This painting? Why was Raven asking about a painting? Was it the one taken from Wolf Marine? She thought Raven was in the barn looking for barbed wire. Why was she asking Jared about a worthless print or painting or whatever it was? Raven should ask where he bought the wire, where he hid the rest, and why he wanted to hurt Karl Wolf. Geez, Betty could think of a dozen questions to ask if the shoe were on the other foot. Not that she wanted Jared to be looming over her with a shovel, but she hoped she'd be a better interrogator if pressed.

"This was stolen during the blizzard," said Raven.

"You're mistaken," Jared retorted.

"Did you take it before or after you strung the barbed wire?" Raven fired back.

Now she was getting somewhere! Bravo!

Jared growled and raised his voice and the shovel. "I didn't do anything with barbed wire!"

Betty couldn't chance what Jared might do next. She raised her own shaky arm and used the best weapon any woman could carry—a heavy, overfilled purse! She slammed her vinyl designer bag down as hard as she could. He was too tall for her to reach the top of his head, but she caught him in the neck.

"Ow!" He yelled and fell forward, dropping the shovel and face-planting on the upside-down metal blade of the shovel, knocking himself out. Betty looked at the lifeless Jared, stunned at her success.

"Great job!" Raven yelled to Betty in a hoarse voice.

"Let's get out of here before he wakes up," Betty called back. "Quick."

Raven reached behind her and grabbed a cream-colored canvas tarp, and wrapped an aging gold-framed picture in it.

"Not without this!" she said, stepping over Jared on her way out of the garage.

Chapter Twenty-Eight

Johnny had called the hospital and learned that Lennie was discharged last night. Darn it! He should have called sooner. He could have driven him home, made sure he had dinner, and impressed upon Lennie that he wasn't alone in the world.

To live at the edge of a precipice, for whatever reason, drove the stake of fear further into one's heart. He knew that firsthand, and once the heart was pierced, it was hard to heal, hard to move forward, hard not to hide further, or worse, hard not jump off the precipice into oblivion. He had lived in a dark hole more than once, alone. If he had had support or had allowed himself to have support, maybe he would have healed sooner. If he could now show support and save one soul from that dreadful trip down, he'd do it every time.

He gulped seeing Tom's sheriff SUV in Lennie's driveway. Why was he here? He hoped that Lennie hadn't already taken the plunge. He glanced over at his passenger seat and saw Karl's debt list that he had lifted from Lennie's truck. He drove up the driveway and parked. He knew he shouldn't have taken the paper out of the truck—it was evidence—but he wanted to give Lennie a chance to explain. Maybe it was more innocent than it looked. Before he could get out of his truck, the front door to Lennie's house opened, and both Marcel and Tom walked out.

"Hey, Johnny," said Tom with a big smile.

Johnny let out a large sigh, and his breath slowed. Tom wouldn't be chipper if something bad had happened to Lennie. Johnny tossed a paper bag from a coffee shop over the debt list just in case they came over to his cab before he could get out. He wanted to talk to Lennie about it before sharing it with Marcel and Tom. Yes, not protocol, and, of course, he knew better, but he was just a citizen now, not a sworn officer of the law.

"How's it going?" Johnny shut his truck door with his free elbow. The other arm held a paper tray with two coffees and wax paper-wrapped pastries.

Marcel touched Johnny's shoulder. "You're a good man. He could use a friend."

Johnny nodded. He could use a friend, too. It was mutual.

He had hoped that Lennie would see him outside the door, but if he had, he didn't let Johnny in. Johnny knocked, and Lennie greeted him at the door with a nod, stepping aside for Johnny to enter.

"I don't know how you take your coffee," said Johnny. "I brought all the accoutrements, or however you say it. Fancy way for me to say 'little creamers and sugar packets.' Oh, and danish. I brought danish. Not the healthiest thing on the planet, but oh, so good. Happy Food, I call it."

He set the cardboard tray down on the counter. "Please, help yourself. Cheese. Lemon. And spinach. That one is pretending to be a healthy one." He pointed to each as he said its flavor.

Johnny laughed. Lennie did not. He looked at Johnny, the way a cat looks at a plastic pet carrier, not believing how extra sweet its owner was speaking, or trusting that the dried fish inside the carrier was worth the risk. Lennie picked up a paper cup of coffee and selected three creamers and five sugars.

"How many do you use?" he asked Johnny.

"None. I take it black. I drink so much on a daily basis that I'd end up consuming pounds of sugar a week, not to mention gallons of half and half." Johnny chuckled, again trying to keep the mood light, difficult to do with Lennie's somber face.

"Was the hospital good to you? You feeling okay?" Johnny unwrapped the danish bag to make sure Lennie felt welcome to take two or three.

"Sore. Stiff."

Sad. Broke. Lonely. Johnny knew that the list of how Lennie felt could continue on, probably for pages. He wondered if Lennie would share the conversation he just had with Marcel and Tom. Did they ask him about the break-in at Wolf Marine? Or if he had strung the barbed wire at Riverview Farm? Or if he figured he could get rid of his debt to Karl by getting rid of Karl himself? Although, why would Lennie steal the debt paper from the door if he was already targeting Karl on the snowmobile? He stole the paper and left it on the front seat of his truck. That paper would only attract attention to his anger towards Karl and make him the prime suspect number one for anything else to follow. No, it didn't add up.

"You saw the sheriffs leaving. They asked me about Karl's sled. If I saw it when I was out driving around." Lennie sat in the kitchen on a wooden kitchen chair. "Guess everyone in town is interested in Karl's record. Everyone but me. I could care less."

"That's understandable," said Johnny, sitting across from him. The kitchen was cozy and functional. He hoped Lennie wasn't going to lose this house to the bank like he lost his boat.

Lennie took a bite of the cheese danish. "He must have made it, though, since his sled was gone when I was there."

"Oh, what time was that? When you...drove by Wolf Marine." Lennie hadn't confessed to Johnny about taking the debt list. Yet.

"I did more than drive by Wolf Marine. I was actually in the store. Around two in the morning." He shook his head. "I did a stupid thing. I took the paper with my name on it, the paper that was taped to the front door."

Johnny nodded. "I see. Did you tell that to the sheriffs?"

Lennie nodded. "I did. They asked if I had left the door open. I hadn't. Did something happen to Karl's store?"

Johnny nodded again, glad that he had told Marcel and Tom. "Yes, someone was in the store last night. They took a few things. Did you happen to also take the notebook where Karl recorded the items on credit?"

Lennie shook his head. "Tom and Sheriff Ouelette asked me that, too. I didn't, but I have to admit that would have been a smart idea. I hadn't even planned on taking the paper. I just thought of it as I drove by, so I stopped. What else was missing?"

"Well, the snowmobile for one. But it sounds like the snowmobile was taken first, way before someone went back into the store after you did."

"Someone stole Karl's sled? He didn't use it first on the trails?" Lennie had perked up. He might say he wasn't interested in Karl's record, but the notion was intriguing overall. Also, there weren't many thefts in Secretly, not much crime in general, so to have Karl's sled stolen and then his store, in a sense, robbed, was definitely a story worth following.

"Yes. Mikey Dyer rode it. That's what I heard, anyway." Johnny sipped his coffee.

"What? He did?" Lennie shook his head and let out a sound that could only be described as disgust. "He can't stay out of trouble to save his soul."

"I've heard that, too." Johnny pulled his lips into his mouth, an old habit to get himself to stop talking and to listen.

"What a pisser," Lennie was still shaking his head.

Johnny realized that Lennie was upset with Mikey, not impressed with him. Maybe they weren't friends after all. Johnny let silence fill the room. Minutes passed.

Lennie looked up and stared at Johnny. "Mikey stole from me, you know. That was the beginning of the end for me."

"He did? Did he steal a lot?"

"About sixty grand," Lennie said in a quiet voice.

"What? Jeezum Crow," said Johnny, not in a quiet voice. He couldn't help but react to that high a number.

"It's my own fault for keeping that much here to avoid taxes on it. My first mistake. He knew where I kept it. My second mistake. I hired him as a stern man here and there. My third mistake. I didn't have cash on me to pay him at the end of the day, so I told him to come to the house with me. I don't know what I was thinking, letting him see all that money. Then one day, I went to pay the boat loan, and all the money was gone. Box and all." Lennie's voice cracked. "At first, I thought I had just put it somewhere else. I tore the house apart. But it was gone. Sixty-thousand dollars."

Johnny had a dark thought, and he dared to say it out loud.

"You actually despised Mikey more than Karl."

"For sure. I do. One hundred percent. I hate Mikey Dyer with my whole heart. Oh, I confronted him about the money. And of course, he denied it.

But I know he took it. It had to be him. Who else could it be? He ruined my life."

"When did this happen?" Johnny held onto his empty paper cup.

Lennie leaned back in the chair and looked past Johnny. "Early summer last year. I was so distraught after that that I didn't go out as often as I should. I could barely get out of bed. I lost some of my traps to that late summer hurricane, and then I lost my boat because I wasn't making the payments on it because I wasn't making any money."

"And what did you do to Mikey?"

"What did I do? Nothing. What could I do? Other than stay away from him. Far away." Lennie picked apart one of the danish with his fingers. "I had no proof, so I couldn't go to the Sheriff. Trust me, Mikey is a creep, through and through. Look at what he did to Karl, stealing his snowmobile and ruining his record. It looks like a little thing, but that's the kind of stuff he does on purpose. To get under people's skin and ruin them because he hasn't had the ambition to do anything with his own life. He probably thinks he can trade the sled for drugs or something, too. Did Karl get his sled back?"

Johnny sighed and stared into the bottom of his empty cup. "I don't know." He cleared his voice. "You're gonna hear this soon enough, so I'm gonna tell you. I'm thinking by the way you're talking that Marcel and Tom didn't tell you."

"Tell me what?" Lennie leaned forward, his elbows on the table.

"Mikey is dead. He died using Karl's snowmobile."

"What?" Lennie's eyes grew wide. "How? Where? He had an accident?"

Johnny shook his head. "Probably not. At this time, the details don't matter. Who could have had it in for Mikey?"

"Besides me? Heck, almost every lobsterman. He ripped off everyone, stealing equipment, asking for a week's pay in advance, and then not showing up to work, keeping the wrong size lobsters without the boat owner knowing, but then the owner is the one who is fined when the marine patrol inspects them. You name it, and he did it. That's why no one would employ him anywhere on the coast of Maine." Lennie sat back against the chair again. "I heard he was getting a passport to get work up in Nova Scotia because he couldn't get work in Maine. They'd shoot him dead up there if they found him stealing out of their traps, another crime I suspect he also did down here."

Johnny also sat back in the wooden chair. Maybe someone knew it was Mikey, and not Karl, on that sled after all. One thing he did believe was that he had read Lennie correctly. He was a good egg. Just fallen on hard times.

"Listen, Lennie, I don't have the kind of money you need to pay off your debts to Karl or to buy a new boat, but I do have a need for a good worker."

Lennie put up his hand. "Oh no, I don't need charity." He looked down at his hands.

"Oh, I know that. Trust me. I know. And what I need help with is hard work. But I pay for hard work."

Silence again. Johnny let the silence hang in the air.

Finally, Lennie looked up. "What is it? What kind of work?"

"I want to build a sugar shack, you know, the building where you boil sap down to make maple syrup. I'm going to tap my maples. I already took a class with UMaine Extension on making maple syrup. I got a certificate and everything. I framed it too." He laughed, hoping again to infuse some lightness into Lennie. "And I'm going to do it the old-fashioned way. Boiling it down. Not this osmosis stuff, or whatever it's called, that cuts the time in half. We're always too much in a hurry. Rush. Rush. Rush. Well, rushing has a price. I'm not going to produce a light-colored syrup. I want to slow boil to create dark liquid gold." He pinched his fingers together and raised them to his lips, making a kissing sound, like an old school Italian chef presenting a freshly prepared meal at a table.

Lennie listened. He actually really listened. Maybe Johnny had him.

"So you need help building the shack? I can't say I have any carpentry skills."

"Yep, that, and clearing out some areas around some of the maples. I'm sure you did minor repairs on your wooden boat. I'm not building the Taj Mahal. As long as it can withstand a windstorm and snow on its roof, it'll be good." He chuckled again. "And I could use help tapping trees and then collecting the sap once it starts running. And helping with Maine Maple

Weekend in March. I did a rough tree count the other day. I think I have a hundred to tap. I am serious when I say that I could really use the help."

"Wow, but are you sure you shouldn't hire someone who really knows what they're doing, if you're going to have all that steam and boiling sap inside? Someone like Craig Fisher, who would know what angles everything should be at?"

"I'll be honest, Lennie. I can't afford Craig. He's the most expensive carpenter on the peninsula. I'm guessing his work is outstanding if he can charge that much, and the sugar shack does not need finish work." Johnny laughed.

Finally, Lennie smiled. A small smile, but still a smile. It was a real smile. "I understand. You need the shack to stand, but you don't need a palace."

"Exactly."

"But why me?" He lowered his eyes again.

Johnny reached across the table and touched one of Lennie's hands. Lennie looked up and met his gaze. "I think you and I are a lot alike, Lennie, maybe for different reasons, but if I'm right, and you are like me, that means you're a good person. And a good person deserves a second chance."

Chapter Twenty-Nine

Raven reached Marcel on his cell and gave him a quick rundown of her encounter with Jared.

"Tom and I are only five minutes away, babe," he said. "Get out of the barn now, and go home. Or go to Betty's if Howard is home. Get her out of there, too."

She looked down at a tied-up Jared.

"I think we're safe for now. Come to the barn when you get here."

She and Betty waited for them at the barn door with Betty clutching her famous purse in front of her.

"That was quite something, wasn't it?" Betty beamed.

Tom's SUV sped into the gravel parking lot, and Marcel hopped out as it rolled to a stop. He grabbed Raven with both arms, and she melted into his chest.

"You okay?" he said to her, pulling back, and then looking at Betty.

"I am totally good, thanks to Betty," said Raven. Betty's smile grew wider.

"I'm good too," Betty said. "Now, for the culprit. He's in there." She pointed toward the other side of the barn, down the inside corridor. Tom ran in that direction as Raven, Marcel, and Betty followed.

In the garage room where Raven and Betty had left him, Jared sat against a wall, struggling with the last piece of baling twine around his ankles.

"Stay right where you are," Tom said, his hand on his gun in the holster.

"I'm glad you're finally here," he snarled. "I want you to arrest those two lunatic women for assault. They hit me over the head and tied me up." He rubbed his wrists and then turned to show a red mark on his neck.

"That's a lie," said Betty. "I'm not tall enough to hit him over the head. And besides, he was going to kill Raven."

"I was not!" His voice, dry and reedy, squeaked like a junior high boy going through the change.

Betty put her hands on her hips. "You were, too. You had that shovel raised, ready to beat her to a pulp. Murderer!" She extended her arm and pointed a finger at him. Raven put an arm on her shoulder. She saw Marcel move toward Betty, too, ready to nix another outburst.

"I wasn't going to do anything of the sort. You're crazy, lady." Jared shook his head and brushed the hay off his clothes, standing.

"Not as crazy as you!" Betty blurted out again.

"Okay, okay. What's this all about?" Marcel now stepped toward Jared, who shrank back against the wall. Betty seemed to take that as her platform to explain her theory.

"Jared killed Karl, except it was really Mikey he killed, and he's hiding the barbed wire and the receipts somewhere in the barn!" Betty crossed her arms in triumph.

"What? You're nuts!" Jared jabbed a finger at Tom and Marcel. "I've told these officers already. They've already asked this. We do not use barbed wire. We do not have barbed wire. I did not buy barbed wire. I did not string any type of wire across the snowmobile trail. Trust me, if I could have put up a bulldozer down there, or a brick wall, or a detour sign driving them into the river, I would have done that, but I did not do any of those things, nor did I hurt any snowmobiler."

"But you did rob Karl." Raven came around Betty, carrying something wrapped in a tan cloth.

"I did not rob Karl. I already told you that. Not that it is any of your business, either." Jared's face was red, and his breathing was heavy.

"That's not true. You stole this." She held up the framed picture of the two girls rowing that had hung in Karl's store. A spot of red popped out from their clothes, highlighted by a stream of light. The rest of the painting was dark. The frame was missing gold teeth in spots, but it was no longer encased in the dust and cobwebs that Raven had seen days earlier.

"Karl gave me that. He was going to throw it out," Jared said.

"That's a lie." Betty was back at it. "He told us himself that it was strange that it was missing. How didn't it make sense that someone stole the painting and not the expensive wetsuits." She stopped talking and turned to look closer at the print. She straightened it in Raven's arms. "Hold it right there." She backed up and studied it longer, and then snapped her fingers. "Oh my! Oh my!"

"What is it?" asked Marcel. All eyes were now on Betty.

She was grinning from ear to ear. "I got it! I know why Jared stole this painting. My upbringing has finally paid off." She clapped her hands and then turned to Jared. "And you recognized it, right? You know exactly what it is."

He paled and seemed to shrink, but didn't say anything.

"He recognized what?" asked Tom, "I'm not following." Raven wasn't following either, but decided to wait for Betty to explain.

Betty had a hard time containing her enthusiasm. "Decades ago, maybe before you were even born, Tommy Boy," Betty reached over and tweaked Tom's cheek, "there was a famous art heist in Newport, Rhode Island. Dozens of paintings, etchings, and small sculptures were stolen in the middle of the night from one of those giant mansions. From one of the Vanderbilts or the Carnegies or someone like that. Somebody super rich from shipping or coal or whatever made men wealthy back in the Newport mansions days."

Raven spoke up, remembering the story. "I learned about this in art history class."

Betty smiled. "Incredible, wasn't it? So clever. A charity fundraising party was planned at that mansion for the newly formed Preservation Society. After the heist, it was suspected that the security company did it because the real security guards had been canceled that day. The company received a call: the party was off, and they weren't needed. They didn't send any guards. Yet, security guards were there! Men, obviously posing as guards, took their spots, and then, when all the guests went home, instead of securing the mansion like they were supposed to, they loaded up their vans with priceless art objects from multiple masters from various schools of art. Monet, Klee,

Degas, da Vinci, and others, and Rembrandt. This Rembrandt in particular." She pointed at the painting in Raven's hands.

A Rembrandt? Raven felt her hands quiver. She was holding a real Rembrandt?

Betty took another moment to admire the painting. "Many of the pieces of art have been recovered over the years. They found some through new owners, some innocent, some not so innocent, submitting works for auction through reputable houses. One painting by Gauguin was discovered by a real estate agent when a cottage along Long Island Sound went up for sale after the homeowner's death. I'm sure some are hanging on the walls of the ultra-rich in Europe and the U.S., never to be seen again. Sadly, neither the da Vinci nor this Rembrandt was ever recovered. Until now."

"How did Karl get this one?" Tom asked. Raven saw doubt in his eyes, believing that Betty had to be wrong. It was even hard for her to believe that she was holding a real painting, a masterpiece, not something she had always thought was a print. But it must be a real painting worth a boatload of money because Jared's face turned paler and paler, and his body sank back into the wall.

She picked up the thread. "Karl told us that someone used it as collateral to buy gas while his grandfather, who ran the store, was still alive. The customer insisted he was coming back for it. His grandfather, and then his father, held on to it in case the guy ever came back with the cash for the gas. He kept it because he liked telling the story."

"Thank goodness he did! Imagine if he were a minimalist," said Betty.

Marcel chimed in. "I've heard him tell that story at least a dozen times to people at the cash register. Holding up the line, of course."

Betty swiveled toward Jared. "You probably heard him tell it. You may have even asked him about it."

Raven nodded. "Yes, you majored in Art History, right? I think that's on the Riverview Farm's website, in the biography section." She shared that she had looked up Jared and Camille when they first got established. She remembered thinking that an Art History major living on a farm in Secretly seemed out of place. "But you ended up at the right place at the right time.

Go figure."

"Well, almost," said Betty. "He got close."

Jared looked at his feet.

Tom picked up the storyline, addressing Jared. "While the rest of us, for generations, thought it was a print or a paint-by-number, definitely something worthless, in Wolf Marine, you walk into the store to give Karl a piece of your mind about the snowmobile trail, and you see it. Maybe, at first, you, too, thought it was just a copy, but when you heard him tell the story and did the math on the possible date, you might even have asked Karl about it. He probably took your interest as an olive branch toward the trails."

"And you were just thinking of your own bank account," said Betty, putting an exclamation point on the story and going back to admire the painting. "Ah, it is amazing. That stream of light in such a dark work. The unique subject matter for Rembrandt. Beyond priceless."

"How much do you think this is actually worth?" Marcel stood beside Betty for a better look, while Tom pulled Jared closer.

"Millions. Millions and millions. Wanna run away together?" She laughed, winked, and elbowed Marcel. "It really is quite remarkable that it's Rembrandt. Dark but less dark than his usual. Not a portrait. That little bit of red on the girls. Priceless."

"Jared! I've been looking all over for you," Camille said as she entered the garage, not wearing a coat, as if she had just glanced out the shop window and saw the sheriff's vehicle in the yard. She looked from Marcel and Tom to Raven and Betty, and then to the painting, and then to Jared, who was still practically cuffed to Tom. Her eyebrows creased together as she tried to make sense of the scene. "What has happened? What is going on?"

"Oh, just a little art history lesson," said Betty. "Care to join us?"

Chapter Thirty

Raven and Betty left Marcel and Tom with Jared and Camille, and the painting, at Riverview Farm.

"What a morning! I think this might be the best morning I've ever had!" Betty hugged her purse. "And you, you little wonder of joy," she said to the purse. "I've never loved you more."

Before leaving, Raven had assured Marcel that she hadn't been hurt at all by Jared. She was also grateful he hadn't asked why she was in the barn to begin with, and why she felt the need to snoop. He was probably waiting until he got home to lecture her. Again.

In the Mini, Betty said, "If we hadn't been looking for barbed wire, we would have never found that painting! He would have gotten away with the robbery and with the murder."

"I'm not so sure he's the killer. I think I'm buying his story about not putting up the barbed wire," said Raven as she maneuvered up the Hart's slick driveway. The sun melting the packed snow, coupled with overnight frigid temperatures, made for icy patches. Thankfully, the Mini, despite what people thought of it, had excellent all-wheel drive traction. She had grown tired of people asking her if it was drivable in a Maine winter.

"You are? I don't believe him for a second. I've never trusted art history majors. It's a feel-good degree. Music majors, yes. Fine Arts majors, yes. Journalists, yes. But art history majors, unless they're going right into museum work, just exist to make you feel inferior."

Raven couldn't think of any art history majors she knew except for Jared. She sort of saw Betty's point if he was the norm.

Betty unbuckled her seat belt at the top of the driveway. "I wish Marcel had let us take the painting with us. I could have shown it to Howard, and we could have studied it under better light."

Howard opened the side door. "How are my two Nancy Drews? Come in and tell me about it." He winked at Raven.

"I saw that wink, Howard, and you have no idea how we just cracked this case wide open." Betty squished past Howard and into the house. As she passed him, she whacked her purse on his behind and laughed.

He jumped forward and looked over his shoulder. "What was that about?"

Raven smiled as she walked past him. "Betty, the hero, will tell you all about it."

"The hero? Did you guys really find the barbed wire? Does it count since you didn't have a search warrant?" Howard pushed his glasses up on his nose as he turned back into the house and shut the door behind him.

Betty scrunched her face at him. "First off, Howard, citizens don't need search warrants."

"No, they need the owner's permission; otherwise, it's called breaking and entering," he said.

Betty shrugged off Howard's point. "Second, we cracked open a forty-year-old case."

"What? Someone died on that farm forty years ago?" Howard asked.

"No, and if you would let me finish, you'd have all your answers. Sometimes, Howard, it's hard for me to believe that you had a big corporate job. You have terrible listening skills."

Raven plopped into one of the plush, flowered, upholstered chairs. The Harts' bickering felt like a warm blanket compared to Jared's anger and her own fright.

"Can you pull up the internet on the TV?" Betty asked Howard.

"Really? You're actually interested in something I do all the time," Howard grinned. Betty stuck her tongue out at him. "Okay, okay," he said, "give me one sec."

The large screen television bolted to the wall blinked on. Howard manipulated the screen. "Okay, what do you want me to look up?"

Betty stood next to his chair. "Use these search words: Newport. Stolen Art. Rembrandt."

Howard looked at her with a surprised expression. Raven guessed that Howard thought Betty would say "Barbed wire. Snowmobile. Maine" or something like that.

Howard didn't question her, and in less than a minute, a picture of the painting of two girls rowing in a boat was on the screen. Their red outfits stood in stark contrast to the otherwise muted colors. That amazing stream of illumination bounced off of them like a spotlight.

"Is this what you wanted?" he asked, his face scrunched in confusion.

"Yes. Perfect," said Betty. "What year does it say that was painted?"

Howard zoomed in on the description. "Sixteen fifty-two."

"Ten years after Columbus sailed the ocean blue," she said.

"Ten? More like one hundred and sixty years after." Howard gave her a little smile.

"Okay, math smarty pants, showing off. I only said that because of the rhyme."

"I always thought of Rembrandt's paintings as dark," added Raven. "This one has that splash of red and the sunlight."

Betty, putting on her teacher hat, said, "He had others with red too. Though they were in portraits. He wasn't known for landscapes, you know, making this painting worth even more."

A knock on the side door made them all jump. Johnny popped into the house before Howard could get out of his chair.

"Hi, everyone. Just saying hi and to remind you all that I'm grateful for you in my life. Especially when things go sideways like they have this week. Glad we all have each other. Okay, bye-bye."

He started to shut the door, and Raven bounded out of her chair.

"Johnny, wait."

He stuck his back in, looking as surprised as Raven felt in saying that. "No time like the present," as her mother always said. She might as well take him back to her house now and show him the cash box.

"Do you have any time today?" she asked.

Johnny came back in and shut the door. He stayed on the mat in his wet boots.

"I don't have anything but time," he said with a large grin.

Howard and Betty looked at Raven.

"Hmm, seems like everyone is on the secret but me," he said.

Raven responded to him. "I have something to show you," and then she turned to Betty and Howard. "I'm going to show Johnny the box."

"Great idea," said Howard, also standing. "And I'm grateful for you too, Johnny." He extended his hand for Johnny to shake. Johnny grasped it with both of his hands.

Betty gave Raven a tight hug and whispered, "Good luck" in her ear.

Raven put her coat on and gave a small smile to Johnny as she passed him while he held the door open for her. She had never asked him to come to her house before; he always had just shown up. She was now inviting her father, yes, her father, to her home.

Both poochies were, of course, elated to get not one but two people to kiss and adore. After letting them have a quick bathroom break, she asked Johnny if he wanted anything to drink.

"You know me, I'd love a cup of coffee."

She moved her hand, giving a "help yourself" gesture toward their coffee machine. He popped a pod in and pushed the button. She listened to the sound of coffee pouring and splashing into the empty mug. There was an innocence to the sound, a status quo. Pouring a cup of coffee was a habit, not a dramatic event. Something that millions of people did every day, around the globe. Johnny was no different than any of those people. No different at all except for one thing. He was her father.

She noticed that he was a patient man. Heck, he had waited almost three years since his return to Maine for her to come around. If she hadn't found the box of money with the notes, would she have accepted him on her own? She kicked herself at how closed and suspicious she was—of him, of Marcel, and now, of her beloved mother. Julia must have had a reason to hide this.

Without a word, she brought the metal box over to the kitchen table and sat down, waiting for Johnny to join her once his coffee was ready. He sat down at the end, to her left, and waited for her to begin.

"I think it is easier to show you this," she said and pushed the box toward him across the tablecloth.

Johnny eyed Raven and then the box. He made no move to touch it.

"I feel like you're making me the treasurer of a secret society." He smiled and took a sip of coffee before setting the mug down. However, he made no move to open the box. Finally, he pulled it toward him.

"We're both getting older the longer I delay." He gave her another smile.

She hid her hands under the table. She didn't want him to know they were shaking. When she looked at his, she saw that his were a little shaky too. Her heart pounded as she watched him lift the lid. She held her breath as his eyes narrowed in confusion, and then grew wide as he realized what he was looking at. He lifted one letter, then another, without opening either. He had written them. He must remember what they said.

His eyes brimmed with tears, causing her eyes to also fill up and then overflow down her cheeks.

"Why didn't she use any of this money?"

Raven shrugged and shook her head. She couldn't find her voice. She sniffled, and he reached across to touch her arm. She pulled her left hand out from under the table, and he held it. For the first time that she could remember, she allowed herself to feel her father's touch. He let go and returned to the box, pulling out more letters and wads of hundred-dollar bills.

He put it all back in and closed the lid. "I was doing the best I could, but it truly wasn't good enough."

Raven leaned forward. "No, no. You tried. I don't know why my mother never told me about your generosity or your concern. I don't know why she let me think you had abandoned us."

"Because I did abandon you both. That's the truth. And frankly, it was the coward's way out to send money. It's easy to send money, Raven. It's hard to live with the day-to-day struggles of raising a child. Okay, so eventually, I asked if I could see you both, if I could move home, but Raven, do you realize how many years it took for me to get to that place? Do not be upset with your mother. She held it together. She raised you to be this wonderful woman. Maybe she kept this money as a rainy-day fund, in case the cabins needed repair or, one day, no one came to rent them. Maybe she never took my sobriety as permanent. She might have always been waiting for the other shoe to drop. I don't blame her for that."

Raven studied Johnny. He was a kind man, a generous heart. She was the one who was cold and doubtful. Maybe she inherited that from her mother, but, as Johnny said, who could blame Julia? But Raven didn't have to stay this way. This was now her opportunity to change as well. If she could forgive Johnny, she could forgive herself.

Chapter Thirty-One

om really wanted to handcuff Jared and drag him to the county jail. He was done with his lies and his attitude. He bowed to Marcel's wish, however, to interview him again first, with Camille, in their house. Jared was read his rights, at least. He was under arrest for threatening Raven with a shovel, stealing a painting, and leaving the scene of an accident. Who knows what else he might reveal now, and it was better to have it all by the book. Jared declined to call an attorney.

Instead of the kitchen, this time, they sat in their living room. No coziness of the wood-burning stove or the niceties of a cup of coffee. This was hardcore, to some extent. What wasn't hardcore, however, was Camille being present, sniffling into a tissue as she sat next to Jared on the couch. Tom and Marcel were in stiff-backed armchairs across from the couch.

Marcel began. "Let's start over, why don't we? Let's revisit the night of the blizzard. Camille, let's start with you."

At the mention of her name, she head bobbed up. Her eyes were red and wet, and her hands shook. She waited for Marcel's question.

"Tell us again what happened that night. The truth, this time."

She looked down at her rumpled tissue and began to tear it apart as she spoke. She didn't look Jared's way, nor did he look at her.

"What I told you was the truth. I woke up, and Jared wasn't in bed. He had been so angry with me for signing the snowmobile trail paperwork, I was afraid he'd do something to sabotage the trail."

"Like string wire up across it?" Tom looked at Jared as he asked. Jared's eyes were on his folded hands.

Camille continued. "No, I didn't think that. I was thinking more along the lines of putting his Range Rover down there, where the trail comes out of the woods, to block the entrance onto our property. We had driven it down there once last summer when we were driving the fields, checking out the boundary lines. I wasn't thinking about the depth of the snow and how that would be impossible."

She coughed and reached for a glass of water that she had earlier put on a side table. She sipped the water, caught her breath, and continued.

"I looked for Jared in the house. I was hoping, like I said before, that he just couldn't sleep and was watching TV, but he wasn't in the TV room. His boots weren't on the mat either, and his coat was gone. I was thinking that he, too, was worried about the wind and the barn roof and that he went out to check on the animals. I got dressed and went out to the barn. I noticed that his Range Rover wasn't in the yard. At first, I thought that maybe he put it in the section of the barn that we are using as a garage—where I found you today—but why would he put his car away and leave mine out?"

She grabbed a fresh tissue and blew her nose. Jared sat in silence.

"But as I got closer, I could see his tire tracks. They led out of our yard. To the road. At first, I thought, 'Why is he driving around in a blizzard?' But then Jared always drives around when he is super mad at me, and that Range Rover better be good in the snow for the price we paid for it."

Marcel asked, "And when he got back, what did you talk about it?"

"We didn't talk about anything. Typical us, we ignored the whole thing. I never asked where he went."

Marcel nodded. "And he didn't offer to tell you?"

"No, he might have even thought I didn't notice." Her voice was thick. "Again, we're both good at ignoring problems."

Marcel continued. "He didn't tell you he had had an accident?"

Her eyes grew wide. "No. What accident?"

"He ran someone off the road."

Camille's head jerked to look at Jared and then back to Marcel. "Are they okay?"

Marcel nodded. "They are now, but no thanks to your husband. He left them in the ditch. Hit and run."

"It was a pickup truck, for goodness sake!" Jared imploded. "A nudge off the road! If he were a better driver, he wouldn't have gone into that ditch. You're acting like I hit a pedestrian."

Marcel shifted his questioning to Jared. "Why were you on the road at that time of night?"

Jared smirked. "You know why. I was stealing the painting. I admit to stealing the painting."

Marcel kept his face blank. "At Wolf Marine, you messed up the store. You made it look like a robbery of the store."

Jared nodded. "Yeah, I planned to, but have you ever been in that store? It looks like it was already ransacked. Why waste time? I just knocked over the rack of faded postcards and made a mess behind the register, pulling drawers out."

"You stole Karl's accounting ledger. Why did you do that?" Marcel asked.

Jared looked confused. "If I did, it wasn't on purpose."

Tom leaned forward. "How could you be sure the painting was still hanging there? Would it be worth the risk of driving in the blizzard to get it?"

Jared sat up straighter, almost like he was proud of his plan. "I went to Wolf Marine the morning of the blizzard. I knew Karl would be pissed to see me because of my fuss over the trails—and, boy, was he. He threw me out of the store—but all I needed was to look at the back wall, to make sure the painting was still there—and it was—and the wheels for my plan were in motion. Everyone knew that Karl would be out sledding, not that he'd be at the store in the wee hours of the morning anyway, but no one else would be out and about either to see me because of the blizzard, except for that idiot truck. But I don't think he got a good look at me. I could have gotten away with it if it weren't for those snooping women."

Neither Tom nor Marcel warned Jared to watch what he said about Raven and Betty. Not necessary.

Tom asked another question. "I'm sure if you had made an offer to buy it, Karl would have sold it to you, maybe even given it to you."

"Actually, I thought of seeing if he'd sell it to me, but I didn't want to draw attention to it. What if he was watching TV one day, and there was a recap of the heist, like on the fiftieth anniversary or something. He'd recognize the painting in an instant. Plus in his story about it, he and his family were still waiting for the guy to come back for it, and he might not sell it for that reason. Little did he know that the guy was never coming back."

"How do you know that?" Tom asked.

Jared appeared in his element. "Those in the art world suspected who was involved, though it was never proven. There were a few photos from that charity event, and some of the guards were accidentally in them. One of the blown-up photographs clearly shows Red Arthur. Red had a rap sheet a mile long from his Boston crimes, including robbing jewelry stores and a private art collector. Well, a month after the robbery, he died in a car accident on Route One around York. He was heading south back down to Boston. The timing fits perfectly with Karl's account of his grandfather taking the painting. I am curious as to why he was this far up the coast, though, with York being about two hours from here."

Jared paused, thinking.

Marcel picked up the questioning again. "You're thinking that maybe the da Vinci or some of the other unrecovered work might be in a house around here still?"

Jared was not a good poker player either. He shook his head no, but it was obvious that Marcel had hit on his thought. Too bad for Jared that he probably would never have the chance to scour the Midcoast to look.

Marcel shifted in his seat and turned back to Camille. "Do you mind getting me a glass of water?" he asked and then waited for her to leave and head down the hall. He leaned toward Jared.

"Jared, I think it's time you told us the truth and admitted that you wanted to kill Karl Wolf, so he wouldn't figure out you had stolen a million-dollar painting from his shop."

Jared straightened again. "No, that's not true. And it's probably more like a $20 million painting."

Marcel cocked his head. "I see. All the more reason to wish he were dead."

"Wishing someone was dead isn't the same thing as killing them," Jared snapped at Marcel.

Marcel didn't give up. "The snowmobile trail ended up being the perfect means, and you pretending to be against it also worked well for your plan."

Jared still insisted he did not tamper with the trail. "No, no, no. I didn't do anything to the trail or the field. And actually, your logic is wrong. If I had wanted to kill Karl on the trail, I would have wanted the trail to come through our field."

Marcel sat back. Tom saw Jared's point, although he wasn't sure; he wasn't completely satisfied with Jared's answer. Marcel seemed to be letting Jared percolate. Tom took over. "What were you going to do with the painting, anyway? Everyone in the art field knows it is stolen goods."

Jared paled a bit and swallowed. "I know a private collector who would pay its real value."

Tom found that hard to believe. "Twenty million dollars? And then you could move from this god-forsaken place. I believe I heard you call Secretly that?"

Jared sneered. "Do I want to move back to Boston? You bet your life."

"And you actually had a buyer," Marcel probed.

"I believe I did."

Marcel leaned forward. "What's the buyer's name? Have you already reached out?"

Jared shook his head. Maybe he thought he might come across another stolen piece of art somewhere else, and keeping the art collector out of it would still afford him a client. Jared didn't realize his future days would all be behind bars if he and Marcel had anything to do with it. If it worked out, by the time Jared was released, he would be too feeble to crawl around old houses looking for art to sell.

"How would you know someone like that? A former art history professor? Someone you knew from owning your coffee houses, Java Jive?" Tom asked.

"Java TIME!" Jared snarled. Yep, he was sick of being asked questions. If he was going to slip up, now would be the time.

Marcel returned to his questioning. "So you string the wire, then go steal the painting. Then all you have to do is wait for Karl to come through."

Jared's face was turning purple. "For the one-thousandth time, I never put up that wire. I don't even know how to do it."

Tom thought of the time he helped a friend put up barbed wire to keep in cattle. He snagged his clothes several times, in several places. He excused himself, went out to the hall, and checked Jared's coat. It looked brand new, no blemishes, just as he'd expect Jared's coat to look. Of course, it could have been a new coat, or Jared could have used a different one, but Tom doubted Jared had a barn coat. He didn't seem like the kind of person who wanted to get dirty. As hard as it was to admit, he believed Jared didn't have anything to do with the wire or Mikey's death.

As Tom approached the living room, he heard Marcel ask Jared, "What about your wife? A painting and a lot of money are more important to you than she is?"

Camille came up behind Tom with Marcel's water, out of Jared's view. Tom knew that she would hear his answer loud and clear.

"Let me ask you, Sheriff," said Jared, with smugness in his voice, "if you had the option of $20 million dollars, but you had to change your life for it, would you do it?"

Marcel didn't answer. Tom shook his head in amazement. If Jared understood the calling to be in law enforcement, he'd know that those in it were not motivated by money, but to serve the public.

Jared added, "Camille has this farm as her investment. I wanted my own."

Camille came from around Tom. Jared's mouth flopped open.

"Good to know your plans didn't include me," she said. She stood before Jared, still holding the glass of water.

"Baby." He reached out his hands to hers. She didn't move toward him. "I was going to tell you a great aunt died and left me money. I knew you wouldn't tolerate my stealing, but I still wanted you in my life," he said.

Camille's snort told Tom she didn't believe him. "Just tell me, Jared, that you didn't put up the wire. I could take almost anything but murder."

"I didn't put up the wire," he said. "I've said I didn't put it up dozens of times already." He turned his head toward Marcel and, in a sarcastic tone, said, "Good for you, Sheriff. You solved the missing painting, but you are nowhere near solving the murder. It wasn't me."

Camille wasn't letting Jared off the hook. "You told me you'd do anything to stop the snowmobilers from going through. Anything!"

Jared sighed and rolled his eyes at her. "I said that, yes, but I didn't mean I would hurt someone. I was just talking big."

"I think you did put up the wire to get back at me. To ruin my love of this farm. You knew you were moving back to Boston because you were going to steal that painting, and you didn't like me making any decisions without you, without you being in charge and in control. The painting was putting you back in the driver's seat, and you could stick it to me in the process."

"Camille—"

She wasn't finished. "So to punish me for signing with the snowmobile club, you put the barbed wire up."

"Camille, I did not."

Tom caught that she had actually signed the official paperwork. "I didn't think Karl made it over here with the contract."

Camille, who had started to cry again, stopped looking at Jared and focused on Tom. After blowing her nose, she said, "He didn't. He sent another officer from the club. The treasurer, I think he said he was."

"Craig?" Tom asked.

"Yes, Craig Fisher," Camille confirmed.

Tom nodded. He remembered Karl saying that Craig was picking up the paperwork. Good to know that Craig had seen Jared in action. He had already mentioned Jared to them. Maybe Craig had more insight into Jared, the farm, and the trail design in general to share.

Chapter Thirty-Two

Johnny left Raven after they both had a good cry. Not that they clung to each other at the door, but for the first time since his return, he felt like he got a real hug from her, his daughter, and because she wanted to, not because Marcel was watching, and she wanted to show Marcel that she was trying to accept him.

Relationships weren't mended in a day any more than they were destroyed in a day, although that did seem more plausible, but their relationship felt like it was on a track, finally, toward something meaningful. He knew neither of them expected storybook perfection the next time they saw each other, which would probably be tomorrow, but tomorrow would be a real new day, not just a fantasy he had been telling himself over and over.

He steered his truck toward home. He must be getting old because he felt he needed a nap, just a quick shut eye, and then afterwards he could...what? It was a cold January day, and he didn't want to simply hang out at home.

Before he knew it, he had turned his truck around and was headed towards the cemetery. He had only been there once since moving back to Maine. With Raven not accepting him, and with Julia never answering his letters, he felt it wasn't his place, that it was almost disrespectful, to visit Julia's burial spot more than that one time, but his recent conversation with Raven opened the door to go back.

The road into the cemetery hadn't been plowed yet. He left his truck on the edge of the street and walked through the deep snow and up a slight grade to the Fossett plot. His in-laws were buried there, too. Good people.

He kicked the snow away from the stone so the Fossett parents' names were fully visible as well as Julia's. He remembered meeting her parents when he was in his twenties, and now he was almost as old as they had been when they passed away.

Time felt like a cruel being, taunting you with dreams that things would get better even as it shaved minutes off your life. It was like bargaining with the Devil: "Help me to survive today. Get me to tomorrow." And then the Devil smiles and steals back days, weeks, and years of your life without a blink of an eye. How many times had he prayed, begged, shouted out loud for help to get to another day? And Time indeed did its part, but it also stole part of his life in the process. The price we are all willing to pay to move forward, Johnny thought. If we were willing to move backward, would Time be generous enough to give back, too? He shook his head at the foolish thought. Of course Time wouldn't, and why would anyone want to go backwards, anyway?

He still couldn't believe what Raven had shown him in that metal box. He had downplayed his surprise to her that Julia had never used the money he had sent. He bet if he did the math, every penny was still in that box. Why did Julia just hoard it? What was she thinking?

She had never acknowledged one payment. She never sent back a single letter, not a school photo of Raven, not an update, and definitely no invitations to come up for a birthday party for Raven or a holiday meal. At one point, he wondered whether the mailman had figured out he was sending cash and was pocketing it. Now he had proof that she received it all.

She had kept his notes, too. Had she hoped that he would just show up one day? Was it too hard to ask him to come, only to fear disappointment if he didn't? He'd never know. She was gone.

He wiped tears from his eyes. "I'm so sorry, Julia. I know I put you through hell, but I hope you know that I never stopped loving you and Raven. I never stopped trying to be a better person, and I promise you that I will do whatever it takes to make it up to Raven. I will never leave her again."

Well, that wasn't true. He hoped Raven would outlive him, but leaving that way wasn't the same as moving away. He never thought that Julia would die before him, and maybe if he knew she was sick and dying, he would have made his way north sooner, but it was too hard to know what he really would have done. Would his arrival have made her sicker and pushed her quicker toward death? Then Raven would have blamed him for her mother's death. Or would his presence have cheered her to see that he had truly come out the other side and was now there for Raven? He would never know. Time had moved past that part of all of their lives.

He thought again about the metal box, a hard, cold object housing his deepest wishes and his love. Is that why she put it all in that box? To hide his feelings because she didn't know how to handle them? He knew Julia knew he cared, and because she kept his letters, he believed it meant she still loved him back. Oh, Julia. All the wasted time.

Julia had also kept the money intact for Raven, maybe for her to have a rainy day fund, or to one day show Raven just what the money and the notes accomplished today—to demonstrate to Raven that he truly hadn't abandoned the family. Raven seemed upset with Julia for not telling her the truth and for letting Raven think of him as a loser. He understood Julia better than Raven did. Julia was hedging her bets.

Today was a good day. It was hard to know how much time he had left on Earth. Did anyone really know how much time they had left? He was heading toward seventy years old soon, and with that decade, it seemed that one's health could hit the skids easily. He didn't have good genes on his side, although his parents' own vices of smoking and drinking probably did them in more than any gene pool.

All he could do was go forward, right, Time? Live as healthy as he could. Be as happy as he dared. Maybe cut back on the caffeine a bit. He heard tonic water was a good alternative to alcohol from someone in the program. He'd try that in the afternoons or evenings instead of coffee, or maybe just switch to decaf. Why venture too far from the proven formula? How much hi-test did he really need? His life truly had turned a corner. He was blessed. He was happy to spend the rest of his days getting to know Raven, having Marcel already as a wonderful son-in-law, making new friends in town, and planning his sugar shack. How could his life get any better?

Chapter Thirty-Three

Through the hall window, Raven watched Johnny turn his old pickup truck around and head down her driveway. She felt warm and safe for the first time in a long time. She wasn't an orphan anymore.

She turned away and heard tires again outside. Johnny must have forgotten something. Peering out the window, she saw it was the 'Carpentry by Craig' pickup, shiny from a recent car wash. Poor Craig, he must want to keep busy in light of the shocking death on the trails he created.

"Hi, Craig," she said, opening the front door once he had started walking towards the house. She stepped out and pulled the door behind her to keep the dogs in.

She wasn't prepared for the hug he gave her, but she hugged him back and quickly let go.

"Sorry," he said, his face turning pink as he stepped aside. "It's been horrible. First, hearing that Karl died, and then learning he didn't. A relief! But all so shocking. And poor Mikey."

Raven nodded. She saw the bags under his eyes from lack of sleep, and he smelled like he had forgotten to shower or change his clothes.

"I was hoping Marcel was here. I wanted to see how the case was going. I feel as a club officer, I'm sort of responsible."

Raven felt the cold start to go through her. "Do you mind if we talk inside. I'm freezing."

"Oh, yes, of course."

Lily and Dukie, of course, were on the other side of the door. Craig ignored them. He either wasn't a dog person, or he was too distracted to notice them.

"Why don't you come in and wait for Marcel. Would you like something to drink?"

Craig stood in the foyer and shook his head. "No, no, I was just hoping to catch Marcel. I can't stay. I'm on my way to pick up Stella's birthday present."

"Aw, that's sweet," she said, grabbing Dukie's collar to stop him from sniffing Craig's legs.

"Nothing but the best for my Stella," Craig said, giving a small smile.

Raven would have liked a little of that attention from Craig on her cabin work. Maybe after the murder was solved, he'd get back to it.

"What did you get her?" She wasn't curious, just making small talk.

Craig pulled his cell phone from his coat pocket and opened the photo app. He showed Raven a beautiful gold bracelet. From the clasp, a small S and a small C dangled.

"I designed it myself," he beamed. "It'll look great on her, too, when we go to Europe this spring."

Wait. Was he going out of town in a couple of months? And for how long? He had no intention of working on her cabins, did he? Instead of confronting him about his work schedule, however, she swallowed and said, "Ah, she'll love it. Did you order it at Starfish?" Starfish was a small gallery in Eelsboro. They had created a new setting for her grandmother's engagement ring, which her mother had worn as a necklace.

"No. They're amateurs. I went down to Old Port."

Old Port. A beautiful section of Portland, but her mother called it "Portland Pricey" for a reason, not to mention the amount of gas to get there. At least three hours worth, round trip, Raven thought. Nothing against Old Port. She just didn't like a neighboring business being ridiculed.

However, she kept quiet. Also, if Craig didn't like Starfish, he could have gone to other stores in Midcoast, in Boothbay, or Camden. Those were very nice towns, much closer than Portland, with just as many good options. Some people were born to waste money, her grandfather used to say, or look fancy, according to Marcel.

"The jeweler closes at five o'clock," Craig said, glancing at the time on his

166

phone. "Sorry to stop by only to run off."

"I understand. I'll let Marcel know you stopped by. I have a question for you before you go, if you don't mind."

"Sure. Shoot." Craig kept his hand on the doorknob.

"When did the snowmobile club decide to reopen the trails?"

Craig's eyebrows knitted together. Raven couldn't tell if he was pondering the answer or thinking she was weird for asking. He answered regardless. "About a week ago. We had our monthly meeting at the clubhouse. I know it sounds nuts, but we had no reason to bother doing anything before that. Four years of no snow along this coast. We kinda lost our mojo for keeping the trails ready to ride for nothing."

Raven nodded. Made total sense. He took a step closer to the door. She continued.

"I know you had to pound new stakes into the frozen ground for signage for those directional arrows, stop signs, and so forth. I was at Wolf Marine when you came in to talk about it to Karl."

"Yeah, that's right."

"You had to do all that yourself, right? Like with a cement drill? Or one of those augers used on the ponds for ice fishing?"

Craig shook his head. "Oh, no, I didn't need to do anything like that. We used the old stakes. They were still in the ground. Some of them still had signage, but we mainly had to add new signs. I even had to make those."

Now it was Raven's turn for her eyebrows to scrunch together. "Oh, I thought I heard Marcel saying he saw you along the state route drilling on Saturday."

"Maybe one or two spots. A couple were rotted or missing. Not many, though. That was rare. We were lucky."

Raven smiled. She felt trapped, in a way, talking to Craig in the smallness of the foyer, but she kept thinking of questions. "One last thing, all the landowners cooperated in letting the trail still go through? Even Riverview Farm? You got all the paperwork up-to-date? That must have been some feat."

"Yep, no problem. I have it all. Will Marcel need to see it?" Craig motioned with his thumb towards the door, probably meaning that the paperwork was in his truck.

Raven shrugged. "Oh, I don't know. That's amazing, you didn't have any problems at all, not even with the farm? No problems with the husband, Jared? I've met him. He is no fun." She didn't mention that he was also not an honest man, more of a creep, actually.

Craig shook his head. "None. Really. There's no doubt that he's a jerk and full of himself. I know I mentioned him when I saw the…." He trailed off, probably remembering the bloody scene in the field. It was hard for Raven to forget it, too.

He continued. "I dealt mostly with Camille, Franklin's granddaughter. She's very nice to work with. She just wanted us to stay closer to the river, down field in a sense, and that's what we wanted too. It kept the trail that came out of the woods, continuing to go straight along the river. Win. Win."

Raven didn't know why she kept asking questions, but she had a feeling it would help her put some pieces together. She felt her brain gears whirling. "Sorry to keep you. One last thing. Did you guys do a test run, even in an ATV, on all the trails, prior to the storm?"

"No, no time for that quality check. I wish we had. Gosh, we might have been able to save Mikey's life. We were out clearing some trails right up until dark. It was already snowing hard when we quit." Craig checked his watch. "I really need to go. I'm sorry."

"Oh yeah, sure. One more question. I don't mean to be so pestering, but I was there when Mikey was found, and I guess I'm haunted by it."

"That's understandable." He pulled the door open.

Raven tossed another one in before he left. "Did you happen to clear any brush or trees near Riverview Farm? Or notice anything else suspicious around there when you were putting up the signs?"

"No, and I regret to say, I had assumed since the farm was giving us permission, and that since they were already a working farm, there would be no obstacles, like that horrible wire." He shuddered. "I take responsibility for that. Naive on my part. I know it cost Mikey his life." He paled. "Do you think the club will get in trouble for Mikey's death? Could Mrs. Dyer sue us for wrongful death? Sue me, personally? Or would the farm be responsible?"

Raven shrugged. "I don't know, Craig. I'm not an attorney."

"Consider yourself lucky then," he chuckled. "A client tried to sue me last month for unfinished work. Me! You know how meticulous I am. Trying to say that I cut corners, that I bought inferior wood, that I rushed the job. I take pride in my work and in my name. Anyway, Raven, I'll be back in town later today and will try to connect with Marcel. Sorry, but I gotta go, or I'll never get that bracelet tonight."

"Drive safely." Raven clicked the door shut as Craig sped down the driveway. Sued for unfinished work. Somehow, that didn't surprise her. She wasn't the only client with a gripe.

Chapter Thirty-Four

After bringing Jared up to the county jail and booking him on all known charges, Tom headed back to Secretly. The day was winding down, and Tom's stomach was growling. No sense going home to a quiet apartment when his sister's diner, Jane Eats, was still open for another sixty minutes or so. He called it a diner, and she called it a diner, and most people in town called it a diner, but it wasn't one of those iconic metal rectangle buildings from the 1950s. Hers was the downstairs of a real home, with five padded wooden booths and a counter on the first floor, and a decent-sized commercial kitchen in the back. She rented out the upstairs as an apartment.

Despite it being a January evening, with darkness settling in early, there were still three cars and a pickup truck out front. With enough light to see the tagline under the diner's painted name. Tom chuckled. Rachel had added the extra line when she bought the diner from a local woman named Jane. The extra line still made him smile whenever he saw it.

JANE EATS

Here, and so should you!

And the original Jane still did eat at the diner, on the house, of course. When Jane ran it, the diner closed after lunch for the day, but Rachel kept it open later to feed the "blue-haired" group, as she called them, providing them an early supper even though they were really the "no hair" group since most of them were old, bald men.

"Hi Tommy," called out a man with glasses and a flannel baseball-type cap from the counter when Tom entered the small eatery, making sure the door shut tight behind him. The wind was picking up, which meant potentially more snow to drift across the roads and probably cause a few car accidents to happen.

"How's it going, Mr. Chase? Might I join you?" Tom sat next to him on a stool, unzipping his thick county-issued jacket.

"Don't mind if you do." In front of Mr. Chase sat the remains of half his dinner on a white ceramic plate: gravied turkey on white bread, with a side of stuffing and cranberry sauce. Real, homemade cranberry sauce, not the canned, jellied version, which Tom actually not-so-secretly loved better. Seeing and smelling the turkey, however, confirmed what Tom would order.

"Your sister does up dinner real nice," said Mr. Chase, popping another forkful into his mouth. His face was clean-shaven, and he wore a knit vest over his shirt, as if he had dressed up for Thanksgiving dinner, though a few white whiskers stuck out along his chin, missed during his morning shave. He also had kept his hat on, but Tom suspected that was more for warmth than lack of old-fashioned manners. Mr. Chase was old school and would, most definitely, be proper if he wasn't chilled.

Tom knew that, besides being open to feed folks like Mr. Chase, Rachel always seemed to run specials on these kinds of dinners, too. Even if the menu said fifteen dollars for an open-faced turkey dinner for everyone else, Mr. Chase's bill would magically be missing a zero. Tom didn't know if his sister actually kept track of the discounted meals as a donation to write off on her tax return, or if she was just happy to see people fed and fed well.

Rachel was in the back of the kitchen and spotted her brother at the counter. He waved a hello, and she came out, wiping her hands on an apron, and walking around to the outside of the counter to give Tom a quick kiss on the cheek.

"I'm Rachel, and I'll be your server tonight." She winked. "What can I get you, Tommy?"

She was two years older than her brother, which meant she was heading towards the big four-oh next year. Or was it this year? Tom had lost track of his own age, let alone hers. Her brown eyes were lined with deep wrinkles, probably from years of laughing too hard on too little sleep, between the diner and her eight-year-old identical twin boys. She worked hard to keep the diner afloat, and he didn't know if the few strands of grey he noticed in her tied-back brown hair were from the diner, her sons, or her husband, Dennis.

"I'll take whatever you need to throw out," said Tom. He meant it. He ate anything, and why waste good food if she had leftovers she needed to get rid of?

"I never have food to toss," she said, and then turned to Mr. Chase, placing her hand on his shoulder. "How was your dinner, Mr. Chase? Anything else I could get you?"

"Oh, gosh, no, Rachel. Lip-smacking good." His bright blue eyes twinkled. "You're the best cook I know, and that says a lot. My Ruthie was good too, god bless her soul, but even she would come in second to you if she were alive today."

"You're too cute, but thank you. Say I have a couple of danishes I hate to throw out, but I won't be able to sell them tomorrow. They'll be stale by morning. Do you think Waldo would like them as a snack?"

"Waldo? Heck, I'll warm them up tomorrow morning for myself, and he and I can share. If he sits nice for them, that is." Mr. Chase leaned over to Tom, who was still standing next to Rachel. "Waldo is my dog. An old boy but a good boy."

"Let me wrap them up for you. I'm glad you can use them." Rachel moved swiftly to the side counter and placed danish from under a glass dome into a white waxed bag. She rolled them up tightly as she walked them back to Mr. Chase.

"Thank you, kindly." Mr. Chase patted his stomach. "And delicious as always. I'll take my check, please."

"All righty." Rachel pulled out her order pad, and Tom saw her move her pen along the lines.

"One Monday evening special," she said as she ripped off the top paper and placed it on the counter next to him. "I can take that whenever you're ready. No rush."

Rachel was smart, Tom thought. Not giving out charity per se. But a deal?

Yes, a definite deal, but would Mr. Chase come every night if Rachel said his dinner was on the house? Probably not. He wanted to pay.

"What's the damage?" Mr. Chase said, picking up the tab and looking at it. "Are you sure this is right?"

"Absolutely. You're just really good at eating my specials at the end of the day." She smiled as she accepted his two-dollar bills.

"I want you to keep that change, now, you hear?" He called after her.

She answered over her shoulder. "Thank you! I appreciate it!"

She put the extra dollar in the tip jar to be split between her, her cook, and her morning server. Mornings were when the diner was really hopping. From six o'clock until around one in the afternoon. Sometimes Rachel even closed from two o'clock until four in the afternoon to run the boys around, but she always opened up, usually, just with herself working, from four until six o'clock or so. Tom couldn't love his sister more for her generous heart. His brother-in-law, well, that was another story, but he decided not to even think generously of Dennis on this evening.

Mr. Chase opened the front door to leave, his paper bag of goodies tightly clasped in his hand, when he almost bumped into someone entering the diner.

"Oh, excuse me," Tom heard Mr. Chase say. "After you, my lady."

Tom leaned back to see who was coming in. It was the new forensics examiner from the Riverview Farm field. Margot, right?

Chapter Thirty-Five

Raven fed Lily and Dukie without fanfare. They were, as always, happy to eat. As she watched Lily lick clean her bowl and then Dukie's, after he stepped away, Raven thought about the hour with Johnny and how quickly her perceptions and thoughts had changed.

Maybe her mother wanted it to be that way. If Julia had spoken well of Johnny to her, would she have believed her? If Raven knew about the money being sent, would she have just felt that Johnny was buying them back? If she sat back and thought about it, Julia did live a peaceful life. Yes, she worked hard to keep Pine Acres running smoothly and to pass it on to Raven, but did she complain? Never. Julia whistled as she washed windows. She hummed as she dusted. She sang, folding mounds of cabin sheets and towels.

"Happiness is a choice," she said over and over, for no particular reason. "Choose to be happy, Elizabeth. You always have that choice."

Raven had been digging herself into a hole—blocking Johnny from her life and suspecting Marcel of preferring his high school sweetheart over her without any cause—why was she choosing misery when there was nothing wrong in her world?

"Don't invite trouble in," Raven told Lily, who hoped that meant she was getting an extra cookie for being a good listener. "Unless it involves being nosey."

That was part of Raven's problem. She had too much time on her hands off-season, when the cabins weren't rented out and bustling with people from away and even some Mainers from other parts of the state who wanted to be by the ocean. Having the time and needing a project were part of the reason she wanted to try renting on Valentine's Day weekend. That thought reminded her she had work to do in the Birch Cabin and also in Pine, Aspen, and Fir. Tomorrow. She'd go back to that tomorrow.

Right now, she had a hunch to explore.

Grabbing her laptop, she sat at the kitchen table and opened up the State of Maine's website. Where was that information on the snowmobile clubs? She found the association, the one that worked across the state with the various volunteer clubs and landowners to ensure that landowners agreed to allow access to the snowmobiles, and that clubs maintained the trails properly and with respect. Both the state, the association, and any club she looked at said the same thing over and over: "Use of the land is a privilege, not a right." Hard to believe there were fourteen thousand miles of groomed snowmobile trails in Maine. Hats off, she thought, to everyone who worked hard to make it happen.

Her grandfather had an old snowmobile that she rode around the yard when she was a kid. It smoked something fierce when he pulled the cord to start it, and her last time on it, she didn't see a washout in the field, where a small stream had softened the snow. One of the skis on the sled went into the hole, and she went flying off to the left. The sled stopped immediately, thankfully, but it made her gun-shy to get back on it again for a long time. She wasn't strong enough to pull-start it herself, and she probably only rode it one more time before he passed away. When she met Marcel, he loved riding, and they vacationed up in the County. They rented her a sled for the day because Marcel already had his own. She didn't realize that snowmobiles now had electric starts, and all she needed to do was push a button. She also sat higher in the seat of the new sled than on the old one, making it easier to spot trail issues like a washout. After a one-hundred-mile day on the trails and stopping for lunch along the way, she had to admit, it was a blast. But then Marcel was elected Sheriff, and his free time dwindled to almost nothing. Getting back into the sport for both of them could be fun, especially if the local trails were open again. Something for them to do again together.

The association's page featured links to nearly three hundred volunteer snowmobile clubs in Maine. Impressive. She and Marcel definitely needed to get back out there. She found the link to the SnowTrack Club in Secretly. It showed Karl as President. Christopher Lane from Lane's Market was Vice President. He probably wasn't out fixing trails before the storm because the store was swamped with people running to the shop. Craig Fisher was Treasurer. Marcel had said he saw him rapidly clearing trails with a team on the morning of the blizzard. Emil Bryant was the Secretary. She hadn't seen him since that chimney incident at the Lane Mansion in the fall. He didn't strike her as someone who would take copious notes at a meeting to earn the title of Secretary.

If the snow came back to the coast in the volume that it had when she was a kid, she'd get a sled and join this club. How fun to keep the trails available. Maybe one could be created through the back part of their land and connect along the side to the preserve. It could then cross the state route and enter the woods just before Riverview Farm and the Baxter River Preserve. Even go across the river, a path to be used when the river froze up.

Raven had paused a moment to fantasize about sledding around town. If there was enough snow, maybe a trail could even pop out by Lane's, or she could sled up to Jane Eats for lunch. Could she attribute this lightness to accepting Johnny as her father? Probably at least part of it. Stubbornness and negativity were heavy burdens she no longer wanted to carry.

She returned to her research. The state website also listed the clubs. Because of the government's transparency, she found the outdoor wildlife budget and how much the snowmobile clubs received from the state. While the formula wasn't posted, she suspected the money was given by trail mileage. In other words, how many trails a club needed to maintain. There were photos of large directional signs and warming huts that clubs had used the state money on. One club showed a man hugging a new grooming machine.

Raven sat back in her chair. Did Karl mention the club not receiving money because of the lack of snow? Something about how they could have at least insulated the walls with the cash? She clicked further back to prior years. Nope, it looked like SnowTrack still received its allotment based on trail mileage even without the snow.

She had Emil's phone number and buzzed him.

"Hey, Raven. How's it going?"

"Oh, it's going. I'll be honest. I hope I don't have a chimney disaster in one of the cabins. A stone was loose from the hearth."

"Oh," he said. "It's probably not connected to the main chimney's structure, but I can come out next week and take a look if you'd like."

"I'd appreciate that, Emil. While I have you, I have a question about SnowTrack."

"SnowTrack? Oh, sure. Shoot. You want to join? We could sure use new members."

"Yes, I think I do. Are you still the secretary?"

"Ha-ha…yes, not that we meet much, or that I have much to write about. It's a requirement of all clubs to have four officers, for checks and balances, I guess."

Raven agreed that it made sense. "I see. I have a weird question. Do you recall if SnowTrack received any state funding for the years that were snow-barren?"

"No, we definitely didn't. Craig said he had no receipts to submit for reimbursement."

"Oh, that's how it works?"

"Yes, we have records from prior years at the clubhouse showing the money we got and what we spent. We were usually in the red because we never got enough to cover new signs, groomer repair, and forget about clubhouse maintenance."

"Those records are at the clubhouse?" Raven had an idea forming in her head.

"Yep. Oh, Raven, sorry to interrupt, but my crew just arrived back from a site, and I need to give marching orders for tomorrow." He laughed as he hung up. She heard moans in the background from his workers as he said that statement loud enough for them to hear. He probably was a good guy to work for.

Raven sat back, thinking about what Emil said. Somewhere, someone got it wrong—either the State thought it sent money to SnowTrack, which it didn't, or SnowTrack actually received it, and if so, where was it? Another money problem. Why was money always the root of all issues, it seemed?

Chapter Thirty-Six

Tom waved to Margot, and she headed towards the counter. Her long blond hair fell around her shoulders and down her back. She had a glow about her, even in the dim light of the diner, that Tom couldn't put his finger on. Maybe it was the confident way she walked or her quiet presence. She didn't need a flashy entrance, long red fingernails, or a lot of make-up.

"Grab a seat. I didn't know you lived around here." He smiled at her, and she returned a partial smile. Maybe he should have taken his dinner to go if she wasn't going to be friendly. He shook that thought off. He was just letting his bruised ego get the best of him.

"I live closer than you think," she said, and her smile broadened.

Before Tom could pursue where Margot lived, Rachel came over to her on the other side of the counter. "Hi, Margot. All moved in?"

"Yes, including Mr. K. He is sulking right now under my bed, but he'll be out and about looking for his dinner soon."

"Oh, you moved to Secretly?" Tom didn't feel like much of a sheriff's detective if he didn't know there was a new woman, and probably a single one, in town, but his sister did.

"You can say that," Margot said.

Rachel laughed. "She's renting above." Rachel pointed over her head.

Tom grinned. "Oh, that's awesome. Welcome to town. Officially, I mean." He stuck out his hand for a shake, realizing too late how silly that looked.

Margot laughed as she looked at his hand, but she did accept it and shook it. Then she took off her coat and draped it over the swiveling, mounted chair.

"Can I get you something before I shut down the kitchen?" Rachel leaned against the back of the counter area, barely missing the variety of small cereal boxes that Tom had loved as a child.

"What about my dinner?" Tom was worried that Margot would be fed, and he'd go hungry.

"All plated and under the warming light. Let me bring that to you right now, Tommy, before you get hangry." She walked back to the red light shining down on a white plate. Soon, a steaming pile of turkey and stuffing with no disgusting, lumpy, homemade cranberry sauce—Rachel knew better—was in front of him.

Margot's eyes widened. "Oh, I'd like a third of that if you still have any left."

"I do. Do you like homemade cran-orange sauce?"

"I love it. Is there any other way to eat it?" Margot adjusted her place setting in front of her.

"Glad one of you appreciates it." Rachel smiled and headed back to the kitchen.

The outside door opened again. Out of the corner of his eye, he saw Dennis coming in. He was glad it wasn't Clark.

"Tommy-boy! Just saw your mom. I dropped the boys there while I help Rachel clean up." Dennis was in his mid-to-late forties but had a boyish charm, probably because he still acted like one. It wasn't Tom's business if Rachel was the main breadwinner. Maybe she didn't care as long as Dennis took care of the boys. But with them now in school full-time, Tom hoped that Dennis would get a job, any job. At least he was here to help her.

Margot pushed up her long sleeves and pulled out her phone. Tom noticed that each arm was heavily tattooed.

"Stare much?" she asked him. Her face bore a bit of a smirk.

He looked up quickly to meet her gaze. His face felt warm. She was laughing. She must be used to people's curiosity.

"Would you like a tour?" she asked.

"Excuse me?" Tom was confused. Margot seemed a bit younger than him.

Was that a new pick-up line? He was out of touch.

"Of my tats." Her face was blank. She was a tease.

He felt his face grow hotter. It took a lot to get him to blush. "Oh, sure. Of course. Thank you, I think."

She laughed again. "Well, at least the ones that are visible in public. I don't want you to arrest me for indecent exposure."

Was she flirting with him? Or pulling his leg? He didn't want to be played a fool. At the same time, he didn't want to miss an opportunity. He thought he'd play along.

"What's that one?" He pointed to a red blob on the inside of her left wrist.

"A cardinal. My favorite bird. A modern, abstract impression of one."

She flipped over her right wrist. Buckle shoes were clearly drawn, and legs were attached to them. The legs went farther up her arm, out of sight beneath her shirt.

"The Wicked Witch of the East, when the house fell on her?" Tom guessed.

She gave him a big grin. "Ah, a *Wizard of Oz* fan. Bonus points."

"I didn't realize I was being rated." This girl liked to spar. He loved it. Too much.

She laughed out loud, quite boisterous this time. Maybe she was actually rating him and flirting with him. He wasn't used to being interviewed as a potential date, however. It felt both stressful and exhilarating.

He pointed again to the Wicked Witch's legs. "So do those legs on your arm end anywhere?"

She started to pull the long-sleeve jersey over her head. In the diner, he thought? There were still a couple of paying customers. He turned to see if they were watching, but when he turned back, he saw she was wearing a tank top underneath. Whew. The effort, besides being shocking in itself to do at his sister's restaurant's counter, also revealed more tattoos than he had ever seen in person. In particular, the legs went up to a very beautiful woman with dark, wavy hair. She resembled Margot.

"My grandmother. She raised me, and I'm named after her," said Margot.

"Does she know you have her on your body?"

"If dead people have souls, then yes, she does know."

Foot in mouth. "Oh, I'm sorry. How long ago did she pass?"

"Almost a year ago." Margot's face changed. The playful light left her eyes. "I used to live with her, too. My mother inherited her house, though, and sold it to the highest bidder."

"She sold it out from under you?" Tom's own family was so loving that it was always hard for him to fathom having an ice-cold parent.

"I guess." She shrugged. She looked over at the tattoo of Margot Sr.

Tom saw a brave woman in front of him, kicked out of the house she grew up in, and starting over. He wondered why the grandmother left the house to her daughter, who obviously wasn't in Margot's life when Margot was a child, instead of leaving it to Margot. That would be a question for another day. Instead, he asked generic questions.

"Was the house in the Portland area?"

She gave a small smile. "Yes, in Cape Elizabeth. Houses fetch a lot down there now. My mother couldn't resist selling it."

"They go for a lot up here, too." Tom didn't know how he'd buy a house on his own.

"I know." She sighed. "So do most rents." She sipped the tap water that Rachel had brought over through a straw. "Your sister is an angel, you know."

"Oh, I do know." He noticed a yellow Volkswagen Beetle tattoo on her shoulder. "You like VWs?"

She shrugged again. "They're all right."

"If they're just all right, why do you have one on your shoulder?"

"Oh, that." Margot touched her right shoulder with her left hand, massaging her fingers over the car. "I forgot about that one. One of the first tats I did."

"So you used to like Beetles, and now you don't?"

"No, I think you're confusing the car with 'Yellow Submarine.'" She took another sip through the straw.

Tom shook his head. Somehow, he was back to pulling teeth with her. What had he said wrong? Was it about her mother or about losing the house?

She looked up at him and grinned. "You sure you really want to know why I have a VW Beetle on me?"

Was this woman nuts or just a lot of fun? He hoped the latter because he definitely liked her.

He swiveled to face her. "I do want to know. I'm wearing my big boy pants today and can handle it."

She laughed. "Okay, I'm not so sure about that," she said, eyeing him up and down. Her looking at him that way gave him a tingle. "But I'll tell you anyway." She paused and sipped another gulp of water. "You ready?" she asked, putting her glass down on the counter.

"Yes. I was born ready." He was starting to enjoy the banter.

"It's Ted Bundy's car."

"Who? What? Wait. Ted Bundy?" Tom's brain whirled. "The serial killer from Florida? From the 1970s?"

"Well, he wasn't from Florida, but that's where he was caught." She picked up her glass again.

"Okay, that's creepy."

"Good." She winked at him.

"You're glad I find that creepy?" He was falling down a rabbit hole. He was positive he was doomed never to get out, most likely because he would want to live down in the rabbit hole forever.

"Yes, I use it as a litmus test. If you thought it was cool, then I'd know that you were really the creepy one."

"Hmmm, I'm starting to think you're too smart for me."

She laughed again, this time by throwing her head back. Her roar was louder than the last time. The last couple of patrons in the diner did stare at her this time, from the register. Were they looking at her tats or just at her hearty laugh? Both were attention-getting.

"Tell me what you do for fun when you're not working and getting tattoos." Tom truly did want to get to know her.

"I volunteer at animal shelters."

"Really?" They just went from serial killers to puppies and kittens. His head was spinning.

She smiled again and looked at him out of the corner of her eye. "Yes, why is that surprising?"

"Well, for one, you have a tattoo in honor of a serial killer."

She made a face at Tom. "It is not in honor of him. It is a reminder to me of how something so innocent and cute as a VW bug can be deadly. If he were driving around in a hearse, how many women would have gotten in to that?"

She definitely was too smart for him. He did agree, though. "Good point. That's nice of you to care about animals in need."

"Animals need protecting."

"You protect animals, but you cut up people. "

She shook her head. "Those people are already dead."

"You know you could do anything for work, I suspect, including being a model, if you don't mind me saying so."

She didn't look at him. "Try a new line. I've heard that one before."

"Gosh, you're confident."

She swiveled her chair with such force that Tom almost jumped and grabbed for his gun as a reflex. In a firm voice, she said, "In my line of work, you have to be confident. I suspect in your line of work, you also have to be."

Again, Tom agreed. "Very true."

"Speaking of work," Margot reached behind to grab her coat that was slouching on the back of the chair, "I have this for you and Sheriff Ouelette. I told Clint I would bring it down to you two."

She held up a clear plastic bag. In it was a large folded paper. She put it on the counter between them. Tom flipped it over and, on the backside, saw the pointy part of a large arrow.

She explained its texture, so Tom didn't have to open the envelope. "It's laminated. I'm guessing a snowmobile trail sign."

"Yes, I think you're exactly right. Where did you find it?" He knew it must be important to the case, but he didn't understand why.

"Clint and I found it under Mr. Dyer's body. Because of the lamination, it didn't get destroyed by the snow or the blood. There are no fingerprints on it, by the way."

"Really? You found this on the trail?"

Tom sat back to absorb what the sign could mean. Mikey must have accidentally grabbed it when exiting the wooded area before the field.

"I'm surprised it looks so new," said Tom.

"Why's that?" Margot asked.

"I heard that the club never went near the field to ensure the signage was accurate, so where did this sign come from?"

"Oh, this is new, for sure." Margot gestured with her chin toward the plastic bag.

"How do you know?"

"Later, when you have proper gloves on, you can take it out and look at the back, but I have a photo of it I can show you now, though."

She pulled up her photos on her cell and leaned toward Tom. She smelled of peaches. The arrow was printed on a used piece of paper. A price list for a local business. Carpentry by Craig. The price list was dated December. Okay, that made sense as Craig was the one repairing the trails and putting up the signage. Did someone move this arrow to misdirect Mikey right into the wire?

Chapter Thirty-Seven

Raven woke up with money still on her mind. The box of cash. And SnowTrack's distribution from the state. She didn't mention it to Marcel, who was headed to Augusta to represent Barrett County at a state-wide sheriff meeting.

All she did say to him, besides 'I love you' and "have a safe ride" and "don't eat too many doughnuts," was to confirm a small dinner party for Sunday night. She still hadn't reminded him that Sunday was also her birthday, but in honor of her day, she'd make the cook's choice for the meal. She hoped Shannon wasn't a vegetarian because Raven loved beef and seafood above all else, and surf and turf or lobster mac and cheese at the end of January sounded like party food for sure.

"That's great about the dinner party," said Marcel. "I'll send Shannon a message to see if she's free. I think she has a new beau, so if she asks about bringing a plus one, would that be okay?"

Would that be okay? That would be fantastic. Raven's pulse quickened. But all she said was "Absolutely, just let me know by Friday morning, before I grocery shop. I'm thinking besides us, we can have the Harts, Johnny, Tom, and Shannon, with or without a date."

"Perfect," said Marcel, and out the door he went.

What was that saying: "Keep your friends close and your enemies closer." She did not plan on being friends with Shannon, but she would look her in the eye and make sure she knew who Marcel chose to marry.

She turned in the kitchen and saw Lily and Dukie, sitting at attention, staring her down. Lily moaned and wiggled. Dukie thumped his tail.

"I know, I know. I owe you two a real walk, but there's still too much snow out there. How about a quick ball toss up the path we have?"

That worked, and thirty minutes later, she and the poochies were back inside. She dressed and headed to the Harts.

"Are you sure you want to invite that tramp into your house?" Betty sat stirring her coffee, still in pink-flowered pajamas. Raven realized she blended into the den chair.

Howard grunted and rolled his eyes.

"We don't know that she is a tramp," said Raven. "And isn't it better to have her under my nose where I can analyze her intentions?"

Howard mumbled, "Keep your friends close—"

"Exactly! Keep your friends close. With friends like her, who needs enemies?" Betty shook her head. "I think it is a mistake to invite her."

"You two are invited also. You can watch her like a hawk for me." Raven smiled. She was joking. She really was, she told herself.

"Yes, we can, and how nice to be included," Betty's face relaxed. Raven bet that she was already thinking of what to wear.

"And maybe I'm more Shannon's cup of tea, and she won't even notice that Marcel exists?" Howard winked at Raven. "She hasn't met me yet."

"You're no one's cup of tea," said Betty.

"Gee, thanks," Howard picked up his newspaper with a huff. He really was a softie, Raven thought. Such a kind and sensitive man.

Betty bounced on the edge of her seat. "Enough about some dumb blonde."

"You were a blonde. Are you dumb, too?" Howard perked up. He was back in the game.

"I still am, thank you very much. A blonde, I mean. And I've never been dumb. I don't really mean she is dumb. I just want to hear about more important things, like how it went with Johnny and Raven and the box of cash."

"Oh yeah." Howard swiveled in chair. "What happened with you and your father?"

Raven felt her body tense. That was the first time Howard ever referred to Johnny as her father, but he was right. Johnny was her father. It felt good to hear the words "your father" spoken in a positive tone. Johnny was her father, yet she still thought of him as Johnny. Maybe one day calling him "Dad" or "Pop" would be natural.

Raven smiled at the thought of yesterday with Johnny and their conversation about the box of money. "It actually went great. He was shocked, of course, at my mother keeping all of the cash without using it, and keeping his notes too." She paused, lowered her eyes, and then looked up. "And it sounds so superficial to say, but now I have hard proof that he really did care all those years, I do feel closer to him. It sounds horrible, but that is the truth."

Howard cleared his voice. "I think that is very acceptable and normal under the circumstances, Raven. Don't be too hard on yourself."

"Yes, totally normal," agreed Betty. "It was also normal to think Johnny was a loser and left you and Julia out to dry, but now you know he was legitimately helping you both. That would make me feel better, too."

"That wasn't exactly what I meant, Betty," Howard started to criticize her. Raven knew Betty meant no harm and cut him off.

"I thank you both for helping me to feel better about it all. On a third note, I researched snowmobile trail clubs in Maine."

"Did anyone need something to drink?" Betty stood up. Raven chuckled at how obvious Betty showed her boredom in topics that didn't interest her.

Howard was intrigued, however. "What did you learn about the clubs?"

"They are paid by the State, through an outdoor fund, for the amount of trail miles they take care of."

"So, how much is that for the SnowTrack club?" Howard asked.

"Maybe five thousand a season?" Raven didn't know for sure, but she had found a newspaper article about another club that thanked the State at their annual club dinner. She then found that club's trail map online and did a rough guesstimate.

"But a club only gets the money when they submit receipts. Isn't that what Karl told us?" said Betty, now interested. She poked her head around the corner of the kitchen.

Raven responded. "Yes, I remember hearing that too, but that isn't what I found. It looks like the State has been sending payments to SnowTrack all this time. I found the record of it on the State website."

Betty walked all the way back into the family room. "So, Karl really was using the cash for insulating the clubhouse walls, like he joked?"

Raven shrugged. "I'm guessing the club was doing something with it. The checks were made payable to the club directly, as far as I could tell. And any club officer could deposit them into a club account."

"Wouldn't that be ironic if Karl kept all that club money, but he had a twenty-million-dollar painting on his wall the whole time?" Betty went back to the kitchen and returned with a tray of danish. "From Jane Eats," she said as she placed the tray on Howard's tray table, after making him remove his laptop. "Karl could have sold the painting on the black market and moved to Rio."

"Is that where you're planning on slinking off to?" Howard asked, winking at Raven, while Betty made a squishy face at him.

"No danish for me, thanks. I'd better get going." Raven stood.

"Oh," said Betty, "one more thing. While I was in Jane Eats, Karl came in. He's going to get a reward for the painting." She frowned. "You know, when I heard him say it, I was glad for him, but you should really get it, Raven. Maybe a little for me too. If I hadn't stopped Jared from leaving, who knows where that Rembrandt may have gone."

Raven shook her head. "No, no. The Wolf family has kept that painting safe for decades, including Karl. I'm glad he'll get that."

"True," Betty agreed. "And it sounds like he is going to put some of it to good use. He said he was erasing everyone's debt, too. From last season. He was apologizing to someone at the diner who was eating with Johnny. Looked about Tom's age with blond hair."

Raven thought about it. Who would Johnny be eating with who fit that description? Then it dawned on her. Lunchbox Lennie.

Howard responded, "Wow, that's amazing that he's wiping out the debts. Very kind of him."

Raven agreed. Now maybe Lennie could start again. It felt like another piece of the puzzle was solved. She needed to check out the next piece.

"Okay, I'll see you, folks, soon." She put her hand on the doorknob.

"Where are you off to? Some place fun?" Betty asked.

"Not really." Raven didn't dare tell Betty that her nosiness was getting the best of her. If she shared her plans, Betty would want to come. She'd have to wait for Betty to get dressed, and it really was going to be a quick in-and-out visit. Emil Bryant said all the records about the funding and anything else connected to SnowTrack were at the clubhouse. Maybe if she did the old-fashioned detective thing and followed the money, it might lead to Mikey Dyer's killer. Not that she wanted to confront anyone herself—she'd pass on the information to Marcel, of course—but she wanted to be sure her hunch was right first.

Chapter Thirty-Eight

Betty watched Raven put her coat on and walk out the door. She rushed to grab her wool coat and her car keys.

"Where are you off to in such a hurry?" Howard looked with bewilderment. "I thought we were having coffee and danish? And you're still in your pajamas!"

"You don't need me to eat, Howard," said Betty, shoving her socked feet into her boots and opening the side door. "I'll be right back."

She waited on the top step of their outside porch, out of sight from Raven's car, and watched Raven back her Mini out of the driveway. She then hustled as quickly as she dared on the steps, being mindful of ice patches, and started up her beige SUV. Her back window was frosted and difficult to see out of. She hit the defrost button but didn't have time to wait. Who'd be behind her, anyway? She threw the car into reverse.

The good part about Raven driving a green Mini Cooper was that it was easy to spot up ahead. Raven had headed away from her own house, as Betty suspected. She wasn't going into Eelsboro to shop either. She was moving into the heart of Secretly. She could be going to Jane's Eats, but she had refused the danish, so she probably wasn't hungry. It was too cold to walk on the beach in Whale Harbor or around the lighthouse. If she were headed to the library, Betty might pass. She didn't want to be snubbed by Marie Claire, the ancient librarian everyone revered as a goddess.

Maybe she was headed back to Riverview Farm, although she heard that Jared was locked up, thank goodness. Did Raven think Camille knew something she wasn't sharing? Of course, she could be just innocently shopping at the farm, picking up those soft, light mittens with the tops of the hands that flopped back to allow the fingers access to cell phone screens. Betty wanted them herself and didn't blame Raven for being obsessed with them, too. What colors did they come in again?

But, no, Raven went past the road leading to the farm. Darn. Oh, maybe she was headed to see Johnny because now that she accepted him as her father, they had a lot to catch up on. If Raven did go up Johnny's driveway, she'd respect that and give them privacy.

But again, Raven went by the cut through to get to the other side of the peninsula to where Johnny lived. Where was Raven going?

Up ahead, she saw the Mini turn left toward one of the preserves. She was going for a walk after all, but it was strange she wasn't bringing Lily and Dukie with her. For once, Betty was glad she drove a boring, tan SUV as her winter car. The Mercedes convertible was not inconspicuous even on a gray day. Well, if Raven was going for a walk, she obviously wanted to walk alone; otherwise, she would have invited Betty. Raven had a lot to ponder—Johnny and the cash box, Marcel's insensitivity to her birthday, and the prospect of that woman coming to her house for a meal. What a shame! The latter was something that Betty didn't think she could tolerate. Raven was a bigger person than she was.

But Raven did not turn down toward the preserve road either. Where the heck was she going?

Then the Mini finally turned left up a driveway and toward the dilapidated snowmobile club's shack. Betty had never seen it before, and wouldn't have known it was the clubhouse except for the paint-peeling sign at the bottom of the driveway. *SnowTrack*. Was it even used anymore? Betty slowed and stayed on the edge of the road, grateful for the snowbanks. Maybe Raven was going to join the club. As a Mainer, she probably knew how to drive one of those machines. They scared Betty.

Betty left her car on the side of the road—it was a side road and didn't look much traveled—and crept up the driveway, using the stone wall and a large pine tree to shield her. It was fun to pretend she was a spy, not that spying on Raven was dangerous or anything. She was just being nosey, as she always was, making a game of it. Too bad the cuffs of her pajama bottoms were dragging a bit and getting wet. Oh, well, a small price to pay for knowledge.

Raven had parked in front of the club. No other vehicles were there unless snowmobiles counted. Betty saw two of them, one black and one red, white, and blue, also in front but more to the side, facing toward what looked like a trail that went behind the clubhouse and into the woods.

Betty watched Raven, noticing the snowmobiles as well. She went over to them, scrutinized them both, and seemed to study their handlebars. Was she looking for IDs on them? She didn't linger long by them and walked to the sagging wooden steps of the clubhouse. She paused at the bottom, looking up at the double doors, and then walked slowly up the stairs. Raven was brave. Betty wouldn't have trusted those stairs.

Betty took the opportunity to quickly walk around the stone wall and into the parking lot. She was almost at Raven's Mini when she heard a yell from inside the clubhouse.

"No, stop!" It was Raven's voice.

Betty ducked behind Raven's Mini and watched through the car windows. The door to the clubhouse flew open, and a man appeared. Betty didn't recognize him. He was pulling something out of the clubhouse that was heavy. Oh, it was Raven! He was yanking Raven out!

Raven grabbed the door frame to hold herself back, but the man was too strong. He pulled her forward, and Raven's boots bounced down the stairs as the man dragged her down in his arms.

Betty didn't know what to do. She had left her purse in the car, so she didn't have a weapon handy. Her cell phone was also in her purse, so she couldn't even call 9-1-1. If she showed herself, she might be of no use at all to saving Raven.

"Craig, you're not going to get away with this," yelled Raven. "Help! Help me! Help!"

Craig. Craig. Carpentry by Craig? Betty and Howard had gotten a quote from him when they first moved to town. He was tens of thousands higher than all the others, and they didn't choose him.

"Shut up," Craig yelled and slapped Raven across the face. She went limp.

"Ah!" Betty screamed unconsciously. Craig froze and surveyed the lot and beyond. Betty crouched lower behind the Mini and then dared to peek through to the other side. Craig had dropped Raven to the ground when he heard the sound. Betty saw her stirring. What to do. What to do. She wasn't even good at making quick oatmeal, let alone quick decisions. How could she save Raven twice in two days?

Before she could come up with a plan, Craig threw Raven onto the patriotic snowmobile like a rag doll, propping her up in the front part of the seat. He hopped on behind her. The snowmobile's engine roared loudly, louder than a lawnmower, Betty thought. Craig revved the engine, and then they took off into the woods.

Brap. Brap.

And just like that, Raven was gone.

Chapter Thirty-Nine

Raven felt herself being placed on a machine. As her eyes focused, she realized she was sitting on a snowmobile. The Polaris that had been out front. She felt a body behind her and saw arms reach in front of her, grabbing the handlebars. If she looked forward past the nose of the sled, the trees swayed. She shut her eyes and slumped forward.

It had to be Craig behind her. She opened her eyes and saw him push the start button for the sled. His right thumb revved the throttle, and within seconds, he gunned the snowmobile with such force that they almost did a wheelie in the snow-packed parking lot.

Her head was clearing. She twisted and turned in the crammed seat, trying to elbow him. "Let me go!" she yelled, her words lost in the wind as they sped along. The speedometer screen in front of her showed thirty miles per hour, but soon it was at sixty-five. She ducked, thinking a low, snow-covered branch would whack her in the head. She thought about the trail's direction. The clubhouse was in the southern part of the peninsula. She didn't know how many miles of the trail were in the woods before it came out onto a road. On these narrow, winding trails, she'd watch for him to struggle to negotiate a corner, especially at the speed they were going. Then she might be able to roll off by ducking under his arms.

If that didn't happen, they would end up smashed into a tree. Under different circumstances, she'd worry about having such an accident, but now it seemed like a crash was the only way she might be able to save herself.

Her face stung where he had slapped her. She might even have a cut, because the wind whipping against her face was hurting that area.

She couldn't check because she needed both hands on the section of the handlebars where they met the stem. She didn't want to fall off and be run over by the sled. Aside from the machine's weight, the track was probably studded.

She started to devise a plan. First and foremost, she needed to get help for Karl. When she walked into the clubhouse, Karl lay crumpled on the dusty wooden floor, a streak of red flowing from his forehead. Craig was standing over him with a metal shovel. She assumed Craig had already bashed Karl at least once and was about to deliver a fatal blow when she screamed. Either Karl had figured out Craig's embezzlement and confronted him, or Craig was hedging his bets and getting rid of Karl once and for all.

Her scream did stop Craig from striking Karl, but the scream also didn't give her time to call Marcel or an ambulance before Craig reached her. Karl wasn't moving on the floor. Maybe he was already dead. But Craig sure as heck could move. He flew over Karl's body and swung the shovel at her. She ran for the door, and he ran after her. The shovel must have caught on a low rafter because she heard it clatter to the floor.

She thought for a split second when she heard the shovel drop that she was home free. She kept running to the door to get to her car, but before she reached the foyer, he grabbed her. She held onto the door frame. He would have to fight to get her out. He lifted her off the ground and carried her down the stairs. It wasn't much of a fight.

She yelled for help outside. She heard him laugh. He was right. There was no one around to hear her, unless deer and porcupine counted. She screamed for help again. It was pure instinct to call for help. Someone might be driving by. That's when she felt a hard knock against her head, and she briefly blacked out. When she had more of her wits around her, she was already propped up on the sled, and Craig had hit the start button. She was trapped. But in a way, a snowmobile ride was better than a back-of-the-head slap with a shovel. She might have a slight chance on the sled.

She held on to the stem to make sure she didn't fall off. Even if the sled didn't run her over, she didn't want to land on a rock. She wondered if she could chance removing one hand to grab her cell and call for help, both for herself and for bleeding Karl. She had brought her cell into the clubhouse, right? If she did, it would be in a coat pocket, most likely her right front pocket, but now she couldn't remember what she did with it, and if she even brought it with her. Did she have it at the Harts? Did she leave it at home or in the car? Why wasn't she glued to her phone like other people? Even if she did have it, Craig would knock it out of her hand. He might then do something worse to her.

Before she could figure out her next move, she heard Craig mumble. "I know just the place to dump you. Then I need to get back to finish Karl."

She knew he didn't mean to drop her off when he said, "dump her." She had to focus on where this trail was headed. Would it pop out onto the state route, and could she signal a passing car? Did it have to stop to cross any roads? Then she'd have a chance. If they kept riding only in the woods, maybe way behind someone's house, it was a long shot to be helped. She was going to have to help herself.

She had no time to waste, either, not knowing what Craig had up his sleeve.

She studied the display on the screen. RPMs, Speed, Gas Tank (*almost empty—maybe they would run out!*), and ETA. ETA? Where was it set to, or was it just a fluke? Or did he set it in advance, thinking he was going to bring Karl there? Or was it from a former ride? What details were listed with the ETA?

She leaned forward, squinting at the screen. The ETA was in time, not miles. Ten minutes until they reached the destination, wherever that was.

She glanced at the kill switch near his throttle. If she were able to push it, the sled would instantly stop, but then what? She still would be his prisoner, and he might decide to do away with her right then. If she could get him to talk, maybe he'd slow down, and maybe the minutes would stretch out, giving her time to think of an escape.

She shivered. She wasn't wearing a warm enough coat for a snowmobile ride. The wind whipped through the down jacket, especially around where she had duct-taped the feathers in. Her hands and ears were frozen. Craig was wearing only a red sweatshirt with the logo "Carpentry by Craig" on the upper left. She turned back to make sure he could hear her. Neither of them was wearing a helmet, and without the helmets, she should be able to plant the words close to his ear, above the noise of the engine.

"Why did you do it, Craig?" she shouted.

He actually responded. "Do what? I didn't do anything?" He did not look down at her but kept his eyes on the trail. It did feel like he took that corner slower, though.

"Why did you embezzle from the club?"

The snowmobile almost stopped. She had rattled him, and his right thumb slipped off the throttle. Her suspicions of the club getting money from the State were correct. Karl had said that it didn't during the non-snow years, but that was because Craig, as treasurer, told Karl that. Craig must have embezzled more than four years' worth of money. He had been treasurer for over ten years. He might have been stealing the whole time.

Craig caught his breath, and the snowmobile lurched. "I don't know what you're talking about." He was pressing on the throttle.

"You could have just told Karl what you had done. He might not have asked for the money back or turned you in. You didn't have to set up the barbed wire to kill him."

"I did not take any money. I did not put up that wire," he hissed.

"You mean you don't have any of that money. You don't have the money anymore. What did you spend it on?"

Craig didn't answer, but his mouth curled into a snarl

"Was it on your new truck?" Raven asked, yelling over her shoulder.

He kept his eyes forward. Raven twisted to get a better look and to be ready to jockey his right hand off the throttle.

"You have a booming business, Craig. You should be able to afford a new truck with your profits."

"That's right, my business is great, so shut up."

But, again, the snowmobile limped along. Another misstep with his thumb. She hit a sore spot. Every second she saved counted.

"Why not just take on more work? You're in high demand," Raven said. "And there is so much work from people from away. They'll pay top dollar for good work."

"You don't know what expenses I have." His lips were pinched together. She could see him thinking of his plan for her, whatever that was. Maybe he'd get sick of her and just dump her off the sled. No, he knew she knew too much. He needed to get rid of her quickly and then dispose of Karl. She had to create her own plan.

Could he really get away with it, killing her and Karl? Why hadn't she told anyone where she was going or what she suspected? Where was he going to put Karl?

Raven willed herself to believe she'd be okay. Another idea floated into her brain. "Stella. You did all of this for Stella."

This time, the snowmobile came to a complete stop. If she thought she could have fought her way off the sled, she would have, but Craig had jerked her around by the shoulders.

"Leave Stella out of this." He growled in Raven's face, his spit hitting her cheeks. His eyes were wide, flashing with anger. She was afraid he was going to slap her again. Wait? Did slapping a woman come naturally to him? Did he also slap Stella, then buy her expensive gifts to keep her with him? Did he pretend to himself that expensive gifts made up for the physical abuse? Raven shuddered at the thought.

Instead of asking Craig about a potential domestic abuse problem, she took the angle of Stella being the problem. "Stella always was the best-dressed in school. She still is. She loves her fashion. Fashion is expensive."

He shook her. "Stop talking about Stella!" Her ribcage bounced off the handlebars.

"That's what this is all about. Stella, and your crumbling relationship with her," Raven continued. Was making him madder a good thing for her because it kept the sled shut off, or shortening her own time on earth in the long run? What if he choked her to get her to shut up?

Tick. Tick. Tick. She felt like she could hear the ticking time bomb that was Craig. But maybe that was a ticking clock in her favor, ticking away the minutes until she was saved.

Maybe someone had seen her car at the clubhouse. Then they went in and found Karl, who told them she had stopped Craig, and now someone knew she had been kidnapped and was looking for her.

No. That was a fantasy. That was unrealistic. She had to save herself.

Tick. Tick. Tick. Craig's eyes were darting. But maybe someone was out looking for her on another sled. Maybe someone would come to save her. Maybe Karl crawled to the door and saw her leave, and was now on his black Arctic Cat. He was just slower than they were because of his injuries. He'd be here any second.

She paused to listen for her fantasy hero, and she almost thought she heard the brap-brap of the engine of another sled coming their way.

Wait. She wasn't hearing things. That was a brap-brap. Another sled was coming toward them.

Craig heard it, too. He whipped her back around and pushed her face toward the display. He hit the throttle before she could yell for help or hold on. Her head bounced on the handlebars. No, who was she fooling? No one would be coming. That had to be her imagination. Even if someone else was out riding the trails, would they even realize that she needed help?

She and Craig sped along the trail in the woods. Raven strained to hear the other sled, but couldn't. Either it was because of the noise the Polaris made, or there really was no other sled.

Just before they popped out of the woods, Raven saw the parking lot for the Baxter River Preserve.

She knew now where they were going. Riverview Farm.

Chapter Forty

As the snowmobile took off, Betty popped up behind the Mini and ran around the side.

"Raven! Raven!" All she heard was the roar of the snowmobile disappearing up the trail.

She ran to the black snowmobile still in front of the building. It might as well have been a monster to her. She didn't even know how to climb onto it, and finally she stepped up onto the side rail. Where was the keyhole? And the gas pedal? How did she even turn it on? She climbed off it and ran, well, walked, as fast as she could, back to her car and to her cell phone.

Her hands shook to open her car door, and then to pull her purse over the console. She zipped open the purse, the object that had saved the day just two days ago, with a clunk on Jared's neck. Now it held the most precious item in the world—her lifeline to Marcel.

"Hey, Betty." His voice rang out as he answered her call.

"Marcel! Some man has Raven!" Her voice shook. She tried not to cry. She needed to be coherent.

Marcel's voice elevated. "What? Where?"

"Where to?" she heard Tom's voice ask in the background.

"That weird building. Where the snowmobilers hang out. It'll look like it's abandoned and falling down. The sign says 'SnowTracks.' It's on that dirt road across from a preserve."

"We've already turned around and are headed that way. We know where you are. Are you okay, Betty? Are you in a safe place?"

"Oh yes. I'm by my car. I'm parked on the road. Take a left into the parking lot just after my car." She marveled at how level Marcel's voice was despite the love of his life being kidnapped. She didn't know if she appreciated his steady-eddie attitude, or if it were Howard, that she'd rather have him hysterical about her being kidnapped.

Marcel responded to Betty. "Yes, we know where the clubhouse is. Can you tell us what happened?"

"Well, I was nosey this morning and decided to follow Raven. In fact, I'm still in my pajamas! She came over to the house and was acting coy. To be honest, I didn't want to be left out, so I followed her to this building. I don't think she saw me." Betty took a breath. "I had crept up to hide behind her car. Because she had gone into the building, the clubhouse. I left that part out."

"Go on," Marcel said.

Betty was sure he was tearing up inside, just acting as a professional. Well-trained. She continued. "So, I just had crouched by the car, and I heard her yell something from inside the building."

"Are there other cars there?" Marcel asked. "Who else is there?"

"No cars. There were two snowmobiles, but now there is only one."

"Okay," said Marcel, "what kind of snowmobiles?"

Betty looked over at the remaining snowmobile. "A black one. And a red, white, and blue one."

Betty heard Tom say, "Craig's sled is the red, white, and blue Polaris. The black one could be Karl's other Arctic Cat."

"I just heard Tom," said Betty. "I did see the word 'cat' on the black one. I tried to start that one to chase after them."

"Raven is on the colored sled?" Marcel asked. "I thought you said someone had her inside the clubhouse."

"No, no. The man took her away. After she had yelled in the building, he dragged her out. She tried to hold onto the side of the door, but he pried her loose. She was yelling for help, so the man slapped her, and she collapsed in the driveway. I think she was okay, though. She looked awake when they drove off." She heard Marcel's breathing change for one moment. An intake of breath. That made her feel better about him.

She kept going. "After he slapped her, he picked her up and plopped her on that patriotic snowmobile. I think that snowmobile is kinda pretty, actually, if it wasn't being used to kidnap Raven, that is. I like the red, white, and blue motif. Well, anyway, they took off into the woods like I already said they did."

"They used the snowmobile trail?"

"That trail leads right to Riverview Farm," Betty heard Tom say. He added, "I'll get back-up to meet us at the farm."

Marcel came back on the line. "Betty, please lock yourself in your vehicle. We'll be there in less than five minutes. It'll be my Jeep, not Tom's SUV."

"Okay. Call me back if you can't find the place."

She disconnected the phone. Her heart pounded in her chest, and her hands were sweating. She opened up her SUV's door to get in, and then remembered that something had made Raven yell when she went into the building. Betty had been there for over five minutes, and no one else had come out. Maybe she should look inside to see what Raven had also seen.

She put her phone back into her purse and walked back into the parking lot. She stood for a moment next to the Mini.

"Hello?" she called out. Silence.

She walked up one rotting step, then another, then another. On the fourth one, she stood in the open doorway. Craig had left the door open after grabbing Raven.

Betty swallowed and took a deep breath. From the top step, she called into the clubhouse. "Hello?" She said.

Silence.

Then she thought she heard an animal sound. Was it a bear inside? She had never seen one in Secretly. Could a moose climb stairs? She had never seen a moose in Secretly either.

She heard the small animal movement again. She strained to listen. She stepped a little bit inside.

A small voice reached her ears. "Help me."

Was it a trap?

She listened to see if she would hear it again.

"Help me. Please."

She poked her head in further. The building was just one large room with a few wooden chairs and an old wooden filing cabinet. Karl Wolf lay on the floor to her right.

Betty ran over to him and knelt down. His head and hand were bleeding. He looked crooked, as if something were broken.

"Help me," he said again.

"Yes, yes, of course I will." She pulled out her phone and dialed. This time, she called 9-1-1 directly to order an ambulance. She didn't want to distract Marcel from his mission to save Raven.

Chapter Forty-One

Tom clutched the sides of the passenger door. He was used to being the driver, not the passenger, and he preferred it that way. This morning, when the sheriffs' gathering in Augusta was canceled—too many of them had snow damage in their counties that needed handling, and the governor agreed that storm clean-up was more important than sitting around listening to bureaucrats pontificate, as Marcel put it—he buzzed Tom and suggested that he pick Tom up for a change.

They had been on their way to talk to Craig. Tom shared the signage that Margot had found. Craig was as good a place to start as any to find out where that sign may have come from—both who made it and where it might have been stapled. Talking to Craig was now moot. Most likely, he was the one who had Raven, which meant he was the one who had strung the barbed wire. Tom's breath caught in his throat. What were Craig's plans for her?

Now, speeding to the snowmobile clubhouse, Tom regretted saying yes to the ride. Marcel's Jeep—not the Jeep's fault—slid through every corner that had sand left from the storm. Marcel did not take his foot off the accelerator, not even to corner. He was sure that Marcel had it as far down as it could go. It probably would break off by the time they parked.

Another call was coming in. The vehicle's screen said it was Betty again. Oh, no. Did she find Raven? Was Raven okay?

Tom punched the green symbol to connect the call to keep Marcel's two hands on the wheels. Her voice floated into the vehicle.

"Hi. I know you're almost here. I just wanted to let you know. I found Karl in the building. He's wounded but alive."

"On it," said Tom. "We're calling an ambulance."

"I already did. I figured you have enough to do. I wanted you to know why I'm not in my car. I'm going to stay with him in the building until the paramedics come."

Tom saw that Marcel was out of words. He responded for them both. "Thanks, Betty. Don't do anything to put yourself into danger. If you have to leave Karl to hide or whatever, do it. Be vigilant."

Betty's voice now shook. Tom guessed that she hadn't thought of Craig coming back for Karl, and thus, her. "I will. I will be careful. I promise."

"Okay, we're hanging up now. We're here."

Marcel entered the parking lot on two wheels and barely had stopped the Jeep when he jumped out. He ran to the black snowmobile and started it up in seconds.

Tom ran to the sled and stood on the running board. "Let me ride with you. I don't want you going alone, and I don't think that one will start." He pointed to a vintage Ski-Doo along the side of the building. One of the club members must have left it.

"Okay, but I'm driving," said Marcel.

Tom was just about to offer to drive. He had more recent sled experience, but he wasn't the kidnapped woman's husband. Maybe he should have tried the Ski-Doo, but if the key wasn't there, or he couldn't pull-start it, or if it had bad gas in it, he'd be left behind, and Marcel would be flying solo against Craig. He got his leg over the seat behind Marcel and hung on to his shoulders. These sleds weren't built for two riders. Marcel revved the engine, and just before they blasted off, Tom saw Betty at the top of the clubhouse stairs, her pajama bottoms sticking out from her coat. She put her hands together in a prayer sign.

Tom hadn't heard the siren of the ambulance over the two-stroke engine, but saw the red lights pull into the parking as he and Marcel blasted off in the direction of the trail. He felt like he was on a carnival ride at a county fair. He was glad to know the ambulance and EMTs had arrived. At least Betty and Karl were now safe.

Craig's tracks were easy to follow. Thank goodness, since Raven didn't leave them breadcrumbs like Hansel and Gretel, or was that Little Red Riding Hood? He wondered how much of a head start Craig and Raven really had on them. Maybe ten minutes. Hopefully less. They could be miles away by now.

Tom held on to Marcel as tightly as he could. Over Marcel's shoulder, he saw the speedometer read eighty miles an hour. Eighty. Eighty was what you did on flat roads in the County that were maintained by professional groomers. It's not what you did on windy, homemade trails in the woods. Even going eighty, did they have any chance of catching up with them?

The fresh tracks on the trail gave them hope. They had guessed they were going in the right direction, but the tracks proved it.

Tom knew enough about sledding and how to corner. Marcel was fixated on speed. Tom knew to shift his weight to the inside of the turn. He leaned over as far as he could to help the sled turn the corner and head where they wanted it to go. If they didn't maintain balance and stability through the turn, they risked tipping over. Then they'd never get to Raven.

But wait, what was that noise?

Tom leaned forward and talked directly into Marcel's ear. "Did that sound like a snowmobile to you?"

"It most certainly did." Marcel went even faster.

They rounded a tight turn and crossed a few planks laid across a stream. "If we can hear him, he can hear us," Tom said again into Marcel's ear.

Marcel nodded.

Did Craig have a gun? Did he even need a weapon when he had a five-hundred-pound sled against Raven, and even them? Would he turn his sled around and crash head-on into them? According to Betty, Raven was sitting in front of him. She wouldn't survive that collision.

Tom didn't have all of the pieces regarding Craig, but he saw the pattern. The new truck, trips, and skimping on work. They'd have to dig more to connect the financial dots, but Tom figured that Craig had taken the snowmobile money for his own. Maybe he thought the Midcoast would never get snow again, and his embezzlement would go undiscovered. And then that customer who wanted to sue him. Craig probably did cut corners to save money, yet still charged the higher cost. Why did he really need so much money? Had to be more than Stella wanting fancy things.

Ahead was a clearing. They were about to pop out at Riverview Farm. They were riding the same trail that had killed Mikey just a few days ago. Did Craig have enough lead time to restring the barbed wire to kill one of them, too?

As they entered the field, they saw the red, white, and blue Polaris still moving in front of them. Despite still flying over the snow, it also looked like a wrestling match was taking place on its seat. Tom saw Craig's back but didn't see where Raven was, but she must have been giving him a run for his money since he was dodging around on the seat, yet still keeping a thumb on the throttle.

Then Tom drew in his breath as he saw Craig's arm pull back. Marcel must have anticipated the punch to Raven's head, too, and gunned the sled as hard as he could, getting the front skis off the ground.

But suddenly, the Polaris skidded sideways and stopped. Craig lost his balance and fell off. He reached out to grab the track, but Raven had turned back to the controls and took off with a brap-brap.

Craig screamed, his hands probably injured from the studs in the track, and face-planted into the snow.

"Let me off," Tom yelled to Marcel, who stopped just long enough for Tom to jump off. Marcel then took off in Raven's direction. Tom put his foot on Craig's back to keep him down. He saw two deputies making their way down the hill to the bottom of the field.

Craig struggled to get up.

"Don't make me draw my weapon, Craig," Tom said, noticing that now the snow was red with blood from Craig's hands. "You give snowmobiling a bad name."

He glanced up the trail and saw Marcel was still chasing after Raven. She might not stop until she's out of gas, he thought.

Chapter Forty-Two

Raven knew reaching Riverview Farm was a bad idea. Very bad. She heard a sled behind them. Could Karl really have recovered? Doubtful. She felt Craig look over his shoulder, but when she tried to look, she couldn't see who it was. Craig must have recognized whoever it was because it only made him go faster.

It was now or never. She tried to gain control of the throttle by yanking at his right hand. He had only a sweatshirt, so she pulled up the sleeve and, with a bare hand, tried to scratch his right arm. She thought that, besides the action itself, it might trigger the bad behavior he would have to use against Stella, and he would fight back.

It worked to some extent, but it didn't help. Even with all of their twisting and turning, she couldn't get his hand off the throttle to stop the sled. She saw him draw back his left arm, his hand in a fist. She head-butted him, hoping to break his nose and his concentration.

It worked. He briefly lifted his hand off the throttle, and she grabbed the brake with her left hand and squeezed as hard as she could. The sled careened to a stop, skidding sideways. She hit the kill switch on the right to stop the sled dead.

Raven shoved her body against Craig's while holding on to the handlebars with one hand to maintain her own balance. As soon as he fell off the sled, she righted herself, pulled up the kill switch, and restarted the sled.

As she pressed on the throttle, she saw his hand come up to grab her pant leg, and then the running board, but the momentum of the sled pulled him with her for only a moment. She gunned it. She dared to look down to her left. He was not holding on.

She kept going on the trail, around the yellow police tape where Mikey had been murdered. She stuck close to the river and wondered if there was another trap of barbed wire to come. She heard a snowmobile pursuing her. Could Craig have gotten on that other sled? Were they working together?

Her hand squeezed the throttle as hard as she could. The trail in this section wasn't as packed down, and she missed seeing where to turn. One of the skis went between two small trees. Thankfully, she used the brake and stopped before hitting another tree head-on.

The other snowmobile came up behind her. She held her breath before she turned to look.

Marcel! She saw it was Marcel.

"Some fancy riding there," he said, winking at her.

She exhaled and breathed deeply. Finally, she smiled. "You don't grow up in Secretly without knowing how to ride a sled."

They turned the sleds around—no small feat with snowbanks and the Polaris being stuck and Raven having to take breaks because her hands were shaking too much from the cold and the whole experience—and went back to the field and to Tom. Craig was being handcuffed by one of Marcel's other deputies.

Marcel shook his head at Craig.

Craig snarled at Marcel. "You'd do the same if Raven wanted what Stella wanted. I'd do anything to keep her happy. To keep her with me."

"Hard to know if Stella would have wanted all those things if she knew the price that others had to pay," said Tom as Craig was taken away up the hill.

Raven didn't share her suspicions about why Craig was really buying items for Stella. There was time enough for that. Poor Stella. She hoped now that Stella could live a better, healthier, safer life.

Then she remembered Karl. "Marcel," she said, turning to him. "You have to send an ambulance to the clubhouse. Craig was trying to kill Karl when I arrived."

"All set," he said, putting his arm around her waist. "An ambulance is taking him to County Hospital, and he is awake and able to speak."

"Yeah," Tom chimed in, "Betty took care of all of that. Do we have to give her a merit badge or indoctrinate her as an assistant deputy?" He chuckled.

"Betty?" Raven knew she had just been through something quite traumatic, but Betty did not go with her to the clubhouse. She was sure of that.

"Yep, Betty. Good ole Betty in her pajamas." Tom chuckled again.

Tom switched the topic to Craig. "I've been hearing that he was getting complaints about shoddy workmanship. I'll bet that was one of the ways he was skimming money, too. I'm sure we'll find other connections also. Oh, and those fibers we found on the wire near the tree. Hopefully, we can match it to a coat of Craig's."

"I don't doubt we'll have a strong case against him." Marcel pulled Raven in tighter. "Money can't buy happiness. When will people stop trying to make it so?"

She felt like melting into his strong arms. She thought of her mother hiding the money. Maybe that was the point. Don't love Johnny for the money itself, but because he cared. Her mother also never equated money and happiness.

Tom looked at Raven. "We had a couple of clues leading us to talk to Craig today. What led you to figure out his embezzlement?"

"I was thinking about the money, too. As Marcel said, money can't buy happiness, but it can definitely cause so many problems—heartache, break-ups, lies, thefts." She thought of Mikey and added murder to the list.

She continued. "And I remembered Karl saying that the snowmobile club wasn't getting state money for all the years that there was no snow. I looked it up and saw that, yes, indeed, SnowTrack had been getting thousands of dollars each year. It had to be either Karl or Craig who had taken it. Chris is too busy with the store, and Emil told me where to look for the records. Why would he do that if he was the embezzler?"

"And you thought, instead of telling your husband, the sheriff, you'd just check it out yourself." Marcel wagged a finger at her and then kissed her on top of her head.

"Well, I didn't want to send you on a wild goose chase if I was wrong. I really thought I'd just go into the clubhouse and look at the files. Fifteen minutes, in and out. I think Karl figured it out, too. Maybe seeing too many new trucks for Craig. I'm guessing that they made a plan to meet at the clubhouse to also go over the records, and Craig acted on his first plan. To kill Karl."

Raven added. "Besides the trucks, Craig was buying custom-designed jewelry and planning a European vacation. How could they want to go to Europe when they live in Vacationland?" She smiled. She always loved Maine's tagline. That, and the "Welcome Home" signs on I-95 North and at the rest stops. Yes, home. Maine was, and always would be, home.

"I'll go up to the farmhouse and update Camille. She'll probably be wondering what happened down here. Again," said Tom.

"Want me to come back and get you up there at the farm?" asked Marcel.

"No, no. My mother or Rachel can come get me. I think I've ridden with you enough for one day." Tom grinned.

"Actually, how about if you come back with us on a sled, and then take Raven's car with you to the farm. I want her to drive home with me," Marcel said.

Raven started to protest. She wasn't a baby, but Marcel shushed her.

Tom nodded. "Okay with me, I can do that. We probably should check on Betty, too. I bet she's still at the clubhouse, waiting for us," said Tom, walking over to the Polaris.

Raven shook her head. "I still can't believe Betty got involved."

"Says 'Little Miss Nosey-pants.' You actually owe her a lot," said Marcel. "We both do."

Marcel and Raven rode back on Karl's Arctic Cat while Tom took Craig's Polaris. Both sleds rode at the appropriate speed for the trail conditions. When they all got back to the parking lot, Betty ran to greet them. Howard was also there. Betty must have called him.

As soon as the Arctic Cat stopped, and Raven got off, Betty threw her arms around her.

"I thought I'd never see you again," she said into Raven's ear.

"I hear I owe my life to you." Raven squeezed her back.

"You've given me life, so we're even." Betty smiled, wiping tears.

Howard gave Raven a bear hug. His voice was choked up. "Glad to have you back, kid."

Betty and Howard stepped back, letting Marcel and Raven figure out their next steps. Raven offered to drive her own car home again.

"It's silly to make Tom run around with my car," she said.

"Nothing doing," countered Marcel. "I told you. Tom will drive your car back after talking to Camille. You're coming home with me. I'm not letting you out of my sight. At least not for a day or two." He again drew her close.

He finally released her, and she got into the passenger side of his Jeep. As she stepped in, something glittery caught her eye. She bent down to pick it up. It was a gemstone earring, a square diamond-like gemstone with smaller gemstones along the edge. The backing has been smashed and bent.

Her heart stopped. She brought it up from the floor and held it between her fingers to show Marcel.

"What's this?" she asked, bracing herself for the answer.

He leaned forward to get a better look. She studied his face. It showed no recognition or guilt.

He shrugged. "Looks like an earring to me."

Of course, it was an earring, she wanted to say. Instead, she swallowed and asked, "How did it get here? In your Jeep?" She knew he never put a suspect in his front seat.

Marcel shrugged again. "I don't know. Must have been stuck to the bottom of Tom's boot. You know how he is. I bet it could even belong to that new forensics-medical examiner woman that he's been flirting with. Is that a real diamond? Do you think it's worth something? Looks pretty gaudy to me."

She didn't respond but studied the earring. Could it be that simple an answer? Could it actually have just come off of Tom's boot?

Marcel took her hands, the earring still between two of her fingers. "Listen to me. No one but Tom, and now you, has been in this Jeep's front seat for a long time. A long, long time."

She could mull over just how long a "long, long time" was, and what that even meant, and who could have possibly been in this front seat to even matter prior to this "long, long time," but before she could get too deep into the darkness, Marcel leaned toward her and pulled her close again. He kissed her gently, and then kissed her again. Nothing felt different between them. His soft lips enveloped hers, and she smelled his woodsy scent. She melted.

"I love you, babe," he said, pulling back and cupping her face in his hands. She felt his warm breath on her cheeks. His expression was serious, and his eyes were moist. "I don't know what I would do without you," he said, his voice having a catch to it.

She squeezed her hand tight and felt the earring dig in. She could let it cause her pain beyond the imprint it was now leaving. Or she could let it go. Let it all go. She almost died today. She was given the gift of another day. Her mother would tell her not to blow it.

So, she did just that. She let it go. She released the earring and let it tumble back down to the floor. She chose happiness.

Mirroring Marcel, she put both of her hands around his face to pull him in even closer.

"Time to go home," she whispered.

Acknowledgements

First and foremost, I thank the Level Best Books community, especially Shawn, Deb, Gwyn, and Tina. My gratitude runs deep.

Secondly, I thank all who made the launch of my first novel in this series, *Blaze Orange*, a success including some pivotal folks: Sally, Bev, Sarah, Jackie, Kathlyn, Ben, Carl, Ann, Anna, Sabrina, Paula, Anne, Gabi, Matt, Jon, Steven, Maureen, Marita, Elaine, Mary Rose, Kim, Renee, Nancy, Jaime, Lisa, Jim, Jonathan, Dot, Cheryl, Jana, Eric, Cori, Bonnie, Ken, Lorraine, Robert, Gary, Dale, and Barbara.

I'm not one for gore, but when I need to pay attention to the details, I'm lucky to have a subject-matter specialist at my fingertips who not only knows her stuff but also enjoys talking about it. (I'm not sure if I should be concerned about the latter.) Regardless, I am grateful to my great niece, Olivia Rivera, for her expert forensic advice, speedy responses, and all-around good sense of humor.

A year ago, I had a delightful conversation with Anna Gilmore Hall, a Mainer, and Brady Barthold, a Minnesotan, about snowmobiling, this novel, and my hesitation about a title. They gave me the confidence to choose the name *Arctic Green.*

I am fortunate to receive extra encouragement, compassion, and advice from three outstanding writers. Thank you, Matt Cost, Jon Lewis, and Cheryl Lawton Malone, for always being in my corner. Thanks, too, to Jim Heffernan for his careful read.

I am grateful to the wonderful state of Maine. Your daily magic is inspiring, and I couldn't imagine being anywhere else. And to the Maine writing community, your support and kindness are immense.

And of course, my greatest gratitude is to Tom Aylesbury. You changed my life in so many ways. My heart to you.

About the Author

Allison lives in Midcoast Maine with her muse, Tom, and their two poochies, Kelton and Roger. When she's not at her laptop, she can be found walking a hiking trail, paddling a river, or reading at the beach.

She can be reached at www.akeetonbooks.com.

AUTHOR WEBSITE:
www.akeetonbooks.com

SOCIAL MEDIA HANDLES:
FACEBOOK: Allison Keeton, Author
https://www.facebook.com/AKeetonBooks?mibextid=LQQJ4d
INSTAGRAM: Allison_Keeton_Author
https://www.instagram.com/allison_keeton_author/profilecard/?igsh=
MWZwbG1jcDNkNnFocA==
THREADS: @allison_keeton_author
X: @akeetonbooks

Also by Allison Keeton

Blaze Orange, Book One, Midcoast Maine Mystery series